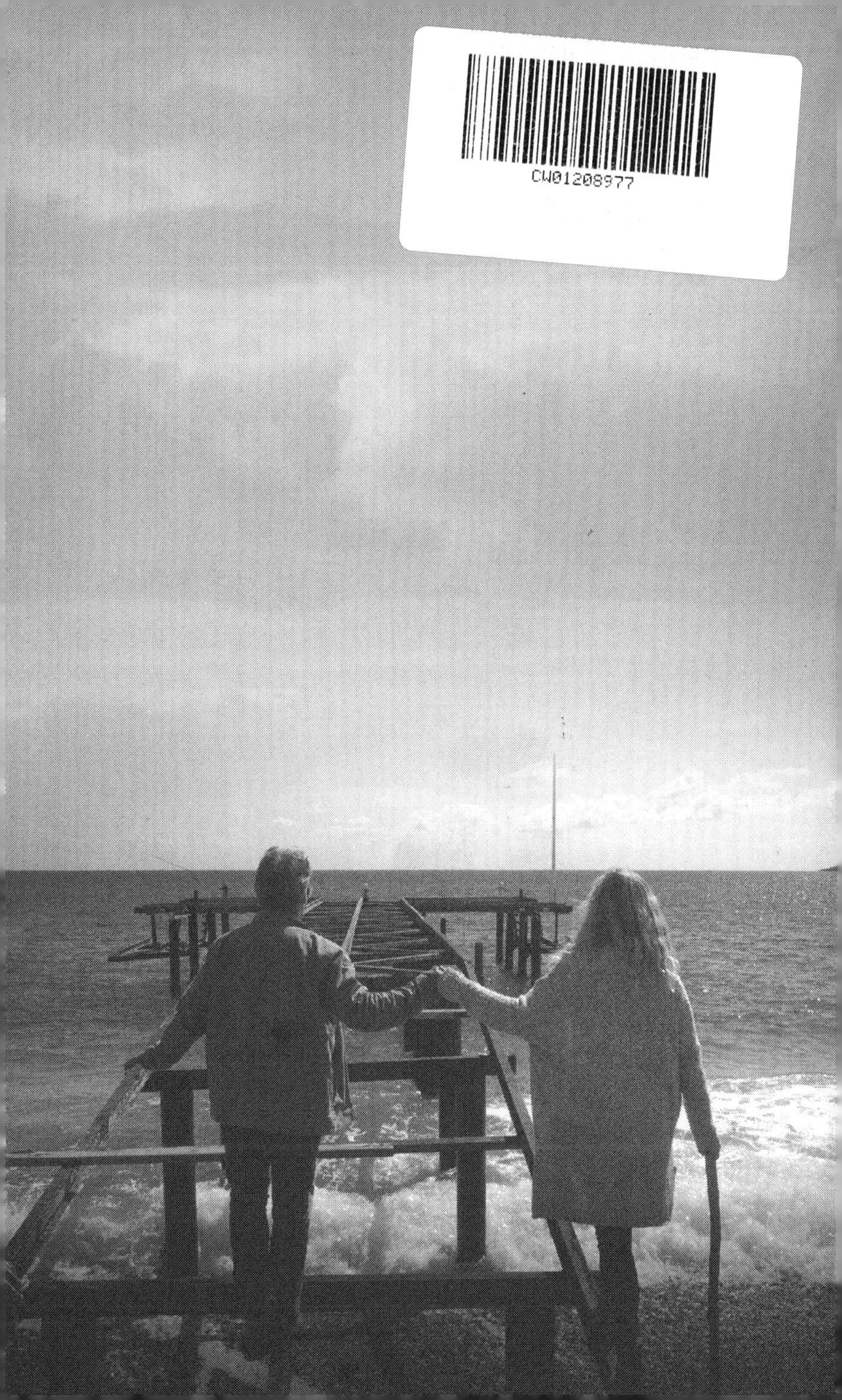

You Will Meet a Stranger

Lynn Florkiewicz

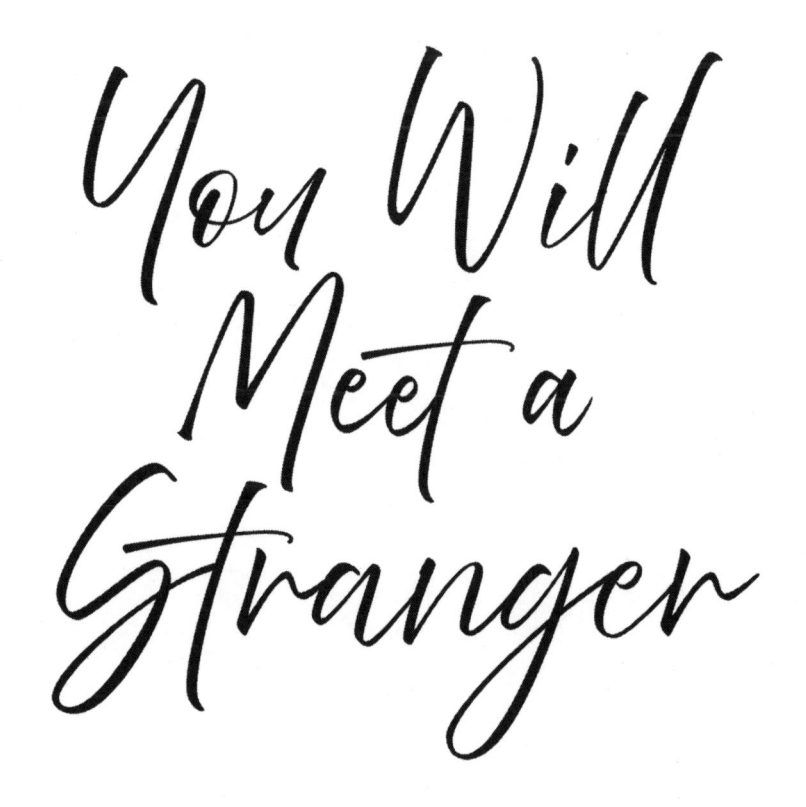

The Book Guild Ltd

First published in Great Britain in 2024 by
The Book Guild Ltd
Unit E2 Airfield Business Park,
Harrison Road, Market Harborough,
Leicestershire. LE16 7UL
Tel: 0116 2792299
www.bookguild.co.uk
Email: info@bookguild.co.uk
X: @bookguild

Copyright © 2024 Lynn Florkiewicz

The right of Lynn Florkiewicz to be identified as the author of this
work has been asserted by them in accordance with the
Copyright, Design and Patents Act 1988.

All rights reserved. No part of this publication may be
reproduced, transmitted, or stored in a retrieval system, in any form or by any means,
without permission in writing from the publisher, nor be otherwise circulated in
any form of binding or cover other than that in which it is published and without
a similar condition being imposed on the subsequent purchaser.

This work is entirely fictitious and bears no resemblance to any persons living or dead.

Typeset in 11pt Minion Pro

Printed on FSC accredited paper
Printed and bound in Great Britain by 4edge Limited

ISBN 978 1916668 669

British Library Cataloguing in Publication Data.
A catalogue record for this book is available from the British Library.

This novel came about through a series of events:

First, my beloved husband, Tad, suddenly collapsed with a heart attack at the age of sixty-one. Over the months that followed, I kept a diary of my feelings, thoughts and emotions.

Second, emerging from the rawness of grief, I began working on a new writing project, the authorised biography of the Italian actor, Rossano Brazzi. During the research, I came across one of his films, *Summertime*, with Katharine Hepburn. This beautiful movie deals with the theme of loneliness and two older characters from different cultures entering a romance.

Third, I had spent two years researching Rossano's life. He was a delight to write about, but I needed to get him out of my head. He, effectively, became my inspiration for the character of Gian.

The contents of my diary, the theme of loneliness and the need to get Rossano out of my head collided. The result is the book you are reading now. Everyone deals with grief in different ways. My way won't be everyone's way, but it worked for me.

This book is dedicated to Tad. I will always love you.

ACT ONE

SUSSEX
SOUTH-EAST ENGLAND
JULY 2020–APRIL 2021

Chapter One
KERRY

I always return to the flickering screen to gaze at those icons from glamorous days. Embracing the style, the kindness, the charm, now labelled false, dated, bizarre.

The little art house in the heart of Brighton's old town was perfect for the film we were about to watch, an Italian classic from 1980. It still had its red velvet seats, though admittedly those deep-sprung seats were well worn. They might not be as comfortable as those you get in the modern complexes, but it all added to the experience. Even the tiny metal ashtrays were still in situ, although, of course, there was no smoking allowed now.

The cinema had also kept its voluminous curtains that swept open when the film was ready to start, along with dark red wallpaper with a decorative pattern woven in. Two ornate columns limited the view for spectators in a couple of seats at the back but not where we were sitting. We'd managed to book seats in the centre, halfway down. Not too close. Not too far away. You had to book for the films they showed here because this tiny venue only seated about eighty people, if that.

I settled back and breathed in. No matter how much they cleaned and aired this cinema, it stubbornly retained that musty odour typical of old buildings. Above me, the arched black ceiling was littered with starlight.

The old projector had long gone. What a shame that everything was digital these days. There had been something romantic about watching the dust motes dance in the column of light that shone out from the projection room behind us. Last week, they'd shown *Casablanca*, with Humphrey Bogart and Ingrid Bergman. I owned it on DVD, but it was so much better on the big screen. And here they only showed classic, vintage or foreign movies, never anything modern. The multiplex on the seafront catered for that audience.

I hoped the 'woke' generation wouldn't ban these beauties from my world. I say that because some of this film was not politically correct enough for modern eyes. It showed men opening doors for women and lifting their hats in welcome. Heaven forbid!

I lost myself in a surreal daydream of an underground movement screening old movies deemed unsuitable for sensitive souls. A secret password would allow entrance into a basement room where aficionados of retro movies could meet incognito, out of sight of critical eyes. Ha! Ha! Although it was an amusing fantasy, it wouldn't surprise me in the least if that did happen one day. I mean, they'd already started putting warnings on old films shown on TV because they included outdated ideas. My immediate response to that? FFS!

I talk as if I lived in the dark ages. I really didn't. I slotted myself into the modern, fun-loving woman category, admittedly getting older, but with my feet firmly planted in this century. I just chose to embrace those things I felt we were missing, and old-fashioned romance was one of them.

Adam, my husband, lovingly tolerated my passion for old movies. That evening was the only showing of *Il Problemo, La Soluzione* and he'd rolled his eyes in mock frustration at the thought of going. The old seats were snug for his stocky rugby-player frame.

Now, in a hushed tone, he continued to jokingly moan to our friends, Tom and Maggie, who were seated immediately behind us. Adam had retained a trace of his Glaswegian accent even though he'd moved down from Scotland a few years before we'd married.

'Thirty years of marriage and still she hauls me off to watch ancient black-and-white movies.'

'Excuse me, Mr Simmonds,' I said. 'This one's in colour.' He was prone to exaggeration. Most of the films I hauled him off to were in colour, the last one being *Cinema Paradiso*.

'I don't see the attraction. It's hard work reading subtitles and watching the film at the same time.' He ran his hands through his hair. Unlike many men in their later years, he'd kept a full head of hair and normally wore it longer than he should, but it suited him. The original nut-brown colour was now predominantly grey.

Tom and Maggie were only five years older than Adam and me (we were both sixty-four), but Tom seemed much more than that, with his elder statesman ways and well-to do accent. Indeed, the friendship between the four of us was unusual because of our backgrounds.

Adam and I had grown up on council estates; our working-class parents had worked in factories.

In contrast, Tom and Maggie were privately educated, widely travelled and had a very different take on class and finance. Being poor to them meant booking a three-week cruise instead of a two-month one. And, tonight, in this retro cinema, the pair were dressed as if for a West-End première. Maggie wore a shift dress and a high-end linen jacket, very Audrey Hepburn. Tom even sported a silk cravat, for God's sake! But that's what I meant about loving the era of the old movies. They were elegant and, yes, it seemed out of place now, but I secretly wished that people still dressed up to go to the cinema.

It sounds as if Adam and I were on the poverty line. We weren't. We began married life like many in the '80s and '90s, happy to make do with pieces of second-hand furniture and odd bits of crockery found at car boot sales. Over the years, we'd slowly got on our feet and now, thirty-plus years later, we were more than comfortable, although nowhere near Tom and Maggie's league.

Tom's rasping voice brought me out of my thoughts. 'I understand subtitles are difficult to begin with, Adam, but this one is a classic. Try to enter the spirit of it.'

'And,' Maggie leant in, 'if you do struggle, just admire the scenery. It's set in the Cinque Terre region. We've been there several times and it's exquisite. An upmarket St Ives.'

St Ives in Cornwall was mine and Adam's favourite holiday destination. It was typical of Maggie to compare our holiday locations, although it was never done with any malice and probably not meant as a comparison. It's just the way she said things sometimes. I supposed the Italian Riviera was more glamorous than St Ives, but I bet they didn't do cream teas there.

Tom suggested that, if Adam got tired of reading the translation in the subtitles, he should admire the lead actress, Gabriella Collina. 'She, too, is very beautiful and upmarket.'

'As is the lead actor, Luca Belfiore,' I said. 'Sex on a stick.'

I sensed Maggie stiffen. That was probably a little too on the nose for her. The word 'sex', spoken in a public forum, had that effect on her. To be fair, though, she did take it in good humour and admitted he was appealing. Appealing! The man was positively hot.

'Have you seen him in anything else?' she asked.

'No, I haven't. Have you?'

'No.'

'Thank God for that,' said Adam. 'That'd mean you dragging me to more of your foreign films.'

'You drag me to *Inception* and *Batman*.'

'Aye, I do, because they're full of adventure and excitement, made in the twenty-first century and I don't have to read anything.'

'And *Il Problemo* is full of romance, character and elegance.' I took in our default summer outfits of shorts and T-shirts. 'Something we could do with.'

I heard him *tut* as the lights went down and leaned in to kiss him. 'I love that you come with me.'

He returned the kiss. 'Aye. It's not so bad, I s'pose.'

The lights dimmed. The sweeping curtains parted. The audience hushed. The screen flickered to life and the credits came up as the theme music brought the coastline of Italy to life.

I squinted when we emerged from the darkness of the cinema. The evening was still light as we joined the hustle and bustle of the Brighton streets. The old town was predominantly the domain of students, so the place buzzed in the evening. Most of the shops remained open until late and there were many open-air cafés and restaurants catering for all tastes. This part of the town consisted of three or four narrow streets leading up to the main part of the city where all the chain shops were but, at this time of the evening, most of that area was closed.

One prominent characteristic of these streets was the scent of spliff. It hung in the air. There was no need to light up yourself. If you stayed there long enough, you'd probably begin to feel the effects.

'That was bloody brilliant.' I didn't need a puff of spliff when I'd been to that cinema.

'Aye, Kerry, it would have been if you hadn't been drooling.'

'Oh, Adam, you're not jealous of an old film star, are you?'

I received a hug in return and, resolutely denying any envy, he quickly suggested fish and chips.

'You enjoyed it, I know you did,' I said. 'I could see how engrossed you were.'

He didn't deign to answer but amusement danced in his eyes.

The aroma of fish and chips reached us well before we arrived at the chip shop door. A few customers were outside, delving into their portions and shielding them from some seagulls perched on the lamp posts. The smell of fried batter, chips and vinegar sent my taste buds into overdrive, and I realised I was very hungry. Adam held the door open for us.

'Has Dan heard about his exam results?' Tom asked.

As a couple, we hadn't originally planned to have children, just to enjoy life and have fun; quite honestly,

Dan had been a mistake. He'd arrived when I was getting on in years and I was worried sick about complications and the whole 'having children' thing, especially at forty-plus. I knew we'd have moments of adversity in our life but not an unexpected child. Amazingly, those doubts were to disappear very quickly. Dan became, and remained, our pride and joy.

'He won't hear until next month,' Adam replied as he put in our order for cod and chips.

'Kerry said he could be sponsored through university.'

'Aye, if he gets the grades.'

I turned to Maggie. 'He's aiming for Southampton.'

'And a little bird told me,' said Maggie, 'that he's courting.'

Courting! Who said that anymore? Clearly, Maggie did.

While Adam collected wooden forks and sorted out payment, I updated Maggie and Tom on the news.

'Chloe, yes. She's really nice. In the same year as Dan. They've been friends for a while, but they hooked up as a couple last month. I don't know how long it'll last. I think Chloe's aiming to get into St Andrews which couldn't be much further away from Southampton.'

Maggie insisted that, if they were meant to be together, love would find a way. 'Like in *Il Problemo*.'

Tom told her the boy was only eighteen and to let him have a life. 'You two didn't get married until you were thirty. Don't marry him off straight from school.'

'You know us better than that, Tom. I'd much prefer him to have a life and do some travelling before he even thinks about settling down. Anyway, it's not up to me. All we can do is set him up as best we can. I always vowed I wouldn't be an interfering mum.'

A portion of cod and chips was thrust into my hands and Adam ushered us outside. He nicked one of my chips.

'Ye'll never stop being a mum, Kerry. And I guarantee ye'll be doing his washing when he's home from uni and spoiling him rotten in between times.'

Yes, I thought, *I probably would.*

Chapter Two
KERRY

My family =
Laughter, happiness, respect and fun,
Tolerance, support, a shoulder to lean on.
Our family. My family. We belong. Together.

The kitchen-diner at 25 Bay Terrace was generally the hub of activity for the Simmonds clan. We had a perfectly decent lounge but, like many families, everything happened around the big oak dining table which had seen better days, although neither Adam nor I ever spoke of replacing it.

Over the years, this large beaten-up oak slab had had things spilt on it; there were countless scorch marks and, after Dan's junior school phase as a budding Picasso, several images of smiley faces carved into it. I remember being livid at the time but now, those scratches and carvings added something personal and made the item indispensable as far as I was concerned.

Two doors led off from our kitchen. One went to the hall, and one opened onto the patio and the landscaped garden beyond. We'd opted for a coastal garden. Low maintenance. We loved the garden. We hated gardening. It was a huge area with a patio, pebbles, a pagoda and a few coastal grasses and shrubs.

Anyone entering our kitchen would see this was our gathering place. Family photos covered the walls, from the sepia images of our great-grandparents through to digital colour prints of me, Adam and Dan, along with a few quotes from my favourite poets who ranged from Shelley to John Cooper Clarke. I loved writing poetry, but I didn't consider myself a poet. I wasn't even sure if what I wrote could be deemed poetry. Just random thoughts, sometimes with no rhyme or reason. But I guessed poetry was a very individual thing. Like art. I wasn't that into art, but I appreciated some of it. It was the modern stuff I couldn't get to grips with. A black canvas with a white speck. I mean, what was that all about?

Adam invariably took the piss out of my poetic ramblings but then I always took the piss out of his collection of ancient *Dandy* and *Beano* comics, so we were even on that score.

Dominating one wall was our massive kitchen dresser, inherited from Adam's gran. It was a great hunk of furniture housing a collection of mismatched plates, mugs and ornaments but they were hidden from view at the moment because of the cards, most with the same generic message plastered on the front: 'Congratulations on passing your exams'.

In the background, Crosby, Stills, Nash and Young sang about travelling on the Marrakesh Express.

The feel-good factor got into my bones. Pride, of course. Dan had studied so hard and now he was one step closer to his dream of becoming a marine engineer. A company, Ocean Marine Inc, had offered to sponsor him through university and, providing he did well, there would be a lucrative job at the end of it.

He stood by the stove, concocting our meal for the evening. He was as tall as Adam now, just on six foot, and had inherited that rugby build from his dad, too. Unlike Adam, he adored cooking and was putting the finishing touches to a Chinese meal.

Maggie and Tom were supposed to join us, but they had a prior engagement. That worked out well for us as they'd insisted on treating us to dinner the previous evening at a swanky restaurant, so we'd already started the celebrations.

Adam picked out a bottle of Pinot Grigio and poured a glass for each of us. The table was laid with various condiments and a plate of prawn crackers. Dan had two woks on the go: beef and mushroom in a black bean sauce and chicken and onion in a sweet chilli sauce. He drained nutty brown rice through a sieve.

'Mum, Dad, you need to sit down. I'm dishing up.'

Soon after, he placed bowls on the table, along with serving spoons. I salivated.

Adam and I locked eyes. He had soft brown eyes that twinkled, and I always loved looking into them. I could see from his expression how elated he was about Dan, but we'd agreed to play it down. Although mature in many ways, Dan was still a teenager and would get irritable if we gushed constant praise at him. I had to say something about the food, though.

'Oh, Dan, this is fantastic.'

Adam reached across for the rice. 'You could change

your mind. Ditch the engineering. I can see it now. Dan Simmonds, Michelin-starred chef.'

Dan's face was a picture. 'You're joking, right? Slaving in a hot kitchen all day.'

'Aye, when you put it like that. But keep your options open.' He stabbed a chopstick at him. 'Don't be frightened of taking a risk, even if it scares the shit out of you.'

That was Adam's go-to line for life in general. I loaded my fork with chicken but then sat back with the realisation that our lives were about to change dramatically over the next year.

'I can't believe it. Our son going to university.'

'My parents, retiring to Cornwall,' Dan said as he took a portion of beef. 'Are you really that old?'

Adam smirked as I sat up straight, almost indignant. '*Early* retirement, if you don't mind.' We were only two years off official retirement age, but I needed to make it clear that it was still early. I drifted into a daydream. 'Oh, Adam, just think, fish suppers at sunset.'

Adam joined me in my musing. 'Breakfasts at The Greasy Spoon.'

Dan grimaced. 'Not that hideous shack by the beach.'

Crunching into a prawn cracker, I reminded him that his father and I had enjoyed many breakfasts there since our honeymoon. 'It's sentimental more than anything.'

'But Greg and Suzie do a brilliant fry-up.'

Ah, Greg and Suzie. They ran The Feather Duck, a quaint bed and breakfast situated in a quiet part of St Ives. We'd been guests there for about fifteen years now and had developed a friendship over that time. And Dan was right, they did do a good breakfast.

'They didnae have the bed and breakfast when we first started going there. We're travelling down in a couple of weeks to do a recce, get a few property details. Are you coming with us?'

'Not this time. I promised to help Chloe's dad build his shed. His MS has got to the stage that he's having to use a wheelchair now and he can't do any DIY. I'll come next time, though. We can do some surfing.'

'Aye, that'll be grand.'

I poured more wine for the three of us. Everything was coming along nicely. There was no denying that we'd been terrified when I'd discovered I was pregnant with Dan. Doubts had lined up on a metaphorical conveyor belt. Would we be good parents? Would we raise a tearaway? Would he resent us? Were we too old? Would we relate to each other? Would he like us?

We needn't have worried. We must have done something right. Yes, he had the odd teenage strop but, overall, he was turning into a wonderful human being. So far, so good. And he'd be the first Simmonds to go to university.

I hoped and prayed it would work out well; for him and for us. Retiring to St Ives was everything we had dreamed and planned for. To spend the rest of our lives in a place we cherished couldn't make for a more perfect prospect.

Dan interrupted my thoughts. 'Dig in, Mum, football's on in about an hour and we don't want to miss it.'

'What, Brighton?'

'Aye,' said Adam. 'They're on the TV. I tried to get tickets, but they were sold out.'

I did dig in and savoured the individual flavours of the sauces that Dan had made from scratch. In between, I swigged mouthfuls of wine. I could almost see the thought bubble above my head: *I wonder how we'll all be doing this time next year.*

Chapter Three
DAN

I was chuffed to get the grades I needed. My mates at school had all done well and none of us were in a situation where we had to retake exams or change our options. Chloe had done well too, and she was having a think about which uni to apply to, although I knew she fancied St Andrews in Scotland. My option had always been Southampton. That was *the* university for marine engineering, and I was pretty sure I'd get in with my grades.

I knew Mum and Dad were pleased but I was glad they didn't make a huge song and dance about it. Dad had suggested going out for a meal, but I liked to cook, and I wanted to do something special. And we'd been out the night before with Maggie and Tom. I'd asked Chloe to come over, but she'd organised something with her mum months ago, before we'd got together, so she couldn't make it.

But that was fine. It was nice to do this, just the three of us. It seemed weird that everything was going to change this year. Me going to uni, Mum and Dad going to St Ives. Bloody retiring. I never thought of my parents being old enough to retire, although Mum insisted it was *early* retirement. Even so, I didn't see them as being in their sixties. My mates at school thought they were cool and were always happy to come over here to hang out.

Dad had built an extension to the side of the house a few years ago and he'd said it was mine, for when I was a bit older and wanted mates around and to have my own space. It was great. I'd put a pool table in there and Dad had connected a TV, too.

I was hopeless at telling Mum and Dad stuff like this, but I knew I'd made them proud. I think that's why I wanted to cook dinner, as a thank you to them. I was proper happy.

Chapter Four
KERRY

When a void opens up and swallows you whole,
Where do you go?

The kitchen-diner at 25 Bay Terrace was as still as a millpond. The golden hues of the onset of autumn failed to lift the atmosphere. The big oak table seemed to be the only source of strength in the room. I certainly had none.

The celebratory cards that had crowded the kitchen dresser just a short time before now held a mass of condolence cards.

On the table, photos of Adam; Adam with me; Adam with Dan; Adam with Tom and Maggie. Recently washed crockery drained by the sink, and it would remain there. What did it matter? Those mourners who had come back here after the funeral had offered to put everything away, but I told them not to worry. As much as I loved them, I wanted them to leave. I needed quiet time. Tom and Maggie had stayed on a little longer, I think, to make sure we were both going to be okay. With a promise that we would call if we needed them, they left us to our thoughts.

Beside me, in a black suit and tie, Dan stared at nothing, his eyes red-rimmed with grief.

I wore my copper-coloured shift dress. It was Adam's favourite outfit of mine.

I stared at the Order of Service in front of me. Adam's twinkly eyes gazed out from the cover; his warm smile lit up his face. My index finger traced the outline of his jaw and touched his lips. I couldn't have asked for a better service, a true celebration of his life and his personality. There were even moments of humour and a blues band had played two songs that Adam had requested for his funeral. We'd made our wills years ago and had typed up a separate document to outline what we wanted for our respective services. I'm glad we'd done that because it meant we'd given Adam exactly what he'd chosen.

Oddly, a scene from *Mary Poppins* sprang to mind: the moment when Mary, Bert and the Banks children jumped into a chalk picture. How I wish I could step into that image in front of me now and be with Adam, to hold him, to hug him, to kiss him and love him completely.

We'd been on holiday in Cornwall when it happened. It was our recce trip to collect property pages and register with estate agents in preparation for the next stage of our lives. Retirement.

A tragic boating accident. That's what the papers said. But it wasn't that. It was the result of a moronic teenager showing off to his friends and behaving like an idiot on a powerful speedboat he had no right to be in charge of.

We'd been enjoying a leisurely cruise on one of the sightseeing boats, to see the wildlife along the coast. We'd made the trip a few times over the years because it was a delightful way to spend a morning or afternoon, especially in good weather. You were pretty much guaranteed to see seals and dolphins and, if you were lucky, a basking shark.

Our boat had about twenty people on it, including young children, and we were pottering around the various inlets, watching the seals play. Then the skipper asked if we wanted to go further out to sea and find some dolphins. Of course, we all said yes. We found them, too. It was spectacular to see those marvellous creatures in their natural habitat, leaping from the ocean and racing one another in the wake of the boat. The children screamed with excitement.

As we headed back to St Ives, I saw a speedboat racing around in the bay. Even then, I didn't think the person driving it was in control. There was a lot of yelling and whooping coming from it, young teenagers having fun. But to me, they sounded under the influence; it was something more than high spirits. They sped by us once and I noticed that none of passengers had life jackets on. Our captain kept his eye on them. At one stage, I saw him grab his radio and talk into it. Whether he was trying to contact the other boat, I didn't know, but I couldn't think why else he would be on the radio unless it was to report them for reckless behaviour.

Two minutes later, the speedboat doubled back, and we heard a bang. I don't know if it had hit something or the engine had blown up, but the front end reared up and a female passenger was thrown clear and splashed down some distance away. The front end smashed against the rear of our boat. Our two outboard engines stopped, leaving both vessels floundering. Fortunately, the actual boats were okay but neither one would be going anywhere soon.

Our skipper hollered all sorts of insults at the other driver. Snatching the radio, he yelled for assistance and dictated clear co-ordinates. The young deckhand rushed from person to person, making sure we were all safe and not hurt. We were all fine, just a little rattled by what had happened. After making his calls, the skipper jumped down from his cabin to check the state of the engines.

Then Adam began stripping off. Before I could say anything to him, he'd jumped into the sea and begun swimming toward the girl who'd been thrown clear. He'd even taken his life jacket off. They were such small garments these days. Later, even now, I wondered if he'd discarded it on purpose or if he'd simply forgotten to put it back on once free of his anorak.

At the time, I wasn't worried. He was a strong swimmer and swam in the sea throughout the year. Another man from our boat followed him in but he'd kept his life jacket on.

Seeing two of his customers dive in, the skipper ordered us to get the oars out from a storage unit in the centre of the boat. We did this in a matter of seconds and the stronger, fitter ones among us grabbed the available oars and began to manoeuvre the boat toward the swimmers. In the meantime, the skipper and his young assistant located several lifebelts and threw them as far as they could, but they all fell short.

I couldn't see the girl in the water much. She kept going under and Adam had to keep diving down to reach her. Then she'd flap around, and Adam would lose his grip and she'd go under again.

That's when I began to worry. Yes, he was a strong swimmer, but the sea was choppy, and he must be losing strength. And why didn't he keep his life jacket on? I kept calling out to him and screaming for everyone to row harder but with every stroke we seemed to go nowhere except up and down.

I couldn't watch any longer. I jumped in. I had to help but I wasn't confident in the sea. The effort of swimming in deep water drained me and my limbs quickly began to ache. The sea was freezing, and, in two minutes, I was shivering and watching my husband struggle. I kept calling his name. Calling, calling, but the breeze carried it away. I lifted one of the lifebelts and tried throwing it toward him, but I had no strength.

Our boat reached me, and I fought hard to fight off the help being offered. I needed to get to Adam. The skipper hauled me into the boat and, when I eventually looked up, I saw Adam just yards away.

Floating.

Lifeless.

The lifeboat arrived at the same time and the crew scrambled to get Adam out. They worked tirelessly on him for what seemed to be an eternity but could only have been some minutes, before pronouncing him dead.

From that moment, all I remember is that I stared at the deck. I don't think I'd suffered from shock before. No hysterics, no weeping uncontrollably, not even a tear. Stunned. Numb. My whole life turned upside down in an instant. My reason for living snatched from me.

I remembered nothing of the journey back to the harbour. I think people were holding my hand and putting their arms around me, wrapping me in a blanket, but I just kept staring at the deck. I don't even remember blinking. I vaguely remember the police meeting us and taking away the occupants of the other boat. They left me alone and said they would speak with me later. Someone had contacted Suzie and Greg. I just kept staring at the ground.

When Suzie and Greg arrived, the tears came. What was I going to do? That's the question I asked them. What was I going to do?

They took me back to The Feather Duck, their arms around me, keeping me safe, telling me that I wasn't alone, that they were there for me, for however long I needed.

But I was, wasn't I? Alone. I'd never been so alone, so lost, so completely desolate.

I remember a small part of me denying that I'd lost him; that when we arrived at the B&B, Adam would trot down the stairs and ask why I was so upset. But, of course, he didn't. He wouldn't be coming down these stairs or any stairs again.

We sat on the patio. Suzie put a blanket around me, and Greg poured me a large brandy. My shaking hands held the telephone as I broke the news to Maggie, blurting out, between sobs, what had happened. She couldn't comprehend it. I remember her being confused and the only question I recall her asking was, 'Kerry, are you telling me Adam has been killed in an accident?'

Suzie took the phone from me and spoke with her. I couldn't talk about it. I couldn't think about it. I couldn't say the words I had to say. Not out loud. If I didn't say it, it hadn't happened.

After Suzie finished the call, a text came through from Maggie.

'You will find a way through this, Kerry. We'll be here for you when you get back. We're going to collect Dan and tell him what's happened. You stay with us when you return, for as long as you need to.'

Oh, Dan. Dan, my beautiful son. How are you going to cope with this? I should have been there with him.

Greg insisted on driving me home. I packed in a dream, mindlessly going from one drawer to another, transferring our things to our cases. Every shirt of Adam's I held close to smell his aftershave.

Suzie insisted on coming too. She'd arranged for a hotel owner to run the B&B while they were away, and she and I sat in the back of Greg's car.

Maggie kept in touch during the journey, but I couldn't remember anything she said. Every so often I began crying and Suzie drew me close and just hugged me. We didn't talk much, only when I felt I wanted to.

Dan and I didn't stay with Maggie and Tom, but Maggie did stay with us. She was a guardian angel that week, helping me with the bureaucracy of death. Registering the date and where it had happened, calling banks, pension providers, doctors and dentists and all those things you simply don't think about, or have no desire to think about.

I raged at the time taken to transfer Adam's body to Sussex. In actuality, it wasn't long, but I wanted to see him, to stroke his cheek, to tell him how much I loved him. And knowing he was in Cornwall while I was the other side of the country in Sussex stressed me out beyond belief.

Maggie did it all. I stood with her, still numb from shock. I couldn't do any of it. Every time I tried to tell someone that my husband had died, I choked. Tom went through my contacts and rang everyone we knew, and the cards began arriving. Texts pinged on my phone. And Dan's.

Heartfelt messages of concern and empathy, an outpouring of support.

Poor Dan. I felt terrible that I hadn't been there when he'd heard the news. He'd reacted in exactly the same way as me; he was stunned into silence, his entire state oblivious to anything beyond what had happened. All thoughts of future plans, hopes and dreams were gone. Cancelled.

Time had, effectively, come to a standstill for both of us.

Sitting here now, at this sturdy table, the tears pricked my eyes at those awful memories; memories that insisted on being front and centre of my mind every second of the day. I rapidly blinked them away. The last thing I wanted to do was break down in front of Dan.

Dear, beautiful Dan. You're too young to lose your dad, a dad you idolised and revered. A dad who should have had plenty more years to spend with his son. I felt in constant danger of losing composure, but I had to be strong for him. I had to help him navigate his way through this. But how? How on earth do you get over something like this?

The garden path is overgrown, the ancient tree is bare
The strong emotions that I have are shifting in despair
I feel so very lonely, the dreams I had are gone
And though I'm very empty, the tears roll on and on.

Reality smashed into me though I struggled so hard to keep it at bay. Future plans and trips would no longer include my best friend and soulmate. What would I do? How could I carry on without him? What was the point? Who would I share a coffee with? Who would enjoy breakfast with me in

The Greasy Spoon? Who would joke with me about foreign films at the cinema? How would I function without him? Who would I play football with on the beach? What about our plans to retire to St Ives? That last one resounded like an echo.

As every question arose the feeling of complete and utter devastation increased.

No. No.

I couldn't descend into the darkness. Dan couldn't see me like this. Instinctively, I reached for his hand. He gripped it tight, but his gaze remained focussed on the photos on the table. He hadn't moved an inch.

'We'll get through this, Dan. I promise. You and me, together, we'll find a way. One step at a time. Your dad wouldn't want us to fall apart. I know we will, but we mustn't let it devour us. We always have to look forward.'

I saw a slight nod. His bottom lip trembled.

'Oh, sweetheart. It's all right to cry.'

He brought his chair closer, leant his head against mine and wept. I couldn't hold it anymore. Tears ran unchecked down my cheeks. Strength be damned. If there was a God, I hoped and prayed that he would get us through this because I sure as hell didn't know how the devil I was supposed to deal with it.

Chapter Five
KERRY

Tonight, you slipped into my dreams,
Skin on skin, spooning.
You wrapped your arms around me, snuggled in,
Held me tight.
I hope you come to me like this every night.

The dream jolted me awake and I tried desperately to reconnect with it. That's where I wanted to be. Asleep, I was oblivious to the fact that Adam was gone, that he was no longer here. The void did not exist in my dream. The second I woke up, the proverbial black dog leapt upon me, baring its teeth, and the harsh truth of my world tore into me.

I reached behind me, knowing he wasn't there but hoping against hope that he was. Hoping that I had woken from the worst nightmare ever and everything would be back to normal.

But the only thing beside me was an empty space. Cold, unwelcoming. The tears began. Not crying. Full-on weeping. Where the tears came from, I didn't know. I had an endless supply of them. I was so, so sure that Adam had snuggled in behind me like he always did. I felt him. I heard his shallow breathing, I felt the stubble on his chin, his hand around my waist. I even felt the hairs on his arm, for God's sake. How was that not real? How could he not be here?

I recalled that first night I'd arrived home after the accident, knowing that Adam was lying in a mortuary, miles away in Cornwall, alone. Suzie had given me something from the health shop to help me sleep that night. I'd said goodnight to Adam and told him I loved him very much. It seemed so surreal. It still did.

In the darkness, I felt for my bedside light switch and scrunched my eyes in its glare while I grabbed a tissue. Adam smiled at me from a photo. It had been taken at The Bellagio in Las Vegas, a very posh hotel on the Strip. We didn't stay there but we had gone for afternoon tea, where everything was served on Royal Doulton china. What a wonderful holiday that was. I remembered us commenting that it was good, but it wasn't Cornwall. America had just about everything, but St Ives had our hearts.

> *I have been welcomed in every café and bar*
> *Overcome that first visit, the hardest by far.*
> *Was it to conquer that dread?*
> *Or was I simply searching for you instead?*
> *What I discovered was proof that you had gone.*
> *And wherever I went, I stumbled along*
> *Trying to hang on to you*
> *Wanting you here*
> *Wanting you near.*

The first couple of months following Adam's death, I became fixated on facing things head-on and visiting every place that had been dear to us. Every café, bar, restaurant, bench seat, view… you name it, I had to visit it. Why, I didn't know. Perhaps it was simply that I needed to get those first visits out of the way, to prove that I could do it, that I could return to those places and function as a human being. I thought if I left it too long, I'd develop a phobia; that a long absence would prevent me from setting foot in those places for fear of breaking down.

Some, like Jenny (who managed The Java Jive café), sat with me. She was in her mid-twenties, with spiky hair, tattoos, piercings and not fazed by confronting death.

'I know this is a stupid question,' she said, 'but, how are you coping? Do you need any of us to help with anything?'

I appreciated her offer and knew she meant it, too. It wasn't a casual enquiry spoken out of some misplaced obligation. She did, however, say something that hit a nerve and sent my internal rage into overdrive.

'Perhaps, one day, you'll find someone else,' she said.

I knew she was trying to be kind, supportive and giving me some hope but, at that time, I could have quite easily punched her. How could she think I would discard his memory so quickly? He wasn't a pile of old clothes to take to the charity shop.

Dan came with me on most of these visits, but I could see, immediately, that he struggled with it. People dealt with grief in their own ways, and I wasn't convinced that his journey included this. But he insisted on coming and I couldn't refuse him although I worried that it would overwhelm him.

Everyone at those various cafés and bars was so welcoming. I didn't think I'd ever received so many hugs in such a short space of time. And the sympathy and words shared with us about Adam were genuine and heartfelt.

I couldn't deny that it was difficult. I stumbled through every visit, forcing myself to be bright and brave even though I was a gibbering wreck of a human being underneath. Once in a while, I wanted to slump in a corner and curl up into a ball or rage at the world about the unfairness of it, knowing that Adam should have been here with us, laughing and joking.

Dan continued to shuffle along behind me, uncomfortable with the sympathy being showered on us. I, personally, needed this outpouring of empathy. It helped me, but it didn't help Dan. He became unnaturally quiet, keeping his distance from everyone and only coming forward when necessary.

At home, he rarely mentioned those excursions, which further convinced me that he only came to ensure I was okay. Without any encouragement from me, he'd given himself the role of man of the house, and as such, he had an obligation to support and protect me. I tried talking to him about grief and loss, saying that he didn't have to make these trips with me, but he wouldn't engage in the conversation. Instead, he insisted he was absolutely fine with it all.

There's never a good time to lose someone but eighteen was a terrible age for a son to lose his father. An awkward age. I remembered my own teenage years and wouldn't go back to them even if you paid me a king's ransom; to be so certain that you were a grown-up when you really weren't. At eighteen, I still had those petulant moods, those occasional tantrums that arose without warning.

Dan was no different. He occasionally closed down, but I was concerned that the emotions he bottled up would come out later in his life, so it was better if they came out now. I wondered if he'd spoken to Chloe or, perhaps, another friend. If he was talking to someone, I'd feel better.

He was normally okay discussing things with me, but grief was off-limits. I knew why, of course.

He didn't want to upset me.

And I didn't want to upset him.

After each excursion, I spoke to Adam about the day and who we'd seen. In public, those exchanges took place in my head but, on my own, I spoke aloud as if he were in the room. I didn't follow any particular religion; however, I did believe in the concept of one's soul surviving and found that comforting.

In the kitchen, I chatted to fresh air or the photos on the wall and, in the bedroom, to a portrait of him in an ornate silver frame. Doing that helped. It changed my view on death, just a fraction. To know that Adam was around in some sort of ethereal form gave me a different perspective on things. I now thought of my relationship as a spiritual one instead of a physical one.

I recalled a scene from *A Matter of Life and Death* with David Niven. He played an RAF pilot in the war. His plane had crashed, and, on earth, he was on the operating table close to death. In heaven, he was surrounded by hundreds of thousands of departed souls watching his case at a celestial court, seeking permission to be allowed to live because he had found love.

It didn't cure me of grief, but imagining I had a band of invisible angels trying to help me process what had happened, well… that helped.

Chapter Six
DAN

Mum kept pushing to do stuff and I didn't get it. Was that what you did when someone died? When my grandparents died, Mum and Dad didn't keep visiting places. I thought it was all too soon, all of it, but still, I didn't want Mum going on her own.

Everyone was brilliant, but I didn't know what to say to them. I didn't know how to respond.

I knew Mum was trying to be strong, but I saw her when she was on her own, when she thought no one was around, that no one could see her.

I saw her.

I saw the tears welling up. I'd see her pop outside every so often with the excuse of needing some air and then she'd come back more composed.

At home, she did the same. She never got upset in front of me. It was always in her bedroom, or she'd make the excuse of going somewhere to get something.

When that happened, I got angry with Dad for leaving us.

Not just angry, bloody incensed. Then I got angry with myself for feeling that way about Dad. It wasn't his fault, for fuck's sake.

Shit, I missed him so much. It was like a weight tugging inside my guts. A huge knot that never loosened and I wondered if it would ever go away. He was on my mind the whole time – whatever I was doing, I couldn't stop thinking about him, thinking about everything we did together.

Mum's tour of cafés mainly took us to the old part of Brighton where the arts cinema was. Everyone who met with us said how much they'd miss Dad. I didn't want to hear it. I just wanted to sit at home and shut the world out.

I hated the fact that people were getting on with their lives while we'd stopped. Compared to everyone else, we seemed to be up to our knees in quicksand with crowds of onlookers gawping at us as if we were in a zoo or something.

Even when I talked with the café owners, I wasn't engaging with them. Not really. I had to keep asking them to repeat stuff. All I kept thinking of was Dad.

In one of those cafés, The Java Jive, the owner insisted on sitting with us while we had a cappuccino. My head was somewhere else. I was staring down the street at the people milling about.

A memory slipped into my head. A fond one.

My parents were big people-watchers and they used to sit in this café and play a game. Mum named this bit of Brighton the bohemian quarter. Full of students and tourists. They loved it here. Lots of individual shops selling stuff you didn't get in the franchises up the road.

The students here wore what they wanted and some of it was a bit weird, even for me. My parents had a word they used when someone was approaching who amused them.

Security.

They'd sit opposite each other, Mum focussing on the street one way and Dad the other. If someone caught their eye, they'd simply say the word *security* to give the other a heads-up. I remember the first time they played it; I wondered what on earth it was all about, but it was funny. It meant you didn't purposely stare at someone. You just waited for that person to walk by. Then I'd see Mum and Dad lock eyes and one would either agree or disagree with the other's observation.

I loved that. I loved those things they did together. The trivial stuff.

I missed it too. I missed the fun stuff me and Dad did. Going to the football. Watching the cricket. Fishing. Helping him with the barbecue in the garden. It was all small stuff, but it wasn't there anymore. It would never be there.

And Mum was missing that, too. That's what I saw with her, when she thought no one was looking.

One day, when we'd come home from a café, I was standing on the landing by the door to her bedroom. It was open and she was sitting on the bed staring at some St Ives property details. It was a property they both loved. Dad had scribbled cartoons over it: a TV on the wall with the caption, 'Adam's TV' and a chair with, 'Your poetry chair' written underneath. And she was crying.

I just stared at the ceiling like an idiot. I knew if I went in, she'd brush the tears away and pretend it was nothing. Then the doorbell went, and I acted as if I'd just come out of my room.

'I'll get it,' I said and trotted down the stairs. It was Chloe.

She looked great in baggy dungarees, a pair of Converse trainers and her hair in a ponytail.

'I wondered if you fancied hanging out.'

I wanted to but I couldn't leave Mum like that. Chloe was great about it. She's so sweet.

'It's fine,' she said and offered to stay.

I didn't think it was a good idea. If Mum came down tearful, she'd be embarrassed, and I didn't want that. I gave her a half-hearted shrug.

'I'm sorry, Chlo.'

She was brilliant. She gave me a hug and left with a promise to call later to see how we were.

After, I went to the kitchen to make a drink and found a prescription for Mum on the table. I examined it closely. She never took pills or anything on prescription. I didn't know what they were at first, so I Googled it. Temazepam. Sleeping pills.

Shit! I stared at it for ages as if they'd give me an answer or something.

She hadn't said anything to me about this and I wasn't sure whether to mention it. I wondered whether to bring it up with Tom and Maggie but thought Mum might not want anyone to know.

Shit, I wished I knew what to do.

Chapter Seven
KERRY

When all you do is cry, the questions push in.
What is my life for? Why am I bothering anymore?
What is the purpose of me sitting here?
Why is my reason for living not clear?

I thought about suicide. The easiest way to do it. How to do it? The method that would not cause any pain. Sleeping pills would be an option if I stockpiled them. I hated pills but I did take one now and again when it all got too much. When the enormity of the accident and what I'd lost was so dominant that sleep wouldn't come. It was as if I was battling against the world. I was Humphrey Bogart dragging *The African Queen* through a narrow, swampy river with no clear end.

But I wasn't brave, and I always thought it took a brave person to take their own life. It went against every instinct. A living thing would always fight to the end to live.

If I was honest, it was just a thought. I knew I wouldn't resort to that. I had Dan to think about and I couldn't do that to him. The last thing he needed was a suicidal mum.

It's just that I didn't see a future. All I saw was a void: a bleak, desolate wasteland and me standing in the centre of it with absolutely no road out.

Chapter Eight
KERRY

Something shifted, the raw emotion changed,
The extreme hurt has been rearranged.
I plan my day ahead, but there's a constant echo in my head.
What will I do today? Adam. Adam. Adam.
The mantra repeating. Adam. Adam. Adam.
A chuckle with friends. Adam. Adam. Adam.
Whatever I'm doing. Adam. Adam. Adam.

A few weeks after Adam died, the brutality of grief eased a little. The shock and desolation had faded from my eyes, but the time of year magnified the sadness. No matter which way I turned, I couldn't avoid it.

From every shop window, along every street and around every corner, Christmas waved its traditional red and green colours at me. Seasonal pop songs greeted me in each store, the Salvation Army welcomed me with carols in the square, children jumped on the spot as they edged closer to a visit with Santa in his sparkling grotto.

Christmas on the TV, Christmas at the cinema. Christmas

novels on the shelf. Christmas food on TV. Christmas decor in the magazines.

All of them hammered nails into my emotional coffin. The perfect Christmas for the perfect family in the perfect home. Happy children, happy parents, happy grandparents. Joy to the world.

I conjured up the image of James Stewart in the final scene of *It's a Wonderful Life*; his wife, children and neighbours gathered around him, happy, smiling, loved.

It had never dawned on me, prior to Adam's death, how Christmas must be for people on their own or having to face that first Noel without a loved one. In some respects, we'd been that perfect family. I had empathy for those who weren't so lucky, but I was in a bubble, embracing the traditions we'd built up over the years and detached from what I couldn't relate to.

Now I swam with those for whom Christmas would never be the same. I was among those who wanted nothing more than to strike it from the calendar, dismiss it from the world and move quickly on to January.

Early in December, a Sunday, I opted to stay home and avoid the season being shoved in my face. Instead, I decided to do something that would be poignant but also lift my spirits. Now that the initial impact of death had lessened, I was ready to do this.

Maggie had suggested a memory box for those things personal to Adam or sentimental to me about him and that's what I found myself making that afternoon. I'd discovered an intricately carved wooden box in amongst a ton of junk in a second-hand shop. I was sure the box was Swiss as it had an image of the Matterhorn on it and some German writing on the back. The wood was smooth and tactile. The box would slot onto the bookshelf so I could dip in and out of it easily.

Our lounge wasn't as large as the kitchen-diner, but it was still spacious, and the log burner filled it with a cosy warmth. Dan closed the curtains on the late afternoon darkness, and we enjoyed some tea and toasted crumpets, a go-to snack on a Sunday afternoon in winter. In a few minutes, Dan would discard the magazine he was reading and put the football on the TV, while I went on working on the memory box.

He so resembled Adam. The same way of sitting, the same dark brown hair, short at the sides but long on top so that it flopped over his forehead like Adam's did when I first met him. And why did men always have eyelashes to die for? I swear to God men had the thickest eyelashes and we women, who would give anything for that, had to buy a ton of mascara to compete.

I was putting various mementos of Adam into the memory box. When I'd sorted through his things, I'd found a school report that confirmed his hatred of studying languages. His French teacher had written, 'Adam rarely starts his work and, if he does, he rarely finishes it'.

Well, he was a good builder so boo sucks to that teacher. Adam had built this house, along with two others in the street, and he always went for quality.

On the new estate up the road from us around two hundred houses were completed within two years. It took that amount of time for Adam and his men to build three houses. Quality was always the key and he'd established a reputation in the area. Buy a house designed and constructed by Adam Simmonds and you knew you'd bought wisely.

I picked up various school certificates, membership cards, his passport. None of these I needed to keep but I couldn't throw them out. They were too personal. His *Dandy* and *Beano* comics from the 1960s were also staying and I'd arranged them in the bookcase. I'd taken two out, which I'd framed and hung on the wall to the side of the fireplace. They were fun, colourful front covers featuring Korky the Cat and Dennis the Menace.

The next item I picked up was a pair of joke thick-lens glasses with black frames. I put them on and nudged Dan. He half-smiled and went back to reading. His reaction clutched at my heart. I'd hoped he'd engage more with this, but he was reluctant to do so. Over the last couple of weeks, I'd asked if he was okay, and he assured me he was, but I didn't think he was being honest with me. I'd tentatively suggested grief counselling and he'd gawped at me as if I'd grown another head.

The next thing I added was the three-card magic trick. Adam used to do this trick with Dan years ago and Dan was always mesmerised by it.

'Dad always said you were his best audience.'

It was like pulling teeth, but I didn't push it. If I did, he'd put the barriers up. This was difficult. For both of us. I hadn't expected to confront this situation so early in his life. Or in my life. Adam and I had each lost our parents when we were around fifty years old. That's when you're supposed to lose a parent. You cope with that sort of thing better at fifty. You're prepared for it at that age.

'You can talk about him, Dan,' I eventually said.

He put the magazine down and sifted through the items but more in a dream than through any curiosity or desire.

I had to admit, my concern was deepening but I think that concern was more about me not being able to deal with the situation.

Chapter Nine
DAN

It was two days before Christmas, and I was in Tom and Maggie's dining room. Mum and Maggie were in the kitchen and Tom was by the cocktail cabinet preparing drinks. They lived in a bloody enormous house on the outskirts of Hove, just along from Brighton. It was one of those red-brick mansions built during the '20s or '30s, with lattice windows and a detached garage with a proper tiled roof. Dad did quite a lot of work for them, years ago, and that's how they'd become friends.

Mum always went on about what an odd friendship it was. Socially, they were at opposite ends of the scale, but they got on well and saw each other loads. Mum and Maggie often went shopping or lunched together and the four of them were always going off to the theatre or the cinema.

Maggie was also a fan of the old films, so I was well pleased that she managed to drag Mum to one last week at the arts cinema. *The Italian Job* with Michael Caine. Actually, I went to that one with them. It's a good film, and fun too. Nothing to get sad about.

Mum's go-to film this time of the year was normally *White Christmas* with Bing Crosby and Danny Kaye. She watched it every year on DVD but not this year. I knew why. I had to sit through it a few times when I was younger. It's so corny, although I admit it was festive, but I knew the ending would upset her, where the two couples get together and it's all happy ever after.

When she asked us to watch it again last year, me and Dad went out. Maggie and another friend came over and they had a 'girls' afternoon in, singing along to the film's tunes. Mum always said she was born at the wrong time. But I told her that if she had been, she wouldn't have met Dad or had me. She got all soppy with me when I said that.

When I was younger, Tom and Maggie were my pretend aunt and uncle and, because they acted so much older than Mum and Dad, they were like grandparents, too. I liked them a lot.

Mum and Dad didn't have any brothers or sisters and my grandparents died years ago, so it was good to have these two as honorary family members.

We've spent a lot of days and evenings in this room. It was a massive square room with an oval table in the middle, French polished. Even our fucking dining tables were polar opposites! Maggie's idea of Christmas matched the pictures you saw in those magazines you got in a solicitor's or a private consultant's office. Everything colour co-ordinated. Christmas place mats, Christmas napkins, a Christmas-themed centrepiece with sprigs of holly dotted about. I had to admit, I preferred our Christmas. It lived in the loft all year round and was a mixture of things collected over the years, some of it so old it was stuck together with Sellotape.

The advent calendar on the sideboard was open at number twenty-three. Even that wasn't from a supermarket. Well, not the supermarkets we shopped in. Christmas was generally delivered to Maggie and Tom by Harrods or Fortnum and Mason. And they didn't have only one Christmas tree, either. They had one in this room and one in the lounge, both colour co-ordinated, with mock presents under each one. I think the trees arrived fully decorated.

We hadn't put a tree up, but Mum put a few Christmas ornaments out. I'd offered to decorate the tree, but she didn't feel it was right to get it out. I must confess, I was pleased she'd said that. Tom and Maggie invited us for Christmas dinner and New Year's Eve, just the four of us. It would be quiet, and they promised to keep things low-key and to treat it as a normal day. We'd been over here a lot recently. I think they were trying to shield us from Christmas. I knew they meant well but it was difficult to forget the season when you were surrounded with it.

Tom came across and handed me a beer. 'How are you, Dan? Honestly.'

I shrugged. 'Okay, thanks.'

Honestly, I didn't know how I was. I felt as if I was suspended in some sort of limbo existence. Just hanging there. Not moving forward and not moving back.

He put a hand on my back. 'If you ever need to talk. Maggie and I… well, we think you're coping admirably. Your mother, too.'

All I could manage was a nod of gratitude. He meant well but that show of sympathy, I didn't want it. If he talked about Dad, I'd be fighting an emotion I didn't want to have. Not with Tom. Not with anyone. I was glad to see the door open and Mum come in with Maggie. There was someone else too. I wondered who the fifth place at the table was for.

Maggie introduced me. 'Dan, this is Colin. He lives a few doors down.'

He reminded me of a teacher from a 1970's film. Unfashionable glasses, a tweed jacket and a bloody awful tie with pictures of Santa Claus on it.

Mum checked the table to see where Maggie had put our name cards. Fucking name cards. There were only five of us. They'd probably been delivered with the Christmas order.

Colin was next to Mum. I'd been put next to Maggie opposite them. Tom took his place at the head of the table.

'I'll let Gervaise know we're ready,' Maggie said.

Gervaise worked for a local restaurant and hired himself out as a chef for private functions. All the time I'd known Maggie and Tom I still didn't know if they could cook. She always got 'the caterers' in when they had guests, even if it was a buffet.

I remember one of the first times they came to us for dinner. Mum had cooked this amazing roast dinner and Maggie was astounded and kept asking insane questions. How did you do that? Where did you get this? It was just a beef joint with the trimmings. We all laughed about it after they'd gone.

I was taking the piss, but they'd been amazing since Dad died and I loved that they were there for me and Mum.

Chapter Ten
KERRY

Solo. One. Alone.
Sleeping on my own.
Will that ever change?
Life as a single seems so strange.

I knew, as soon as he was introduced to Colin, that Dan would baulk a little. Like a lot of people, especially youngsters, he formed an impression based on appearance, what people wore. I couldn't deny that I did that, too. I mean, that's basically what Adam and I did all the time with our people-watching. But, in reality, we did look beyond appearances.

Colin, apparently, was a retired dentist who collected novelty ties. I didn't even know that was a thing. He had over two hundred of them. I remembered those ties being all the rage a few years ago like Kinder toys and Beanie Babies and now all these things were either on the skip or being sold on eBay.

I pressed my lips together when I saw Dan's face during the introductions. He almost reeled with astonishment. He took after Adam in the fashion stakes. Tonight, he'd opted for retro 501s he'd found in a vintage shop and a classy turquoise open-necked shirt. He did own a tie, but he wouldn't have given an inch of room to the kind of tie Colin had around his neck.

Collectors sometimes get labelled as being geeks and Colin could be said to be one. Out in the kitchen I'd been given the low-down about the collection and did my best to feign interest, though I had to stifle a yawn now and then. Oh God, I hope he didn't start talking to Dan about them.

Maggie saved us from that with a barrage of questions. What did we want to drink? Were we okay to eat now? Could we take our seats at the table because dinner was being served? I was seated next to Colin with Maggie and Dan opposite me. Tom placed a bottle of red and white wine on the table, and we helped ourselves. Dan stuck to the beer he'd been given.

Gervaise provided us with a gastronomic delight: a beautiful leg of lamb with plenty of rosemary and all the trimmings. The evening was relaxed and convivial; we chatted about holiday destinations, weather, films, TV, books. I didn't know if anyone was deliberately steering the conversation to general topics, but it was good to be involved in discussions that distracted me from my thoughts. Even Dan was enjoying himself. He'd been subdued, of course, but he insisted he was fine; that I wasn't to worry.

I did worry, though. I'd discussed it with Maggie and Tom a few days ago when I popped in for coffee. Tom said he'd keep an eye on him and had arranged to meet up with Dan for a pub lunch after Christmas. Perhaps that would help. Two men together was probably better than a mother and son.

As the drinks flowed and we finished our crème brûlée desserts, Colin edged his chair a little closer to me.

'Of course,' he said, in the middle of giving us a lecture about steam trains, 'the restoration railway societies can't afford coal now. It's increased in cost by about thirty per cent. Ridiculous. Soon, they won't be able to afford to run these trains. A great shame, don't you think?'

I flinched as he snaked an arm around the back of my chair. Opposite, Dan's eyes took on a sudden hardness. I shifted my chair so that Colin couldn't engage with me like that. He was a nice guy, but I didn't want that sort of attention. Once I'd moved, Dan relaxed. I allowed myself a small smile. How lovely that he was so protective of me.

After dinner, we went through to the lounge where the fire spat out a warm welcome. The lights on the tree twinkled and it felt homely. What a shame Adam wasn't here. Being in such a snug environment gave me a sudden twinge of loss and I quickly nudged those thoughts to one side.

Maggie suggested Colin sit with me on the sofa. Again, Dan stiffened, and I managed to insist that Dan join me.

I thought I was the only one who'd noticed how Maggie was trying to matchmake. I was getting on well with Colin but then, I tried to get on with everyone. I wasn't paying him any special attention, just being sociable. However, I was in no mood to be paired off with anyone. If James Bond had walked in, in the guise of Sean Connery, I still wouldn't have been interested. Not in a romantic way. Perhaps I was being over-sensitive. Perhaps Maggie wasn't trying to be a matchmaker at all but it's certainly how it felt.

Much later, in the kitchen, Tom ordered a taxi to take me and Dan home.

'Kerry, you know we're here for you every day. Christmas will be difficult for you and if you want to stay over for the week, you're most welcome to. New Year too.'

I kissed him on the cheek. 'I know, Tom, and I appreciate the offer, but we like being at home. We'll come for dinner, of course, but...'

'The beds are made up if you change your mind.'

He rubbed the back of his neck as if searching for the right words. 'Have you thought about what you're going to do? I mean, your plans?' He winced. 'I'm sorry, my dear, I shouldn't be asking. It's far too soon to be thinking ahead like that. I was just curious, that's all.'

'It's fine. Really. And I have thought about it, yes. I think a big part of me still wants to move to St Ives. I don't want to spend the rest of my life here. Dan has to be settled before I do anything. Once he's at uni, I can think about my own plans.'

Dan had put his life on hold since Adam had died. He hadn't even applied to Southampton so nothing would happen until next year and, in a year, we might be in a different place emotionally.

'We'll miss you if you do go but, of course, Maggie will probably get me to buy a holiday home down there, so you won't get rid of us that easily.'

'You know I don't want rid of you. You are the two people I will miss more than anything and, if I do move, I want you to come and stay as often and as long as you want to.'

A few minutes later, Colin shrugged his overcoat on and said his goodbyes to Tom and Maggie. He asked me to go to the hall with him. I followed him out about a minute later. Dan was already there when I arrived, and I sensed an atmosphere. They hadn't had a lot to say to each other over dinner and there was an awkwardness about the pair of them now. I linked arms with Dan and was enthusiastically jolly with my question to compensate for the uneasiness.

'Everything all right?'

Two hesitant nods.

Colin spoke directly to me. 'There's an antique toy fair at the Brighton Centre next Sunday morning, I wondered if you fancied coming with me.'

Dan's grip on my arm was noticeably tighter.

Keeping my tone overly jolly, I answered, 'Thanks, Colin, but not at the moment.'

The grip loosened. Colin gave a tentative response. 'Okay, well, if you fancy a coffee some time, let me know.'

Another awkward silence. I didn't want coffee with him. I wanted coffee with Adam. I knew he was being kind, but it sounded as if he was asking me on a date and I didn't want that.

Colin's eyes darted everywhere. I felt bad. I should have filled that gap with some trivial comment. Dan certainly wasn't going to.

'Okay,' said Colin, overcompensating himself now. 'Perhaps when you're feeling up for it. Hope you're able to enjoy Christmas Day. I know it'll be difficult for you.'

Bless him. He was a bit of a geek but harmless. As soon as the door shut, Dan stared at me.

'You're not gonna go out with him, are you?'

'No! I'm not going out with anyone.'

The relief on his face spoke volumes. I drew him close and put my arms around him. I sometimes forgot how young he was.

I found Maggie in the lounge. I had my coat on, ready to leave.

'Maggie, you and Tom are wonderful friends, but don't ever do that again.'

She feigned ignorance but couldn't keep it up for long under my scrutiny. She grimaced. 'Oh, I'm sorry. I thought it might be nice for you…'

We didn't have to say anything else. We were back on an even keel. She wouldn't try that again and she knew, deep down, that it was my decision and my decision alone as to when, and indeed *if*, I ever began a new relationship.

Chapter Eleven
KERRY

Why can't I cry?
I want to cry, to mourn, to grieve
The tears are around but they don't want to leave
I feel guilty for adjusting to life on my own
I want you here, I want you here in our home.

One day, I lay on the bed staring at the ceiling. Motionless. Still. Silent. I was no longer sobbing my heart out every second of the day, but neither was I in kilter with the everyday world. Life raced on for those around me but my journey, at best, was taking place in slow motion and I didn't have a clue about how to pick up speed.

The long nights of winter had endlessly drifted into one another. Dan and I had lived from day to day, sometimes aimlessly, sometimes with some effort but never with any real purpose.

The arrival of spring, however, injected some resolve in us. Nature had exploded and colour returned. In neighbouring gardens, tulips, bluebells and daffodils emerged from their hibernation. The magnolia tree in the corner of our plot had those soft, velvety buds that were getting ready to burst open any day now. And in the mornings, the first sounds to reach me were the joyous chirps of birds chorusing their greeting across the rooftops.

The sky was clear but also deceiving. Through the window, it looked like a hot summer's day. In reality, it remained cold.

My gardening outfit was a pair of scruffy jeans and one of Adam's jumpers that he used to wear when doing DIY. I could still smell him in the fibres of the wool, and I hoped that never went away. I'd kept his aftershave in the bathroom cupboard and every so often, I'd spray a little into the air, to inhale the memory of him.

Today, I wanted to tackle a stubborn shrub in the garden that I'd never liked. At the back of my mind, I was considering our plans to retire to St Ives, and I was thinking it was best to keep the house and garden up to scratch in case I did decide to sell. With Dan deciding to go to university later in the year, I'd long since decided I didn't want to be in this house without Adam. Returning home every day was becoming increasingly difficult. It was as if the house itself was in mourning and couldn't function without the man who built it.

I opened the kitchen door to the garden. The hedges round the perimeter were ready to be cut back and Dan had offered to do that for me. Together, we were determined to make this day a productive one.

Dan had put some post on the dresser and a blue envelope caught my eye. No prizes for guessing who this was from. Here was I thinking about St Ives and bingo – a letter postmarked St Ives. Serendipity. I opened it and extracted a familiar, decorative card. On the front was a drawing of a whitewashed house with olde worlde charm. Above the sketch was an elaborate and artistic piece of calligraphy telling me this was from The Feather Duck Bed and Breakfast and providing contact details. On the back, a handwritten note:

We know it'll be difficult, but we'd love you to come and stay. Suzie and Greg. xx

Closing my eyes, I plummeted back to where I didn't want to be. Back on that boat, searching the sea, calling his name, calling for Adam and feeling the strength drain out of me.

The doorbell distracted me from that memory, and I made my way into the hall. Dan was halfway down the stairs, dressed for the garden tasks ahead.

As I opened the door, my peripheral vision revealed that Dan was on the alert.

It was Colin. He'd dressed a little more fashionably than he had at Christmas, but I still couldn't imagine him being anything other than an acquaintance. Yes, an acquaintance. Not even a friend. We didn't have much in common and he simply didn't float my boat, for want of a better phrase. He'd dropped by once before, but we weren't in, and he'd left a note with his telephone number.

I hadn't rung. Now I felt bad for not doing so, though you'd have thought he might have taken the hint.

'Hello, Kerry, I was just passing. I wondered if you'd like to go for a coffee…' he flipped the palms of his hands up, 'not necessarily now.'

'No, she wouldn't,' Dan responded, or rather mumbled. I'm not sure that Colin heard but I certainly did. I glared at

Dan. I knew how he felt about Colin but there was no need to be so rude. He had the grace to look embarrassed. I turned my attention back to Colin.

'I'm sorry, Colin, I can't. Dan and I are getting stuck into the garden, and I honestly don't want to make plans at the moment. Perhaps later in the year. Do you mind?'

Colin shuffled his feet. I'd put him off. I'd brushed him aside. That's how it had come out and that's how he'd taken it. All the same, I didn't want men pestering me for coffee and thinking that my grief had disappeared after a few months. It hadn't. I thought it did disappear once, just for a few hours, but it rose up again and dug its claws in.

Colin cleared his throat. 'Okay. Take care, then. Bye.'

I felt dreadful for letting him down, but I didn't want him to get the wrong idea, either.

Closing the door, I said, 'Dan, I know you don't like him, but he's just being kind.'

'Mum, he's a dick. He's not your type, anyway.'

I tried to remain stern, I did, but I couldn't help but chuckle at the description.

Colin wasn't the only man to come calling at my door. I had a neighbour, five doors down, who decided that he would like to ask me out. His name was Lee, and he was, admittedly, good looking and had a vibrant personality. However, with both Colin and Lee, I found myself comparing them with Adam. Everything from looks, manner, body language and personality were scrutinised and neither lived up to Adam. I wasn't interested and, as gracefully as I could, I made it clear to both of them that I was not on the dating scene.

An hour later, I was becoming more and more frustrated with the shrub. What I'd thought would be a ten-minute job was turning into a nightmare. Every effort to get the roots out foiled me and I began yelling at it as if it had a brain.

'You're too bloody stubborn for your own good. It's no use you hanging on here, you're coming out and that's the end of it.'

I wiped the sweat from my brow and stood up straight, feeling the muscles in my back burn.

The yelling-at-the shrub thing was funny to begin with, but defeat and anger lurked beneath the humour. As my attempts continued to fail, the maelstrom swirled and my tears came to the surface. The fun had turned to despair.

Suddenly, it was as if nothing was going right in my life. I couldn't even dig out a poxy shrub, for God's sake. I dropped to the pebbles and stifled a sob. I tried to stifle it because I didn't want Dan seeing me like this.

Bless him, he came over in a second and sat down next to me. 'Leave it, Mum, I'll have a go at it. You do the hedge.'

We stared at its roots for a while, half in the ground, half sticking up like a mad stick insect. It was a symbol of my life at the moment. One foot stuck in a swamp, the other foot out, unable to move either way.

'Shall I put the kettle on?' Dan asked.

Before I had a chance to change my mind, I blurted out, 'I'm going to visit Suzie and Greg.'

His mouth fell open. 'What! Mum, I'm not... I mean, don't you think...'

'It's never going to be a good time, Dan.'

I could see he wasn't happy about it, but he didn't protest.

'I'm going to call Suzie and Greg now before I change

my mind. I'll make the tea.' I quickly got to my feet to avoid further discussion and, on the way to the kitchen, shouted back, 'Did you send your application off to Southampton?'

'Uh… huh.'

At the kitchen window I picked up the phone and watched as Dan began pulling at the shrub. I heard him swear as he yanked at the roots, the exact words coming out of his mouth that Adam would have used.

'Fucking come out, you fucking bastard.'

Tears pricked my eyes as Suzie answered the phone.

Chapter Twelve
DAN

We were on the concourse of Brighton railway station, and I still wasn't convinced that Mum should be going to St Ives. Since Dad died, she'd gone headlong into confronting all the things she knew would upset her.

Why didn't she just wait?

And St Ives? Fuck. We did talk about it, but she told me she needed to do it. I couldn't tell her she couldn't, could I? I thought it would... shit, I mean, it would just open everything up again.

I've got closer to Tom over the last few months. We started going for a beer every so often and he said that everyone dealt with grief differently, that you had to find your own way of dealing with it. Well, my way wasn't to force myself into doing stuff I didn't need to do.

This trip nagged at me from the day Mum said she wanted to go. Where we live, I'd got my head around the reason for her visiting cafés and restaurants and stuff like that. But St Ives was where it all actually happened.

I ended up texting Greg. It was the first time me and Mum had been separated since Dad died. She was worried I'd fall apart but I was worried *she* would, especially down there. He texted straight back and told me not to worry, that they'd look after her. I knew they would, but I still didn't feel comfortable about it.

Eventually, I decided I'd go down later in the week, while she was there, for the weekend. I liked Greg and Suzie; they were cool, and it'd be good to hang out with them and make sure Mum was okay.

She seemed fine now, but I thought she was putting on a brave face.

'I'll call you when I arrive,' she said, 'and you must call me.'

'I'll be down in a few days.'

'I know, but this is our first time apart since… I worry.'

'Well don't. Mum, I'll be fine.'

She pulled me in, and we hugged. I held her a little longer than I normally would.

'You know where I am,' she said, as she prepared to go through the barrier 'Day or night. I love you lots.'

'Love you, too.'

I wouldn't normally, but this time I waited until the train moved off before leaving the station.

ACT TWO

CORNWALL,
SOUTH-WEST ENGLAND
MAY 2021

Chapter Thirteen
KERRY

*Grief is like the tide; it ebbs and flows
but sometimes it crashes in so hard, it causes my spirit
to sink low.*

At Paddington, I boarded the Great Western Railway service to Penzance in Cornwall, as far west as any train would go. My only change would be at St Erth, the last station before that, where I would transfer to the St Ives line.

I'd booked first class because it was a long journey and, in contrast to our scrimp-and-save days of years ago, I could afford it now, especially with a senior railcard. I wanted some comfort, and it was nice to have that extra bit of room and a regular drinks and snacks service. There weren't that many people in my carriage, perhaps half a dozen, so the atmosphere was relaxed and quiet. There were two men on the other side of the aisle perusing a document.

My overactive imagination decided they were scheming together. Like in Hitchcock's *Strangers on a Train* where each man agrees to kill the other man's wife.

Kerry, stop it!

Train travel has always instilled in me an enormous sense of nostalgia and pleasure, speeding through towns and countryside, watching the world whizz by, not having to worry about driving, traffic, roadworks or diversions. I was fortunate that I rarely encountered delays so, all in all, this mode of transport was a delight, particularly in first class.

I pulled out my John Cooper Clarke poetry book and some sandwiches from my rucksack. I'd booked a single seat. I was normally okay socialising with other passengers, but I wanted the option to remain in my bubble because I didn't know how I was going to feel, especially as I got closer to St Ives.

Leaving Dan at the station had been a wrench. He'd moved forward a little, emotionally. We both had but, to my mind, he was holding too much in and that wasn't healthy. Tom and Dan had recently gone for the occasional drink, which heartened me. He'd hinted that Dan confided in him at times and that I wasn't to worry.

'Dan is dealing with it in his own way, Kerry,' he'd said. 'Not everyone can confront things the way you do. Let him do it in his own time. He's a sensible lad and he knows he can talk to me at any time.'

To me, that didn't sound as if Dan was giving much away, probably worried that it would get back to me. It was clear he'd donned the mantle of man of the house, even though I'd told him it was unnecessary. It was sweet and thoughtful, but he didn't need that responsibility at that stage of his life. Not when there was no need.

I wondered if he opened up to Chloe. She was the same age, they got on well and with her dad in a wheelchair, she had empathy about how life events could impact people. I hadn't spoken to Chloe about Dan and perhaps I should. I almost headbutted the window. If Dan found out I'd talked to Chloe… well that didn't bear thinking about. Mentally, I screwed that thought up and threw it in the bin.

The bookmark in my poetry book was a photo of me and Adam at The Greasy Spoon. I fondly disappeared into a daydream, one that took me back to the last time we'd visited.

The Greasy Spoon was located in a quieter part of St Ives, overlooking Polperrion Bay, one of the smaller beaches. The café's name told you everything. The tiny kitchen was probably not that clean although I suppose it must have passed basic hygiene rules. The veranda was wooden, the floor uneven with some planks that needed replacing and the paintwork was flaking badly. The place screamed out for a complete overhaul, but we couldn't remember it being anything other than rundown, almost dilapidated. The plus side was, that when you sat down for breakfast, the meal delivered was hearty and set you up for the day.

Adam and I always ordered the full English and a mug of tea. During that last visit, we took with us the property pages and a few details of houses and apartments that had taken our fancy. Adam sketched cartoons on them to help us visualise where our furniture could go: TV there, radio there, table here. He practically moved us into every house we had details of.

We'd been visiting St Ives for the last thirty-five years and had always promised ourselves that we would escape the hustle and bustle of Brighton and enjoy retirement in this quaint little seaside town. The view we had from the veranda that day just cemented those feelings as we surveyed the turquoise sea, golden sands and rocky cliffs, all giving us a sense of calm and tranquillity.

'Hot drink?' The voice of the train's catering manager brought me out of my musing. I ordered a coffee from the trolley and made a start on one of my sandwiches.

In between eating, drinking and reading my book, the stations sped by: Reading, Taunton, Exeter, Newton Abbot, Totnes, Plymouth. Pulling out of Plymouth, I settled back to wait for the view that would shortly greet me. The train slowed to a snail's pace to cross Brunel's grand Tamar Bridge which crossed the wide River Tamar. When we reached the other side, I would wait until I saw the sign announcing my arrival into the county of Cornwall before returning to my book.

On the bridge, my nose to the window, I gazed down at the boats below and very quickly pulled my head back and closed my eyes. Shit. I'd forgotten it was so high. I didn't do heights. To get over that, I focussed on the horizon where a Navy frigate was moored. Another memory came to mind.

A few months before Adam died, he and Dan had gone to some sandstone rocks in the middle of the Sussex countryside to go abseiling. I went along with them to take some photos and we were going to have a picnic afterwards. While they were preparing to leap off cliffs, I was questioning where best to position my chair to enjoy the scenery and jot down some poetry.

I remember Adam calling to me. 'Come on, Kerry, it's not that high.'

I took my notebook out. He came over and jokingly tried to pull me toward the edge. I snatched my arm back.

'Don't you dare.'

'Come on, Mum. It's perfectly safe. You can be between us.'

'You can scribble your poetry anywhere,' Adam said.

'Yes, funnily enough, I thought I'd do it here. On the flat. With no sudden drops.'

'Take the risk—'

I completed the sentence before he could. 'Even if it scares the shit out of me. Adam, you're so predictable.'

We all laughed, and I ordered them to stand with the instructor for the obligatory photo before they began their descent.

I came out of my memory with a chuckle. Abseiling. How on earth could someone just walk down the side of a cliff? My knees turned to jelly just thinking about it. I returned to my book and requested a fresh cup of coffee.

Before I knew it, we'd pulled into St Erth, from which the small branch line ran to St Ives. The train was waiting for us. On the platform, my stomach tensed, and I repeated a few affirmations. This was it. No turning back. Get on and think of good things.

I chose a seat on the right-hand side. This short, fifteen-minute trip was advertised as one of the most beautiful train journeys in the world. It took passengers from the tidal lagoon at Lelant, to a view of the Hayle estuary where the sands of the Gwithian Towans stretched into infinity. In the distance, out of the cobalt blue sea, the brilliant white Godrevy lighthouse stood on a rocky outcrop. I heard my fellow passengers murmuring their appreciation. It was always the same on this trip. It made such an impact on the senses.

I thought I was doing okay, really, I did. My affirmations were working. The train was busy, and I had a marvellous distraction. Sitting immediately in front of me was a handsome cockapoo and his soft brown eyes had made me fall in love with him. I happily made a fuss of him and thought this would see me through to St Ives.

But he and his owners got off one stop before, at Carbis Bay.

As we rounded the bend, St Ives came into view. My throat tightened.

I was there. The speedboat raced toward me; the bang shattered the air. The girl was thrown clear, and I stared in horror as the front end of their boat reared up.

The sudden darkness of a short tunnel brought me back. My chest felt tight, and I had a sudden urge to crawl under the seat and hide. I could quite happily have collapsed on the floor of that train and sobbed my heart out. My vision blurred. I wiped my eyes and stared hard at nothing in particular. *Focus on something else. Focus on something else.* I prayed to a God I wasn't sure I believed in to give me strength. *Please don't let me break down in front of strangers.* I prayed that no one had seen my eyes brimming because if anyone asked me if I was okay, I wouldn't be able to stop this emotion from bursting free. A number of people began preparing to get off and I sat back to gather myself.

Fortunately, I made it off the platform and down to the taxi rank. In my head, a movie director had yelled 'cut' and that awful scene in the carriage was a wrap, in the can, never to be repeated.

It was a glorious day and, although it was out of season, there were quite a few tourists milling about and my people-watching skills diverted me from earlier thoughts. The traffic, as always, was busy and I wondered why they still allowed cars to drive through the town. It was inevitable that the taxi would get stuck in a queue, and it did. I was in no rush, though, and continued to enjoy the sights.

St Ives was originally a fishing cove. The main street, Fore Street, running parallel with this one, was now full of unique, independent shops you didn't see anywhere else. Window displays invited me to make the most of my holiday and explore what was on offer.

A poster caught my eye, promoting a writing, music and poetry festival.

And it was running this month!

I hadn't even thought to check if anything was on. Fantastic. That would keep me occupied. Suzie and Greg were sure to have some programmes for it at the B&B.

As we inched our way along, my attention was drawn to an older man. I say older – he was probably the same age as me and he was deep in conversation with someone. In his arms were two of the cutest miniature poodles I think I'd ever seen. One black, one white.

I couldn't deny he was handsome but there was something else about him. His stance? His clothes? I wasn't sure to begin with but decided it was his clothes. Everyone wore shorts and tee shirts and, at the risk of sounding like a terrible snob, I thought most tourists defaulted to the cheaper brands. Thin cottons that lost their shape and colour after the first wash.

This man was in shorts and a shirt but everything about him screamed quality. I'm sure the clothes were tailored. He stood around six foot, maybe a little less, greying at the temples. He had a Continental air about him and an old-fashioned elegance. I found myself taking every bit of him in and wondered if I'd met him before. I had no idea why I would think that. He was good looking for a man of his age. By that, I mean he didn't have the obligatory belly that many men developed over the years.

I think I'd remember if I'd been introduced to him.

The taxi resumed its journey and just a few minutes later we climbed Boscawen Hill and pulled up outside The Feather Duck. I quietly exhaled with a rare feeling of joy. After more than seven hours of travelling, I'd arrived.

While the driver retrieved my bag from the boot, I gazed at the hanging baskets, vibrant against the brilliant white wall. A silhouette was painted at the base of the building depicting a family of ducks waddling. It had always amused me and still did. The family of ducks continued around the corner and invariably caused passing children great delight.

The duck theme continued inside. Suzie had loved the Beatrix Potter books as a child and had brought that love of ducks and geese into her business, hence 'The Feather Duck'. The themed decor, however, was subtle and in excellent taste.

The reception area was modern, with works of art and ornaments by local artists. The wooden floor was made of beech and a winding staircase led up to the bedrooms, four in total, all en suites. When Greg and Suzie had taken over this place, it had had seven rooms but, like Adam and his building visions, they opted for quality over quantity. They charged extra but that ensured they welcomed the clientele they wanted.

Every room had a different colour scheme, normally pastel and, like the reception, tastefully executed with little extras that enhanced your experience, such as individual soaps, a selection of teas and coffees and a welcome half-bottle of Prosecco.

While I was waiting at the counter, I spotted a business card advertising Rico's Bar. Must be new. I'd not heard of it and wondered where it was. I thought the owners had missed a trick. They should have called it Rick's, like in *Casablanca*. That said, most people probably wouldn't have made the connection. Harry's Bar would have been better. All the major cities around the world had a Harry's Bar and these were generally listed in the tourist guides. I dragged myself out my daydream before it formed into an entire screenplay with a cast that would include Frank Sinatra.

Alongside the business card was an old-fashioned bell to attract attention. Suzie would be around somewhere, so I gently tapped it and its trill rang out.

Just a few seconds later Suzie appeared at the top of the stairs.

Only one word described Suzie. Hippyish. She reminded me of an extra in the classic '60's film, *Blow Up*. I could imagine David Hemmings capturing images of her as an iconic model. She came from London and, if she'd been old enough, I'm sure she would have been one of the 'in-crowd' flitting up and down Carnaby Street and hanging out with The Beatles.

She suited the bohemian lifestyle that used to thrive in St Ives in the sixties. They had their own version of the

Swinging Sixties when Donovan and the like used to hang out at the harbour with his fellow folkies and beatniks.

Suzie was forty-two years old, with long, flowing hair and flowing outfits. She even seemed to flow down the stairs.

When she reached the bottom, she opened her arms wide. 'Kerry.'

The welcome caused me to dissolve into tears. I'd held them back since getting on the train at St Erth. As her arms enveloped me, I detected a hint of flowers.

'Oh, Kerry, my darling.'

I couldn't speak. I allowed myself to be loved and held.

Greg came through from the dining room. He was a gentle, bearded Cornish giant, a few years younger than Suzie, dressed in cargo shorts, tee shirt and sandals. His unruly, thick hair was bleached by the sun. Seeing us, he didn't need to say anything. He'd assessed the situation and gathered us in his arms.

'Hello, my lovely,' he said in his strong Cornish accent. We stayed in this embrace for some time.

Drawing back, the next thing he said caused me to chuckle back my tears. 'Would a large gin and tonic help? Light on the tonic?'

Chapter Fourteen
KERRY

Occasionally, emotions cause me to stumble
If I put it right, I hope not to tumble any more...
Any more than I have to.

The notion of a gin and tonic on the patio meant the formalities of checking in and unpacking were postponed. My bags were stored in a little office, and we headed through the double doors to enjoy the weather and shake off the effects of the long train ride. I'd booked a three-week stay here and I already knew I'd made the correct decision. Yes, I'd be confronting my most painful memories, but I had Suzie and Greg and The Feather Duck to support me.

The inside of the bed and breakfast was a haven, but the patio was an exotic oasis. It was the perfect place in which to chill out. The quality insisted upon inside the main building extended to the patio. Suzie had opted for expensive rattan furniture, a double lounger, a double swing chair and a selection of giant candles and antique-style lanterns. In the evening, the place was transformed into a magic grotto, especially when the little fairy lights that ran the length of the terrace were switched on.

Potted plants and cushions added colour to the area, and beyond the surrounding wall there were far-reaching views across the bay. The ocean twinkled in the early evening sun.

Suzie had also invested in a 1930's drinks trolley. I remember her telling me about this during one of our phone calls. Greg had restored it, and it now housed a good selection of spirits and mixers.

We made ourselves comfortable with our drinks and toasted my arrival.

'Darling, I've put you in the room you always had with Adam. Are you all right with that? I can always change it. We don't have anyone else staying while you're here.'

'Really?'

'No, lovely,' said Greg. 'When you said you were coming, we wanted it to be private. We weren't sure how you'd feel about other people being here, so the only other guest will be Dan when he arrives.'

This random act of kindness almost set me off again. How lovely of them to think of that. And generous, too.

'Right, my lovely,' said Greg, 'what you got planned?'

'Well, I see there's a writing festival on so I'm signing up for some poetry talks, if there are any. But it would have been our anniversary on the 26th. Will you celebrate with me?'

'Try and stop us,' said Suzie. 'Shall we do it here, just the three of us? Will Dan still be here?'

'Unfortunately not. He'll just be down for this coming weekend. And The Greasy Spoon is a must.'

I couldn't miss the furtive look between the pair of them. It transmitted a clear message, and not a good one.

'What? What's the matter?'

'Oh, darling, it closed down.'

A knot tightened in my stomach. My tears welled. I immediately thought that the whole trip was a mistake, that I shouldn't have come down, that everything was going to be shit. Nothing would be the same anymore. Suzie virtually leapt across to sit beside me and hold my hand.

'But that was *our* place,' I said. 'That was one of the reasons for coming down.'

'It's Rico's now,' said Greg.

I almost sneered at the name, as if the place had been turned into some seedy pornographic den.

Greg leaned forward. 'They've done it out right nice and Rico and Tina are proper friendly and it's not full of tourists. They wanted something more for the locals.'

'They reserve tables for the locals,' added Suzie. 'That was Tina's idea. She was born here and wants to do her bit for the community. And Rico's dad moved over last year and is teaching Greg Italian.'

I stared at Greg. 'Italian?'

'I'm going to Italy with the senior rugby team later in the year, so I thought I'd learn a bit.'

I gritted my teeth. I hadn't expected this, but I had to confront it. 'Right. Well, the best thing for me to do is go there. Now. Get it over with.'

'We'll go with you,' Suzie said.

'No.'

'Oh, darling, you can't go on your own.'

'Suzie, I have to do it. Just me.'

Greg picked up his mobile and punched in a number as I described how, over the past months, I'd made the effort to visit all of the places dear to me and Adam. 'I'll take a book. I'll be fine,' I said, to reassure them. 'Honestly, if I get upset, I'll check out some funny videos or something.'

I could see Suzie wasn't happy, but she accepted my decision, providing I contacted her if I had a sudden need for company.

Greg reached the person he was trying to phone. 'Rico? Greg. You got a table free, mate? If so, can you hold one?'

My next revelation was difficult to divulge to Suzie. I jutted my chin toward the sea. 'I also want to…'

When I'd told her, she turned and faced me full on, reached for my other hand and locked eyes with me. 'Are you absolutely sure?'

'I have to do this, Suzie. It's the reason I'm here.'

None of this sat well with her but she was very good about it and repeated that she and Greg would be there for me if I needed support.

'Just pick up the phone. Wherever we are, one of us will be there.'

Greg, meanwhile, had given me a thumbs up as he gave Rico my name. 'She'll be down in about fifteen minutes.'

I put my jacket on and picked up my rucksack.

Greg got up with me. 'I'll take your bags upstairs, lovely.'

'Darling,' added Suzie, 'I mean it! Please call if it all gets too much.'

The challenge of visiting Rico's and the kindness shown to me by Suzie and Greg was overwhelming; so much so that I completely forgot my phone and left my poetry book on the table.

Chapter Fifteen
KERRY

Life is a memory of things that used to be
A great big tapestry weaving stories I've lived.

St Ives was a pretty little town. Quintessentially Cornish. Quaint, traditional, timeless. As I strolled around the narrow, cobbled streets I drank in its ambience and reacquainted myself with the amusing road names: Salubrious Place, Virgin Street, Teetotal Street, The Digey. I smiled at the signpost directing me to The Island. It wasn't an island at all, just a small, rocky headland. The independent shops were a delight and made a nice change from the generic shopping areas that had sprung up around the country. If I was in one town centre, I was in them all – but here, the majority were local businesses selling clothing made within the county, bakeries selling huge cinnamon buns and scones made on the premises, restaurants and cafés serving local produce. It was an absolute joy to ramble about, examining what was on offer.

I tossed a few coins into the open guitar case of a busker before stopping by a side street, Piran's Lane. There, on the wall, was a sign fashioned out of driftwood advertising Rico's Bar, along with an arrow directing me down the alley. Part of me wanted to walk on but my doggedness took over. It was an unforeseen hurdle to get over and if I didn't do it, I'd beat myself up. I left the bustle of the main street behind me and walked along the quieter alley until I reached the end where it opened up to another of the many small beaches. Polperrion Beach.

There it was.

The former Greasy Spoon.

Now Rico's.

Every fibre of my being wanted to loathe Rico's but, instead, I felt uplifted.

The building had undergone a complete transformation. The flaking woodwork was now gleaming in bright, vivid colours and the veranda itself had been extended to the size of a double garage. (The Greasy Spoon's had been no bigger than a single.) The entrance to the kitchen and the tiny office next door had been redesigned and no doubt both of those areas had been renovated, too.

Around the veranda were concertina doors that, at the moment, were open wide. Fairy lights hung around the outside, and over the speakers I heard James Taylor singing about going to Carolina. The place was almost full. Some customers were playing dominoes and chess. Conversation was quiet and not intrusive.

I waited by the entrance. I could see a young couple, in their thirties by the look of it, by the kitchen door. They must be Rico and Tina. He looked Mediterranean with smooth olive skin, very dark hair. Handsome and slim. Tina was about the same height as him. She had a pixie haircut and was glowing with that healthy outdoor radiance. They wore cotton shorts and their polo shirts each had a tastefully embroidered Rico's Bar logo sewed onto them. Tina caught my eye and nudged Rico.

My anxiety, which had all but gone while I was taking this in, revived as he came toward me.

'Good evening,' he said, in an Italian accent.

'Ah, hello. I think Greg called you.'

'Oh yes, you are Kerry. Yes, come through. I 'ave a table for you. Best in the 'ouse.'

I followed him. I found his accent endearing. I was sure that the promise of the best seat in the house was guaranteed to everyone. I couldn't imagine a bad seat in the house. Everyone sitting here could drink in the sea view and the activities on the beach below.

I was given a table with a 'Reserved' notice on it. He removed it.

'*Prego*,' he said.

I draped my jacket over the back of the chair. It was a sturdy wooden chair with arms and a comfortable, deep cushion on it.

'What can I serve for you?' he asked.

'A one-shot cappuccino, please.'

'One-shot cappuccino. *Va bene.*'

He left. James Taylor finished singing about going to Carolina and was replaced by Dean Martin singing 'Sway'. I couldn't deny it, I was entranced by this little gem of a place and my upset over the demise of The Greasy Spoon was fading fast.

I searched my rucksack for my book and phone and found, instead, a sense of panic.

Shit.

I rummaged some more in the hope that I'd missed them. I hadn't.

Shit.

I still hadn't got to grips with sitting in a café on my own. I had to have a book, a notebook, a crossword. *Something*. Something to make it appear that I was perfectly at ease with life. With a book, I had the excuse of disappearing into my poetry. With the phone I could message or check Facebook. Without my phone, I couldn't even call Suzie. Shit, shit, shit. I couldn't leave. That would be embarrassing.

The menu solved the problem. I grabbed it and studied it thoroughly, as if I would be tested on it later. It looked very good. Nothing like The Greasy Spoon's, which was probably just as well otherwise I'd have made comparisons. This was a mixture of Italian and English snacks to enjoy with drinks. They also had a lunch menu, and I was delighted to see one of my favourites on there, Caprese salad: slices of tomato, buffalo mozzarella, basil and olive oil. It was a limited menu but, judging by the snacks being delivered to the tables around me, whatever you ordered here would be excellent.

Taking a break from the menu, I gazed out at the beach. Polperrion wasn't a huge one, not like Porthminster or Porthmeor. I love it because it was quieter and there were fewer amenities. My foot tapped. I did that when I felt anxious. If I didn't have something to distract me, I couldn't keep my foot still. I hoped the habit would disappear in time.

'A one-shot cappuccino,' said Rico, placing a cup and saucer in front of me.

'Thank you.'

'*Prego.*'

Now, this was what I meant about quality. Not only did I get a well-prepared coffee, but I also had a selection of biscotti on a plate with a napkin and a small glass of water. Very Italian.

Below me, a group of people had started up a game of football and I gazed fondly at the scene.

I decided to check out the clientele. To my left were tourists studying maps and checking out leaflets. The locals were easy to spot. Not only did many of them have that outdoor complexion but they seemed to know one another, and a few had the unmistakable West Country accent with its rounded vowels and Rs.

Looking to my right, I did a double take. Seated a little way along was the man I'd seen from the taxi when we'd stopped in traffic earlier. He was reading Carducci. Impressive. Carducci was an Italian poet from centuries ago. He must enjoy poetry like me. Those two adorable dogs were sitting at his feet.

I couldn't help it. I studied every bit of him. He had an old-fashioned air about him. It was difficult to explain what that was but if time travel were possible, I'd have said he'd walked in from the late '50s or early '60s. Something about his body language, his hair. I didn't know. But that's what he reminded me of.

He wore stone-coloured trousers turned up a little. No socks and a pair of deck shoes. His short-sleeved shirt was a deep bronze and suited his complexion. He screamed elegance. I wondered if he was on holiday. Then I wondered if he was married.

I mentally pulled myself out of those thoughts. Why did I wonder if he was married?

The certainty that I'd met him before re-emerged. I'd had that feeling in the taxi. *Had* I met him before? I dismissed the thought almost immediately. Surely, I'd remember it if I had.

He put his book down and took a sip of wine. My God, why couldn't I be that chilled when I was on my own? All I did was fidget and panic, absolutely certain that people were examining me, knowing I was a widow and whispering about it to one another.

He looked at me. A small smile appeared as he nodded a greeting.

I nodded back.

I turned to finish the dregs of my coffee and my biscotti. It'd been a long day, but I was buoyant, proud of myself. I'd managed to travel to St Ives and get over the initial upset of being here without Adam. And I'd come to Rico's Bar, the place I wanted to detest but would now consider a regular haunt.

I caught Tina's eye and mimed the universal code for the bill. In a few seconds, she returned with a card machine.

'You're staying with Greg and Suzie, aren't you?' She spoke with the local accent.

'Yes, that's right,' I said, presenting my card.

'You here long, then?'

'Three weeks, so I'll see you again. I like what you've done with the colours and the lights.'

'It gives it a cosy feel, don't it? Well, I'm Tina and that's Rico, my husband.'

She gave my card back. 'Well, it's nice to meet you, Kerry.' She handed me a business card. 'You know where we're to.'

When I first heard that phrase, I thought it sounded odd and I suppose it did to anyone that wasn't Cornish. But it was clear what she meant: you know where we are and you're always welcome. She accepted my tip with a cheery thanks and the hope that I'd return first thing tomorrow for a coffee. Her hand rested on my shoulder for a second as she went to the next table. It was as if she and Rico had already accepted me as a regular.

I got up, put my purse in my rucksack and made my way towards the door.

'*Signora!*'

I swivelled on my heel. That elegant man came toward me, his dogs at his feet. He lifted my jacket from the chair.

'Your jacket, *Signora*.'

'Oh, goodness, thank you.'

I took the jacket and wished him a good evening. I couldn't help but let my gaze linger on him a few seconds longer. He had the bluest eyes, faded a little with age, but blue all the same.

As I turned to go, Rico and Tina shouted, '*Ciao*,' to me and I waved.

On my way up the hill to The Feather Duck, I recognised that my mood had changed. An hour at Rico's had calmed me. The place seemed to wrap its arms around me and say, 'it's okay, we have you and you can do this'.

Chapter Sixteen
GIAN

She intrigue me, I tell you truthfully. She seem uneasy when she arrive but I cannot tell you why. My instinct, however, is good, so perhaps it is my sixth sense that speak to me. The thing I notice is the foot tap, as if she is anxious that something will happen to her.

I do not see her before, so I think she is a tourist. She study everything and everyone. She is not beautiful, you know, but she is pretty. And stylish. She wear elegant linen trousers and a cotton jacket, coral colour, it suit her very much. She drape that jacket on the chair.

But the nervous foot tap is what I focus on, and I wonder what cause her to be uncomfortable. She seem a little lost in her thoughts and she read the menu two or three times.

When she receive her coffee, she relax a little and she look at the customers.

I think she also study me, but I do not stare at her all evening. That would be rude, so I read my book. I read Carducci. He is a poet from my country, Italy.

When she concentrate on something else, I take in everything about her; her hair, her earrings and the way she is, you know, her mannerisms. She read that menu at least four times but she no order.

She study everyone again and her eyes, they come to me. Brown eyes. I nod to her, and she nod to me. I think she is *simpatica*, you know. A nice lady.

When she pay Tina for the coffee, she get up to go and forget her jacket.

'*Signora*,' I call out to her. I nearly trip over my dogs but, fortunately, I do not embarrass myself. I tell you, my dogs do not give me an inch. I lift her jacket from the chair. It is tailored, lined with a satin-type of material. I hand it to her.

'Your jacket, *Signora*.'

She is relieved not to forget this and then she examine me, as if she know me but then she decide, I think, that she does not. I have not met her. I think I would remember if I had.

I don't return to my seat until she is out of sight.

Chapter Seventeen
KERRY

Something small will trigger tears and blur my vision
Shopping for one, a show on the television.

I realised, on returning to The Feather Duck, that I hadn't been to my room since I'd arrived. It's weird the way certain things hit you when you least expect but opening the door to our double room was, quite honestly, heartbreaking.

Like all of the rooms here, it was light and airy. The colour scheme in this one was light peach with some cream accessories and, on the bed, high-end Egyptian cotton sheets. It really was very tastefully done. Even the kettle and cups matched the decor.

A small TV was mounted on the wall with a digital radio to the side of it. Double doors swung open to a balcony just about wide enough for the table and chairs positioned there.

But I'd never been here without Adam. The sense of loss was palpable. I hung up my clothes and put out framed photos I'd brought with me. One was of me and Adam in Krakow where we'd enjoyed a city break. We had been a little drunk and this photo captured us in a fit of hysterics. The other was the portrait of him taken three years ago, the one I kept by my bed at home. He hadn't realised I was taking photos and I'd managed to capture the image of a very contented and happy man. This was the photo I liked to talk to, so it had to come with me. While I unpacked, I told him about the journey down and how welcoming Greg and Suzie had been.

'I think you'd like Rico's Bar. I know we liked the fry-ups and everything, but this is completely different. They're not competing with the same demographic. It's upmarket, modern, welcoming. And they reserve tables for the locals. How great is that?'

I always felt sorry for the locals in this town during the summer. The 'six weeks of madness', the residents nicknamed it. They must get frustrated because the place was always overrun by visitors.

'I should think that'll guarantee them regular custom during the winter, too,' I continued. 'And they fitted some double-glazed concertina doors, so it'll be much warmer during their off season.'

It had always been bloody freezing on that veranda when The Greasy Spoon was there. They never closed in the winter, but they didn't have the luxury of shutting out the elements. Rico and Tina had obviously invested heavily in the property but hopefully it would pay off for them.

After sorting myself out, I made a call to Maggie just to check in.

'I'm so pleased you rang,' said Maggie. 'We were wondering if you'd arrived safely.'

I told her about The Greasy Spoon's demise and how wonderful Rico's was. 'You would love it, Maggie, it's very you.'

'It certainly sounds very Continental,' she responded. 'By the way, we popped round to see Dan earlier. He's fine and told us he'll be going down at the weekend. How lovely for you and I think it'll do you both good. The change of scenery.'

Yes, I thought. I could already feel a layer of something coming away. I wasn't sure how to describe it, just that an emotion of sorts had slipped away. I wasn't naïve enough to think it wouldn't come back but, the fact that I'd recognised the difference was heartening.

After the call, I returned to the patio. Drinks were in order, and I also needed to speak with Dan. I'd texted him to tell him I'd got here safely but promised to check in later via FaceTime.

The patio opened its arms to me. A few of the large candles and lanterns flickered and the twinkling fairy lights gave the whole place a romantic atmosphere. Greg was out but Suzie was locating a good bottle of wine for us.

I, meanwhile, made myself comfortable and connected with Dan on my iPad. He was in the kitchen and getting ready to go out with Chloe. When I told him about The Greasy Spoon and my decision to hate every bit of it, he frowned. Because I was being so upbeat about it, he was convinced I was putting on a brave face and secretly wallowing in despair.

'You sure you're okay, Mum, with the café? That was something quite special for you and Dad.'

'I truly wanted to slate everything about it but it's a little gem. The couple that run it are lovely, too. You'd like them. We'll go there when you come down.'

He brightened, happy that I'd not sunk into some sort of depression over it. I was a little hesitant to tell him the next thing because I knew what his reaction would be.

'I picked up the property pages.'

There it was. In his eyes. A flicker of alarm. He would think it was too soon and, if I had been intending to buy a house this week, I would agree wholeheartedly. But I wasn't.

'I'm not signing a contract, Dan. I won't do anything until I've discussed it with you. I promise. And, when I do seriously look, it would be nice to have you with me.'

'Okay,' he said, reassured.

Our doorbell chimed in the distance.

'I've got to go, Mum, that's Chloe.'

I blew him a kiss and told him to enjoy his evening. I loved that he was so protective and concerned about how I was doing down here. Neither of us were sure about our futures at the moment. Dan had delayed his application to uni until this year and I wasn't sure yet whether I could retire to a place that was supposed to be mine and Adam's.

Often, when I was in a fix about things, I wondered how I would have advised Adam if it were me who had died, and my answer was clear: 'Do what makes you happy. If you are happy, I am happy. Why would you not move to a place just because I am not here?'

Adam's stock phrase wormed its way in: 'Do it, even if it scares the shit out of you.' I picked up the property pages with renewed enthusiasm.

Suzie returned with a bottle of Pinot and two glasses. She placed them on the table between us, a table they'd picked up in a junk shop for a fiver. Covered in blue and white Portuguese tiles, it added to the Mediterranean ambience.

She poured each of us a glass and gestured at the paper. 'Anything?'

I pulled a face and signalled *maybe*. There were some

luxurious properties here and I was fortunate that Adam left us well-provided for. He'd invested well in his pensions, and I had yet to receive my own pension from the bank, which was also sizeable. Price wasn't the issue. Mixed emotions were the issue. Regardless of the pep talk I'd given myself about what I would say to Adam, it didn't convince me.

'The trouble is, Suzie,' I said with a sigh, 'everything is so different. Everything I do, every plan, every desire, every thought, every second of the day… I was part of a couple. Then, suddenly, well, it's just me.' I paused. 'Dan thinks it's too soon.'

We swirled the wine in our glasses, and I asked Suzie if she'd ever had second thoughts about moving to St Ives. She was a London girl, a city girl, who'd left the thriving metropolis to live in this quaint Cornish town with a population of twenty thousand.

'Oh, my darling, I had them all the time. I can't think of a person who wouldn't. Not everyone can adapt to living here. You see tourists, all the time, stopping by the estate agents, gushing over this property and the next one. How lovely it would be to live here all year round. Poppycock! You know a lot of people who make that decision decide it's the wrong one and move back to where they came from. They endure one winter and they're off. We're at the end of the line, cut off like an island. It takes two hours to get to the border with Devon, for heaven's sake.'

'You sound as if you're trying to talk me out of it!'

She held up a finger. 'You are not one of those people, Kerry. You and Adam came here every year, not just for your annual holiday, but on weekends and not just in the summer. You endured the constant downpours, the gale-force winds and the icy winter we had just a few years ago. You know this place out of season and you still fell in love with it. That's the difference, darling. This isn't a tourist resort for you, it's home.'

She was absolutely right.

'And I did the same,' she said. 'I stayed here during the highs and lows. You have to. Oh, yes, I had a reason for coming here. Greg. But it was still a wrench to swap London for St Ives and I battled with that decision all the time.'

'But you still came down.'

'Because Greg said something incredibly wise that put everything in perspective.'

I frowned. 'What?'

Suzie mimicked Greg's lovely accent. '"My lover," he said, "you're never less than a day away from anywhere in this world. If you want to go back to London for a weekend, get on a plane at Newquay and you'll be there in half an hour."'

'You study those property pages, darling, and we'll view a couple. Together. If nothing else, we can be nosy and exceptionally critical of other people's decor and furnishings.'

We laughed and clinked glasses.

Chapter Eighteen
KERRY

Even on good days, an underlying sadness lay
dormant
Like a sleeping volcano
Waiting.

After enjoying a delicious breakfast on the patio with Greg and Suzie, I rang the writing festival line and booked a place at a poetry workshop. I was delighted to see this festival was on because I had wondered if I might be at a loose end and, whenever that happened, I always started thinking too much. And when I thought too much, it never ended well.

Suzie and Greg had planned to do a few things with me but there were some excursions I wanted to do on my own, to see if I *could* do them. The Greasy Spoon, of course, had been one of those. But there were also restaurants and shops that we used to frequent, and they were all on my list.

I didn't know what it was about wanting to face things alone. Perhaps it instilled a sense of achievement in me.

It was certainly not to hear people telling me I was brave, that I was coping well and that I was an inspiration. God knows I heard plenty of people express that opinion. It was lovely but I hadn't chosen this path to garner approval. I was coping the way I felt I could cope. I couldn't hibernate and wallow in self-pity. Adam wouldn't want me doing that. I wanted to make him proud of me and this was the best way of doing it.

On the second day of my visit, however, the black shadow had descended. Anyone in my position would know what I was talking about; I often ambled along for several days with everything on an even keel then, wham bam, I'd wake up and, overnight, my emotional journey had made a U-turn.

Along with that came vulnerability, the fear of loneliness, the need to be wanted. Unfortunately, it coupled itself with anger, a bitterness wanting to rise and make itself known. Not a good combination.

The result of this was that the least little thing would upset me beyond reason.

This was one of those days.

I had a counter system in my head. Ten counters. If I was having a good day, all ten counters would be in an imaginary left-hand column and remain there. If I was tripped up by something, a counter went over to the right-hand side.

I had a poetry workshop at eleven and this would definitely keep all of my counters together.

For my mid-morning coffee fix, I couldn't think of a better place to go to than Rico's. I'd felt at home there and the coffee was amazing, although I suppose I shouldn't expect anything less from an Italian.

I wondered if that man would be there?

The thought startled me. Why was I even thinking that? I wasn't here seeking a new romance. That's the last thing I needed or wanted.

I wasn't ready for that.

Yet, when I reached the entrance, I couldn't help but look toward the table where he'd been sitting the previous evening, and I couldn't deny the disappointment I felt when I saw he wasn't there. In his place was another man setting up a chess game.

Tina approached. 'Kerry, lovely to see you. Table for one?'

Inwardly, I groaned. Table for one. How sad did that sound? Meal for one, table for one, coffee for one. Every bloody thing for one.

A counter leapt to the right-hand column.

Outwardly, I thanked her and took the table offered that had a reserved sign on it. Having had Greg initially introduce me as a friend, I was now being treated as a local. On days like this, that helped.

Rico came to my table, his arms outstretched.

'*Buongiorno, Signora* Kerry, 'ow lovely to 'ave you back. I think, for you, is the one-shot cappuccino, *si*?'

Impressed by his memory, I told him yes, that would be lovely. This morning, I was fully prepared. I had my phone, the festival guide and the property pages. I had the distractions I needed today. That underlying sadness simmered and would continue to do so.

Had he arrived at his table? Fuck! Why did I do that? The man was probably married. What did it matter? I wasn't interested. Jesus!

While I waited for my coffee, I scanned around to see who was on the veranda. I still loved to people-watch and continue my silent conversations with Adam if I saw anything that I thought would make him laugh. But, today, I found it difficult to connect with any humour.

The tables were occupied, by couples mainly. Some local, some tourists. My jaw tightened and a flash of resentment ran through me.

Another counter leapt across.

Why do you get to stay a couple?
Why do you get to stay as two?
Why couldn't we have stayed together like you?
We never hurt anyone, we just had fun.
Why couldn't that have gone on?
Why do you get to stay a couple?
Why do I get to sit here, just me?
Just one.

Rico brought me out of my musing. 'For my newest regular, *si*?' He placed a coffee and biscotti in front of me.

'Thank you and, yes, I think I am a regular.'

'That is good to 'ear. Enjoy.'

To move from anger to a more tolerant frame of mind, I flicked through the festival guide and ticked off a few talks and workshops that interested me. This settled me down and I felt more composed.

'Good morning.' A male voice. An accent.

He stood beside me. I couldn't deny it. I was pleased to see him.

'Oh, hello. How are you?' His two dogs were up on their hind legs craving attention, so I made a fuss of them. 'And how are you two?'

'They are well, thank you. I am well, too. And you?'

I didn't want to tell him I felt like crap because everyone here was part of a couple and it incensed me beyond reason. I didn't want to ask him how he stayed so chilled and relaxed when he sat on his own. No, none of that came out.

'I'm good, thanks,' I replied.

He excused himself and made his way to the table he'd sat the previous night, to greet the man who had set up the chess game. Rico delivered an espresso to him, and he was immediately focussed on the game.

While I sipped my cappuccino, which was bloody lovely, I flicked through the property pages. Suzie was right, why not do some browsing and, like Adam always said, take a risk. Although looking at houses was hardly a risk. All I was doing was marking off those I liked and reconsidering those I'd ticked off last night. I wasn't moving my furniture in.

I'd almost finished my coffee when I spotted a couple beyond that man's table. A couple in their late seventies, very smitten with each other. The simmering tears I'd held back were immediately on the surface. So close, I hiccupped when pushing them down.

Four or five counters leapt over to my right hand.

I went to the railing to take in the view across the beach. Best to concentrate on something else, anything; the colour of the sky, the brightness of the sun, that stupid Dalmatian running around like a maniac in the surf. Calm descended. The expected flood of tears ebbed away.

I mentally placed a couple of counters back into my left hand.

'Are you all right, *Signora*?'

Shit. It was him. Concern was etched across his face. God, he had the bluest eyes. The dogs stared with love-me eyes.

'Yes, yes. Really, I'm fine. Thank you. It's just…' I didn't know what to say. It's just that I missed my husband so much I wanted to throw myself off that cliff over there; that it wasn't fair that everyone was having a lovely time, and I was on the verge of a complete meltdown.

'You are visiting?'

'Yes, I arrived yesterday.' Beyond him, I spotted the elderly couple and panicked. I couldn't allow more counters to transfer.

'I should be going,' I blurted out. Then realisation. 'Oh, God, I haven't paid.'

'Please, this is my treat. Compliment of the house.'

'Oh, I thought Rico was the owner.'

'He is. I am Gian. Rico is my son.'

Why hadn't I connected the dots before? 'Ah, you're the one teaching Greg Italian.'

'You know him?'

The change in topic almost made me giddy. The panic subsided. The tears ebbed away although I felt sure they would appear again later. More counters slipped back to my left hand.

'Yes,' I answered. 'And Suzie. I'm staying with them at The Feather Duck.'

'You are here for the festival?'

'No, I had no idea it was on, but I've signed up for a poetry workshop.'

'You write poetry?'

'I dabble.'

'*Cosé?*'

I couldn't help but chuckle. The word obviously confused him. 'Sorry, "dabble" means that I make a feeble attempt at it. Do you? Write poetry?'

'I read it more than write it.'

Beyond him, the elderly couple continued being sweet with each other and that hollow feeling opened up. Gian turned slightly. He'd seen my upset but had no idea what was causing it.

'Would you like to join me, *Signora*? You can help me beat my friend at chess.'

Oh, bless him for being so diplomatic. 'No, thank you. I've got a workshop in a little while so…' I went to get my purse out.

'Please, let me pay for your coffee.'

'Thank you, that's very kind.' I had a sense about him. I'd had it before, and I had to ask. 'Have we met before?'

His expression told me that he was sure we hadn't. I shrugged. 'Well, thank you, for the coffee.'

'*Prego*. We will see you again, yes?'

'Yes, definitely. Thank you. Bye.'

'*Ciao.*'

Ciao. Why did the Italian language sound so cool?

I kept my eyes front. If I turned and saw those lovely eyes were still on me it'd scare the shit out of me.

Part of me was flattered by that thought. Part of me wanted that.

A big part of me didn't.

Chapter Nineteen
GIAN

I was in the office when I see her again. My friend, he was setting up our morning chess game. She wait at the entrance, and she seem a little sad. I was on my mobile. I speak with a client and watch her until I have to write something down. So, I move away from the window.

At the desk, I write notes with my fountain pen. My wife, she give me this pen. She say it make me write more slowly and pay attention to what I do.

When I live in Italy, I work as a lawyer. I am retired now but I do occasional work, you know, as a consultant for a legal firm. This was a client on the telephone.

When I end the call, I return to the window, but I do not see her. But I see my friend, Peter; he is waiting. I like that Rico and Tina decide on this theme for their bar. Nice music, chess and dominoes to play. It remind me a little of the bars in Santa Margherita. That's where I come from; a small town that perch on the side of a cliff close to the Cinque Terre region. The residents, they paint the houses different colours. When we were children, we call it the town where the rainbow fell. I think that Burano, near Venezia, they call the same because of the colours.

When I come from the office, I see her. She is two tables from me. On my way to Peter, I say hello to customers, and I stop to greet her. My dogs, they need to greet her, too.

She study the festival guide. She seem happy to see me, but I sense something with her. Something beneath the skin. Something that distress her.

I join my friend. Peter is a very keen chess player, very competitive. I only beat him a few times. Rico, he bring me an espresso and, while Peter examine the board, I sit back and watch her.

She has shorts on today and an elegant cotton blouse. I notice that when she is reading, she seem calm. When she has little to do, there is the nervous foot tap.

Then she stare at the table to the side of me and something happen with her. I look to the table and see an older couple. I don't understand and when I look back, she is standing at the balustrade.

I put my hand on Peter's arm. '*Mi scusi.*'

I go to her, and I ask, 'Are you all right, *Signora*?'

She say she is fine but, I don't think she is fine. She say she has to go. Then she realise that she has not paid so I offer to pay. I discover that she stay with Greg and Suzie and that she enjoy poetry.

We talk for a little but she focus beyond me, and I see tears within her but I do not understand.

'*Signora*,' I say, 'would you like to join me? You can help me beat my friend at chess.'

But she can't sit with me because she must go. I insist to

pay for coffee. She thank me and ask if we have met before, but I don't remember her. I think I would remember. I have only been here just over a year, and I don't remember her.

She leave the bar and my eyes, they follow her for a while. Before I return to Peter, I notice she leave her festival guide and property page on the table. I notice, too, that she make a mark by some properties. Not holiday homes. Residential.

Chapter Twenty
KERRY

*My friends are loving and giving
But this hole in my heart is so unforgiving.*

The poetry workshop was informative, cathartic and a wonderful diversion.

I had come to accept a while ago that there would be days when grief bubbled to the surface no matter what and today continued to be one of those days. The wobble at Rico's this morning proved to me how vulnerable I still was, especially when people showed concern, as Gian had.

When I'd arrived yesterday and wandered around this town without Adam, I was perfectly fine.

Today it was all wrong.

After the workshop, I'd arranged to meet Suzie and Greg for lunch. On the main street, I spotted Gian with his dogs. He was with someone and suddenly threw his head back and laughed. My first thought? I wondered if I would ever be that carefree again.

Two things happened when I lost Adam. (I was getting very good at analysing what went on in my head.) Many people in my position said that it felt as if a huge chunk had been taken away from them.

That was true, but it was more than that.

Yes, there was the chunk but there was also the spark.

The chunk represented the grief and that chunk, over time, reduced a little and became more manageable. I thought that was the basis of the phrase 'time heals'.

The spark was Adam. It ignited in me the day I met him.

The spark represented passion, elation, the joy of being alive with that wonderful man. Now, the spark was extinguished and, in its place was the sadness that was always in me but that I kept buried deep.

The fact that I had lost that spark and the worry that I would never get it back was what many people termed the dark night of the soul. Those times when the ghost of that flame burned bright reminded you of what you had lost.

Suzie and Greg had immediately picked up on my mood during lunch. They didn't push me to talk, or pry or try to buck me up. When we returned to the B&B, at my request, they left me in peace on the patio. I'd already written the day off as a sad one and, here, if I wanted to break down, I could.

The patio was so tranquil compared to the hustle and bustle of the town and the view across the bay matched anything I'd seen advertising far off climes. The sea had streaks of cobalt, turquoise and navy. I could understand why this area was a haven for artists.

'Good afternoon.'

I spun round to see Gian standing there. His dogs ran to greet me. God, they were adorable. He handed me a newspaper and a guide.

'You leave these behind. At the bar.'

'Oh, goodness, thank you. You needn't have worried.'

He shrugged it off as being no bother and took in the view. He'd changed into chinos and a linen jacket. Quality. I wondered if he did his shopping in Italy.

'It is very beautiful here, yes?'

He had a rich, resonant voice. I was envious of his easy-going nature. I was wound up like a jack-in-the-box waiting to be released. It was nice to see him, but I couldn't trust myself to remain composed and I couldn't just turf him out. That would be rude.

'*Mi scusa*, I don't know your name.'

'Kerry.'

'Kerry, I wonder if you will join me for a drink at the bar tonight.'

I had to turn away and focus on the rooftops. Why did I have to have an off day in front of someone I'd only just met? I furiously blinked back the tears. I thought I'd done a good job but, when I turned to face him, I clearly hadn't.

'Oh. I have upset you.'

Oh God. The poor man. I adopted the big pretence that I'd become so good at. 'No, no you haven't. Please, take no notice. It's just me being me.'

'No, I don't believe this is you.'

I moved along the terrace, aware that he was following me but keeping his distance. The dogs had switched their interest to the comfy double lounger. I swallowed hard and decided to bite the bullet and just tell him. I swung round.

'I lost my husband last year.'

When you tell people straight like that, the whole thing gets awkward. People don't like being confronted by grief. I expected him to be the same, but he moved toward me.

'I'm so sorry.'

If I ignored the empathy, I wouldn't break down. I didn't want him feeling sorry for me or having to listen to my tragic tales of woe. I concentrated on being bright and breezy and mentally awarded myself an Oscar for good acting. 'Most days, I'm fine but... well, this was our favourite place.'

'That couple. At the bar.'

'I always thought that me and Adam would grow old together.'

I sought out another part of the terrace and he stayed with me. As I took in the colours of the ocean, I was convinced that this would now be the awkward moment; that he would be stumped for words and that I'd feel bad about landing my emotions on him.

'Kerry, these dark days. They will be a part of you. I understand. I lost my wife three years ago.'

Something akin to relief cascaded through me. An invisible hand lifted the heaviness that had descended. Here was someone who understood. Here was someone who had gone through it. I turned, aware I probably had eternal hope in my eyes.

'Really?'

I so wanted this to be true. He gave a brief nod.

'I loved her very much. I miss her every day. Your husband, Adam. He would not want to see you so unhappy.'

I sat down on the double lounger, and he sat opposite me. The dogs vied for attention, and I instinctively fussed over them. Having someone here who had gone through this conveyed a sense of calm to me. A kindred spirit. I wasn't alone. Everything would be okay.

For several weeks after Adam died, I studied the obituary

columns to see if any other men had died at Adam's age and if they were married. It wasn't a morbid thing. I just needed to know that someone else was going through the same thing as me. At the same age. That I wasn't the only one suffering.

Gian patiently waited. He didn't seem perturbed by silence. He wasn't pushing me to speak but suddenly I wanted to open up. I wanted to know if he felt the same.

'Some days... today... I just feel completely lost.'

Sensing my melancholy, the dogs shifted closer. I stroked them.

He sat forward. 'And there is nothing you can do. You have to let it happen. If you need to cry, cry.'

The pause was comfortable. He shifted forward a little further.

'Kerry, you would prefer that I go? I know that solitude is something you need on these days. But sometimes you need someone. I am happy to sit with you. We don't have to talk.' He motioned at the drinks trolley. 'Would you like me to prepare a drink for you, a glass of wine perhaps?'

'Yes, yes, that would be nice. Just a small one, though.'

Gian selected one of the miniature bottles kept on the trolley, enough for two glasses. He poured drinks for both of us and returned.

My thoughts were all over the place, but I suddenly remembered why he'd come. Not only had he brought back the stuff I'd forgotten, but he'd also asked me out. Was that a date or just to go out for a drink like friends did? What did you do about dating now? How on earth did you meet people these days? Why was I even thinking that? I didn't want to date anyone. I wanted Adam.

But the company would be nice.

I'd like to sit in Rico's with someone and talk. That thought prompted me to make my decision.

I locked eyes with him. 'What time? Tonight.'

His lips parted and the delight reached his eyes. 'You choose.'

'Seven?'

He confirmed the time with the slightest of nods. His gaze became intense. 'You feel a little better?'

'Yes. Thank you.'

He swigged down his wine and got up. The dogs leapt off the lounger and were by his feet in a second.

Before he left, he rested his hand on mine. 'These days will become less, Kerry. Remember this.'

Chapter Twenty-One
KERRY

It'll pass, it'll pass, it's a process I know
It'll come, it'll stay and at some point, it'll go.

As the day went on, I felt in danger of descending into the shadows again, but I'd learned that getting out and about would stop that from happening.

I checked my wardrobe. I hadn't brought much with me. I didn't want Gian thinking this was a date, so I put on a pair of flared trousers and a cotton shirt. I wanted to be presentable, but I also wanted to appear off limits, and this ticked both boxes.

'It's not a date or anything romantic,' I told Adam's photo. 'It's just that he's lost his wife, and I've lost you and we are two lonely souls seeking some company.'

Gian didn't seem terribly lonely to me. I'm not even sure that lonely was the right word. I considered myself independent and social, but I'd been part of a couple for so long, I'd forgotten the rules for being single. I was in a wilderness.

At Rico's, Dean Martin sang 'Mambo Italiano' over the speakers, a jaunty number which transported me to the era I loved so much. Adam had been sure I'd been born in the wrong era and constantly teased me about it.

Gian was at his table; he rose when I walked toward him and drew out a seat for me. I knew a lot of women would now be sneering at this man for standing up when a woman approached but this was what I meant about that '50's era, the manners and the courtesy that went with it. I liked having someone show that respect although I never expected it.

Gian had opted for casual clothing, wearing an open-necked shirt and a pair of linen trousers. Like me, he still wore his wedding ring. I couldn't bring myself to take mine off.

The dogs competed to greet me, and I bent down to stroke them.

'This is Tosca,' Gian said, pointing to the white one, 'and this one is Figaro,' pointing to the black one. 'They are named after characters.'

'From the operas?'

'Yes! You have seen the operas?' He raised an eyebrow at my reaction. 'You don't like opera?'

'I've never seen an opera in my life. It's very highbrow.'

'Highbrow?'

'Opera, to the working classes, is for posh people.'

He threw his head back and laughed. 'That is very amusing. In Italy, opera is for everyone.'

He lifted Tosca onto his lap. Figaro curled up at his feet. Rico brought us a bottle of white wine and some blinis with cream cheese and salmon, and we settled into a phase of safe chit-chat. Where was I from? Sussex. Where had I worked?

At the local bank, as chief cashier. How old was my son? Eighteen.

He was easy to talk with and genuinely interested in what I had to say. We began a game of dominoes. I hadn't played for decades but the rules soon came back to me and playing saved us from any awkwardness if we weren't talking. He seemed quite content to be quiet for a while and having a game to play helped with that. He placed a tile down.

'Tell me about your husband.'

'Oh, God, you don't want to hear about him.'

'But I do want to know. Where did you meet?'

I pictured it immediately. 'At a party. I hate parties. The music's too loud and there's always far too many people.'

We were in Brighton, my hometown. I remember it clearly. It was 1986 and 'Take My Breath Away' was in the charts, from *Top Gun*. A friend of mine, Ann, was going out with a student from the local college and he'd invited us both to a party one Saturday night. It was being hosted by one of his classmates at some digs in Springfield Road, a long street with old Victorian houses, many of which had been converted into flats for students. The party was in the ground floor flat, and I discovered a whole load of people had been invited. I'd always loathed large, noisy gatherings because I couldn't hear what people were saying. I struggled to be heard myself and, all in all, the whole experience was a chore, although when I was in my twenties, I tended to feel obliged to play along.

I much preferred interacting with only a handful of guests but, back then, I didn't feel I could say no to people's invitations because I didn't want to upset them. At that age, I thought that attending these boisterous evenings was what you did, that it made you part of the gang. I later discovered that most people I knew weren't that keen on them either. We'd all thought it was the cool and hip thing to do.

During this particular evening, I craved some peace and quiet so snuck out into the little courtyard at the back of the house. Adam was there, drinking from a chipped cup. He wore jeans with a shirt and jacket and had beautiful shiny hair that flopped over his forehead. I hadn't seen him in the house, and I wondered if he'd made his escape and been out here since the start.

He grinned at me. 'I couldnae stand it either.'

'Why did you come, then?'

'Nae choice. My housemate wanted a party. Why did you come?'

'Coerced into it.' I examined his cup. 'Are you drinking tea?'

'Aye. D'you want some?'

'Oh, yes please! I'd much prefer that to this awful bloody lager.'

'There's an all-night café round the corner. D'you fancy that, instead?' On seeing my pleading eyes, he got up. 'Come on, we can get out through the back here.'

Gian topped up my wine glass, encouraging me to continue.

'Well, we went on a few dates and got more comfortable with each other. I mean, you reach a time where you can be yourself, don't you?'

That process hadn't taken long. Adam and I seemed to muddle along as if we'd known each other for years. One thing that quickly cemented our relationship was our sense of humour. We both liked to see the fun in things and that was our foundation. Enjoy life, if you could. I remember one summer's day, early on in our relationship, we had a game of one-on-one football. It was real rough-and-tumble stuff. A typical tomboy, I'd grown up with the twelve boys in our street. The only other girl was Helen next door and if we did anything remotely girly, the boys soon knocked it out of us. I'd grown up climbing trees, fishing for tadpoles and playing football.

I remembered the expanse of Littlehampton beach, just four miles along the coast from Brighton, and how, much to Adam's frustration, I'd scored the first goal. I ran around the beach waving my arms around shouting, 'One-nil to the Albion!'

'Don't get smug. Rangers haven't even started yet.' He supported Glasgow Rangers, of course. He immediately pushed me out of the way to equalise and go on to celebrate.

I pleaded a case for a clear foul, but he was having none of it.

Later, we had brunch in a café and the most jaded waitress I'd ever encountered approached us, chewing gum all the while. I wondered if she was chewing a wasp.

'With the eggs,' she mumbled, 'do you want fried, poached or scrambled? And, with the bread, do you want brown or white, toasted or fried?'

'Blimey,' I said, 'it's like the Spanish Inquisition.'

We instinctively chorused the classic Monty Python line, 'Nobody expects the Spanish Inquisition.'

This was followed by several seconds of hysterical laughter, made even funnier by the reaction of the waitress, whose expression never changed.

If Gian was tired of my rambling, he hid it very well. He constantly asked questions and was interested in everything I had to say. We inevitably got onto the topic of my son, Dan.

'You had him late, yes?'

'He was a mistake. We hadn't planned to have children but now, of course, I think it was a wonderful mistake to have made.'

The sun had set. Tina had turned the patio heaters on and many of the tables had emptied.

'And the property page. You are thinking of moving?'

'Moving here is the next step but… without Adam, it'll be like walking off a cliff.' I emitted a hoot. 'And that's something I'll never do. And I know he'll be at university, but it has to be right for Dan, too. I need to know he's settled and fine with it.'

When I spotted the time on the clock on the wall, my jaw almost fell to the floor. It was gone ten. The dogs were asleep. It wasn't the hour that alarmed me but something else.

'Oh, God, I've spent all evening talking about Adam. You must be bored stiff.'

'But I ask you to.' He grinned. 'Now I know more about you. That football team you support. Is that Brighton?'

'Yes. What's yours?'

'Milan.'

'AC or Inter?'

'Oh! You *do* know your football. AC.'

The chemistry between us that night sent a streak of guilt through me. In an instant, it felt wrong, and my instinct told me to stop enjoying myself. I didn't want to be impolite because I'd had a lovely evening but, having such fun also injected a sense of angst into my veins, that I was betraying Adam's memory.

'It's getting late. I should go.'

'Of course.'

The dogs were immediately alert as we got up. Gian draped my jacket over my shoulders. We said goodbye to Rico and Tina, and he gestured for me to go ahead of him.

'I live just up the hill from The Feather Duck so, if you permit me, I walk you home.'

The dogs trotted along at his heels. I'd enjoyed his company and I hoped that we would do this again. I wasn't looking for romance, but it was wonderful to have a friend to meet, especially one who had gone through the same trauma as me.

We arrived at The Feather Duck, where two delightful old lamps on the wall sent out a twinkling light. I think they might have been the old gas lamps from years ago which had been converted.

I turned to Gian. 'Listen, Gian, thank you for asking about Adam. I don't get to talk about him much.'

'He is part of your life, Kerry. You should talk about him.'

'Then you need to tell me about your wife.'

'May I take you to a sculpture park on Wednesday? At Tremenheere. It is just three or four miles away. There are places to sit and nice artwork. I can tell you about Lucia.'

'Yes, I'd like that.'

'I pick you up at two?'

That was perfect.

My heart thumped. Shit. This was the awkward moment. Goodbye after an evening out. Had he viewed this as a date? I hoped not. I was ready to dash inside with a speedy goodbye. If he leant in to kiss me, I knew I'd step back and that would be a disaster and could potentially spoil a budding friendship.

He took my hand. 'Goodnight, Kerry.' A pause. 'What is your last name?'

'Simmonds.'

'Goodnight, Kerry Simmonds.'

He let my hand go. Thank God for that. I had had the dreadful notion that he was going to pull me toward him.

'Goodnight, Gian… what's your last name?'

'My name is Gianluca Belfiore. Everyone knows me as Gian.'

I think a small yelp escaped from my constricted throat. I must have been staring at him like a prize idiot. 'Gianluca… Belfiore? Luca Belfiore? *Il Problemo*, *La Saluzione*?'

Now it was his turn to gawp.

I almost punched the air. 'I *knew* you looked familiar. My God. You're living in St Ives!'

'I have to live somewhere.'

'I'm sorry,' I said, 'it's just a surprise, that's all.'

'A pleasant one, I hope. You've seen it? *Il Problemo*?'

'Yes, it's a classic.'

A shy smile appeared. He appeared very humble about it all. 'Until tomorrow?'

He reached into his pocket and brought out a packet of cigarettes and gold lighter. I frowned as he put one in his mouth.

He gave a helpless shrug. 'I try to give up. In Italy, we still smoke but, here, I am friends with the devil. But I reduce to four a day, from thirty, so that is good, yes? Soon, I reduce to zero.'

To be honest, I was so gobsmacked about learning who he was, the number of cigarettes he smoked didn't register. I watched as he walked up the hill. I'd just spent the evening with Luca Belfiore. *Wait until I tell Maggie*, I thought.

That thought stayed with me from the street through to the patio. I'd spent the evening with Luca Belfiore. Fuck. I mean, really... fuck.

Greg, a beer in his hand, scrutinised me from his chair. 'You look like you've been given the world's most complicated riddle.'

'I've just spent the evening with Luca Belfiore.'

His face was blank. 'Who?'

'Luca Belfiore. Your friend Gian is Luca Belfiore. Gianluca Belfiore.'

'Right,' he said, none the wiser.

'*Il Problemo, La Soluzione.*' I sat down next to him. 'Where's Suzie? She'll know who I'm talking about.'

'She's popped out to the local businesses' forum. Back in about an hour.'

'Okay, I'll go and get changed and tell her later. Bloody hell, Greg, how do you not know that film?'

'I don't do foreign films.'

I kissed him on the cheek. 'I forgive you.' I turned to go.

'Wait a minute,' he said. 'You telling me Gian's a film star?'

'Well, he was. I don't know what other films he did. We're talking about 1980.'

'Bloody hell, he kept that quiet.'

Upstairs, I turned the bedside lights on, plonked myself down on the edge of the bed and FaceTimed Maggie. It wasn't late. I knew she'd be up.

'Is everything all right?' she asked, her face almost on top of the camera as she tried to gauge my mood.

We didn't normally call each other when we were on holiday, but this was a matter of some urgency.

'I've just spent the evening with Luca Belfiore.'

'What! When? What, now? Where?'

Giggling at her reaction, I gave her a brief overview of what had happened and how he was related to Rico. I smirked as I told her that, yes, he was still very handsome and, yes, he was very nice, but this wasn't what stood out for me. He'd been a lifesaver that day because he was dealing with his own grief and knowing someone in the same position was almost like having a crutch to lean on.

'Honestly, Maggie, it made all the difference today. I felt so low earlier and he didn't shy away from it like a lot of people do. It just helped, you know?'

'I'm pleased for you. Are you going to see him again?'

Knowing how she'd tried to steer Colin toward me I quickly told her that I saw him as a new friend. She wisely chose not to twist my words. With a promise that I'd keep in touch, I ended the call.

I lay back on my pillow. I'd had a fantastic evening. It had done me the power of good. The sadness that had simmered inside me the whole day had gone. Talking about Adam and sharing my memories of him had lifted me more than I could have imagined. I stroked the photo of Adam, then picked it up and kissed it.

'I love you, my darling, and I miss you loads.'

Chapter Twenty-Two
GIAN

I collect Kerry in my car, a Fiat 500 that I bring over from Italy. I see many of these cars here in Cornwall but then I realise they are easy to park and drive down the narrow lanes, so it make sense.

The sculpture park at Tremenheere, this is outside of St Ives on the road to Penzance and has many modern sculptures and a stunning view across Mount's Bay. I like it very much.

Kerry, I think she has a wonderful soul with a sense of positivity, of fun. Even yesterday, when I discover she lose her husband, she did not want me to see her sad. I like that about her. She remind me a little of Lucia in that respect.

At the park my dogs run everywhere. They are very curious but always check to make sure I am here. Our family, we always have dogs, even when I was a boy. They are good companions, especially since Lucia left me because, if my mood is low, they sit with me and do not leave.

Me and Kerry take a leisurely stroll and we talk about holidays we have taken. I learn that she and Adam always come here, to St Ives. Me and Lucia, we always visit the Amalfi Coast and sometimes the islands: Capri, Sardinia, Ischia.

Then, Kerry, she tell me about a memory box that she make to keep items in. Items personal for Adam. She is passionate about this, and she say she go through this often. I make the mistake of telling her I have one for Lucia but then she ask something that cause me to be silent.

'Memory boxes are great, aren't they? Do you look at Lucia's very often?'

I do not answer, and I think she see the subject is sensitive for me. I didn't mean to be rude. I just cannot bring myself to open it. I try several times, but I can't do it and I think, you know, that Kerry is braver than me. When she tell me of the cafés and bars she visit, after Adam leave, I could not do that. I run away from these places. I cannot torment myself by visiting them.

I am grateful that Kerry does not ask me why I not look in the box. Instead, she ask if I have a photograph of Lucia.

'*Certo!*' I said and I show her the one I have on my mobile. She is the first thing I see when I open my screen. She's wonderful; the best wife I could hope for. And her cooking? *Mamma mia*, my wife is the best cook in Italy and, like Kerry, pretty, not beautiful. For me, a good heart is important. A good soul.

'She looks fun,' Kerry say.

'My Lucia, she is the bundle of fun.'

'And that place where you lived, what's that like?'

'Santa Margherita? I was born there. It's very small, very elegant, very picturesque. It is on the west coast of Italy, north of the Cinque Terre ports and has many colourful houses that hug the coastline, so close, you think they will tip into the Mediterranean.

'Lucia was born there, too, and we marry there, have our children there.' I turn to her. 'You know, I only act in two films. I didn't like acting and it is a precarious occupation. I already pass my exams to become a lawyer, and this is what I choose. I had a wife and family to think of and acting, well, that is not a safe profession.

'I have my practice in Santa Margherita. Lucia and the children often walk me to my work on the way to Rico's school. My daughter, Carlotta, she was too young for school... she...' I swallow hard. This is tough for me. The pain never go away. The thought of her make my heart ache.

We have stopped and I see that Kerry is concerned for me.

'We lose Carlotta to leukaemia. She was four years old.'

Kerry put a hand on my arm. 'Oh, Gian, I'm so sorry.'

'That was a very difficult time for me. For us. We want more children, but we were frightened, you know? That it will happen a second time. We could not bear the thought of having to go through that suffering again.'

We continue with our walk. 'We miss Carlotta very much, but we have to carry on, you know, for Rico's sake. He miss her too, and we remember her on birthdays and Christmas, and we go to the church to light a candle. We talk about her, and she is still in our life but in a different way. Even today, me and Rico, we speak about her and remember her. And Lucia, too.'

Kerry understand this and tell me that she feel like this with Adam. That her relationship is now spiritual. It is good to have someone here who understands this. I continue talking.

'As a family, I thought we would remain in Santa Margherita. Then Rico, he marry Tina and move here, and we were happy for him but, without the children nearby, it was different. And, then Lucia, she did not feel so well.'

Speaking these words take me back to the hospital. Lucia is diagnosed with cancer and the prognosis is bad. I only have her with me for a few months after we see the consultant. I visit her in the hospital every day, for hours, and we talk and remember things. And Lucia, she say to me that I must be happy, that I must get on with my life and find another woman who will love me. I tell you, I cried. We both cried. I did not want another woman. No one would take her place. But that is what I so love about Lucia. She only ever want me to be happy and, even then, when she is in her last days, she is thinking only of my happiness.

One day, I read to her. She is very tired, and she close her eyes. So, I read and hold her hand. Then the nurse come in and I take no notice. They come in and out all the time to check everything. But, this time, she lean across the bed and stop me from reading. She shake her head and I know that Lucia, she is taken from me. My world falls apart.

After I tell Kerry this, we just stroll quietly. I appreciate that she does not ask me anything or try to converse with me. I think we are both in our own thoughts for that time. When I feel ready, I continue.

'After Lucia, I couldn't stay. Every inch of my town remind me of what I have lost. Rico and Tina, they said to join them here. They have a café in the town but when this one by the beach come up, they see the potential and move there instead. So, I invest in the bar with them, but it's theirs. I am what you will call here a silent partner. I am fine with that because I have a permanent table there, I make friends and I still get good Italian coffee, yes?'

We laugh at that.

'And, you know, I learn last night that I will be a grandfather.'

She turn to me. 'Oh, Gian, how lovely. Congratulations. When's it due?'

'At the beginning of December. Tina is just two months in. I think I should not be telling you this.'

'Don't worry. I won't say a thing. I'm so pleased for you.'

We stroll for a little and then she ask me if I miss Italy.

'I go back. My brother is in Rome. I just don't go to Santa Margherita.'

There is a bench ahead and I suggest we sit down. You can see across the bay from here. It remind me a little of Italy when the sun is out like this. I take out biscuits for the dogs and hand them to Kerry.

'Do I have to ask them to sit?'

'They'll sit if you want them to.'

Kerry give the biscuits and is now their best friend, like anyone who feeds them.

'Your son, is he... after his father? Does he cope?'

She does not answer for a while. 'He's holding back. I know he finds it difficult, but I can't get him to tell me how he really feels. I'm hoping he confides in Chloe, his girlfriend. They seem close and she's someone his own age. I don't want to push him because he closes down. You'll meet him tomorrow. He's coming for the weekend.'

'It is never easy to lose your father. I lose my parents

several years ago and I miss them very much. But it is difficult for your son at such a young age.' I turn to her. 'And you? Do you find that your poetry help you?'

'Oh, God, yes. More than I realised it would.'

'Will you recite one for me?'

She is surprised. 'Seriously?'

I don't know why she would think I do not want to hear. She reach into her rucksack and bring out a notebook. Then she check to see that I am serious. I say to her that I am serious, why wouldn't I be?

'Okay. Well, this is one that I wrote just a little while ago.

'We may not see each other, we may not touch,

'We may not speak.

'But you're with me every minute, every day of the week.

'My emotions will sometimes shatter and break,

'I wish life didn't offload such heartache.'

I tell you truthfully, when she say that last word, a seagull fly over and does its poo. It land on the notebook. I do not want to laugh because I don't want to upset her, but it is funny, you know?

She stare at the mess for some time, but then she see that I am trying not to laugh but I have to. And, you know, she laugh too. It was very amusing.

Chapter Twenty-Three

DAN

I opened the fridge, picked out two San Pellegrinos and handed one to Chloe. The kitchen was a mess, and I could see what Chloe thought of it the minute she arrived. Shit, I wish I'd tidied up before she came. I hadn't washed up last night's dishes. I was sorting out some photos of Dad and they were scattered all over the table.

It had only been a few days but, not having Mum here, well, everything was different. The house was so fucking empty without Dad. And now with Mum being away, it was just horrible.

Greg had kept in touch and texted me occasionally to tell me Mum was doing okay and that I wasn't to worry. But I'm glad I said I'd go down for the weekend. I thought I'd be fine with her gone for a few weeks, but it had turned out to be harder than I expected.

I noticed Chloe eyeing up the state of the kitchen. She must have thought I was a bloody tramp. She kissed the top of my head and went over to the sink. I watched as she ran the hot water.

She piled the plates and saucepans to the side, then added some washing-up liquid. Shit. That made me feel even more guilty. I wanted to tell her to leave it, that I'd clear it all up later, but before I could she turned to me.

'Shall I come with you? To St Ives? Will there be room?'

I could have easily done a footballer's knee slide across the floor, which felt weird. A second or two of complete elation – I hadn't had that in ages.

I went over to her. 'Yeah.' I didn't know what else to say.

She hugged me and I blinked back my tears.

Chapter Twenty-Four
KERRY

*I would give all my worth to spend one more day with
you on this earth.
We would find a comfy chair, and while away the
memories we share.*

The visit to the sculpture park was fabulous, although some of the installations didn't make a lot of sense to me, or to Gian. Like any modern art, however, the structures made you think about what they represented, and the park's setting was a bonus. The views across the bay were far reaching and I loved the way the sun sparkled on the ocean and how the light caught on the sculptures, depending on where you were standing.

Adam and I had rarely visited galleries or anything artistic like this. I was open to that sort of thing, but Adam was definitely not, and I'd learned early on in our marriage not to drag him along to this sort of exhibition. Similarly, he wouldn't insist I spend an afternoon at a cricket match because I found it so mind-numbingly boring. Those were the big differences between us.

We were polar opposites in some respects, even down to how we liked our food cooked. We both loved toast, but I preferred it just as it was browning; he loved it burnt. I loved steak medium to rare; he loved it cremated!

The big differences, well, we found a compromise for those. That was part of marriage, wasn't it? Compromise. It was part of our individuality and it made us closer. I knew some couples were joined at the hip, but that lifestyle would have destroyed us. We both sought hibernation at various times and each respected that need for solitude.

In Cornwall, our together time was spent on the beach, walking, trying out new restaurants and seeking out some of the standing stones. We loved ancient civilisations and, of course, Cornwall was a Celtic county so there were numerous sites dotted about to visit. If I wanted to visit the Tate in St Ives or some other art studio, Suzie would partner up with me while Greg would join Adam for a pint and a pasty.

When we returned from Tremenheere, Gian parked up and came into reception with me. It was late afternoon and Suzie and Greg didn't appear to be around. It was another awkward moment for me. I didn't understand why he'd come in. Why hadn't he dropped me off and driven home?

Again, I wondered if he had considered this a date. Was he going to try and kiss me? I hoped not. He didn't seem fazed at all. The dogs scampered about and explored every available nook and cranny while he checked out the various paintings on the wall. We eventually found ourselves facing each other and, for once, he seemed a little unsure of himself, a little nervous. He scratched his head and rubbed his chin.

'Kerry, there is music at the bar next week. Latin American.' He held up a finger. 'Not loud. I promise. Would you do me the honour of accompanying me? Suzie and Greg are coming.'

How I yearned to say yes. Yes, yes, I'd love to. I want to dance and leap in the air as if I hadn't a care in the world.

My instinct, however, screamed no. No, you can't do that, it's not right. That invisible thread of guilt tugged at me whenever I was in a situation where I thought I would enjoy myself; that it would be crime to have fun now that Adam wasn't here.

As if reading my mind, Gian said, 'Don't be frightened of living, Kerry.'

I bristled. 'It's all right for you. You're enjoying life, having fun.'

His eyes took on a hardness I'd not seen before, and he raised his voice. 'You think I don't grieve? You think it disappears?' He clicked his finger and thumb. 'Like that? It does not work like that, Kerry. This grief stays with you.'

I wanted the floor to open up and swallow me whole. I hadn't meant to be so flippant, so dismissive. It went without saying that grief didn't disappear on the flick of a switch. I knew that. I couldn't believe I'd even suggested it.

His voice softened. 'I know what you are feeling, Kerry. You stand in a boat on the river, out of your depth, with no direction, no knowledge, no indication of where to go, floating but going nowhere. Even now you think, what is the purpose of this? What is the purpose of life?'

He gently held my forearms and the fierceness in those blue eyes softened.

'Kerry, I am in a boat, too. I am just further up the river.'

I pulled away, more out of embarrassment than anything. I found myself staring out of the window by the patio. It was all so beautiful and colourful and here was I acting with no sensitivity. I felt him step up behind me and rest his hands on my arms.

'This grief will not disappear, not completely. You think everything is fine, that you are dealing with it, but then you hear something, you see something, then it rips into you like a blunt knife digging into your heart.'

Shit, yes. And when that knife sliced through, it is then twisted slowly to create as much pain and torment as possible.

He turned me to face him. 'I would give anything to spend one more day with Lucia. But I can't. She is gone. Carlotta is gone. Adam is gone. We have to learn to live life without them.'

I'd had a small glimpse of the Latin temperament that Italians were famous for. Had I been Italian, we probably would have had a raging argument. I'm glad it didn't escalate to that because I was hopeless when it came to confrontation. And I was beginning to value his friendship. I didn't want to fall out with him over a stupid comment. A comment made without any thought of the impact it would have. Just because he was ahead of me in the grieving stakes didn't make it any easier for him.

'I'm sorry, Gian, I didn't mean to sound so dismissive.'

For him, the comment was history. After a brief pause, he asked again. 'Will you come? To the dance?'

I wanted to do this. I really did. I wanted to have fun and go dancing. I felt as if I hadn't danced in years.

Again, I flipped the tables. If it was Adam standing here with Lucia, I'd be yelling, 'Go, go and enjoy yourself, go and have some fun. You're alive. So live. Live every day and embrace what life gives you.'

'Yes,' I finally replied. 'I'd love to come.'

Chapter Twenty-Five
DAN

We arrived at The Feather Duck around three in the afternoon. Mum paid for the train tickets. First class. Bloody brilliant and it was so great to have Chloe along. She's so full of life and energy and I was keen to do stuff with her and show her the town. She'd never surfed or done any bodyboarding, so we planned a load of things to do. We wouldn't have time for it all but, in my head, I was already planning another trip to make sure she didn't miss out on anything.

It was awesome to be back. I'd forgotten how great this place was. Not just the bed and breakfast, but St Ives in general.

Suzie and Mum ran to meet us. You'd think they hadn't seen us for years. Well, I suppose that Suzie hadn't seen me in a year, but she was always really welcoming.

I liked Suzie. She's so cool, always wearing clothes that seem to move in the slightest breeze. Very 1960's, like one of those dancers off the old reruns of *Top of the Pops* that Mum and Dad used to like watching.

To be honest, I had been dreading getting here but having Chloe with me made it easier. Mum seemed chilled and she had a bit of a tan as well. The writing festival, she said, had been good for her. I was pleased. She seemed more like Mum again. Not so sad. More upbeat.

Greg came through from the patio with another bloke.

'Look who's arrived,' Suzie said to Greg.

Greg came straight over and gave me a bear hug. He's fucking massive. He spoke quietly to me so no one else could hear. 'Your mum's fine, mate.'

I gave the briefest nod just to thank him. I hadn't mentioned the sleeping pills to anyone. I didn't want Mum thinking I'd been talking about her behind her back, but I knew I could tell Greg if I needed to.

Greg turned to Chloe. 'Hello, my lovely, you must be Chloe.'

'Yes, hi. This is so amazing. I love all the ducks.' She meant it, too. I could tell she was taken by this place the moment we entered. She's always so interested in everything and everyone and didn't hold back on examining the art on the walls.

'Thank you,' said Suzie. 'You will have gathered I'm a duck fan although I try to keep the obsession to a minimum. I'm so glad you could make it down, too. I'm sure Dan appreciates having someone his own age here. And I love your jeans.'

Chloe glanced down at her flares and then at Suzie's outfit. 'Thank you. I love your outfit, too. I was pleased to come and it's nice to have a break, especially here. I remember coming once on holiday, when I was about ten, and loving it.'

The bloke standing by Greg was watching everything until Suzie pulled him toward her. 'This is Gianluca, Gian to his friends. He's a big film star.'

He looked uncomfortable about it and seemed to want to play it down. I didn't recognise him or the name.

He grinned. 'I appear in two films, forty years ago. In Italy. That, I think, is not the big film star.'

Mum made the introductions. 'Gian, this is my son, Dan, and his girlfriend, Chloe.'

He seemed like a nice guy. Greg nudged Chloe.

'Say *piacere* to Gian.'

Chloe went on the alert. 'What?'

'*Piacere*. Go on, say it.'

She ran her hands through her hair as if she were preparing for something, then repeated it, although she hadn't a clue what it was all about. Neither did I. I thought it must be some private joke between them.

Gian cleared up the confusion. 'That means "pleased to meet you". In Italian. *Piacere*.'

Mum told us that Gianluca was teaching Greg Italian, and that Greg was going to Italy with the rugby team. I was well impressed. I loved rugby and wouldn't have minded doing that myself.

Gianluca took mine and Chloe's hands. 'I must go but it is a pleasure for me to meet you. I will, I think, see you over the weekend.' He turned to everyone else. 'Greg, Suzie, Kerry. *Ciao*.'

Greg responded. '*Ciao. Arrivederci*.'

It was funny hearing Italian spoken with a broad Cornish accent. Suzie's chuckle made it clear she was thinking the same as me.

Chloe's gaze following Gianluca as he wandered outside. Then she whispered to me, 'He's fit. For an old bloke.'

I couldn't believe she'd said that. He was old enough to be her dad, for God's sake. Granddad, even.

Chapter Twenty-Six
DAN

One thing I loved about Mum and Dad was they didn't treat me as a kid. When I got to an age where adult things were coming into the frame, it didn't faze them. Not like some parents. Talking about relationships, sex, that sort of thing. It was me that shied away from it when Dad started on about girlfriends and intercourse. I was fucking mortified whenever he spoke about it and wanted to curl up in a ball until he finished. But then it became the norm. I didn't know if I'd become immune to it, or perhaps I'd grown up a bit but and I found it easy to talk to them about those things.

Because of that, Mum didn't bat an eye when me and Chloe checked into the same room. I knew she'd bring it up when we were on our own and I knew what it'd be: if we had sex, use protection.

And, here we were, on our own. It was the first morning after we'd arrived, and I was in Mum's room waiting for her. We were all heading off to the beach. She was getting something from the bathroom and the advice came through loud and clear.

'I hope you're being careful.'

'Mum, I'm not an idiot. Of course, I'm being careful. Anyway, Chloe's on the pill. And we're not rabbits, either. Young people aren't like you lot were in the '70s.'

She laughed at that.

The drawer to the bedside table was slightly open and I slid it out because I recognised what was in there. Those fucking pills. Several blister-packs. Unopened. What was she doing, stockpiling them?

Mum finished up and I quickly nudged the drawer to before she saw me. In the bedroom, she put on some lipstick.

'You all right, Mum?' My throat felt tight. I didn't want her to tell me she wasn't. I wouldn't know how to deal with that. In a microsecond I'd already decided I'd talk to Suzie if she offloaded on me.

'Yes, good, thanks, and I'm glad I made the decision to come down. I'm glad you're here, too. And Chloe.'

She grabbed her bag. 'Right, come on, let's hit the beach.' She headed for the door. 'Greg's hired some bodyboards for you.'

I paused by the drawer before leaving. Should I mention them to Greg? I mean, why was she saving them?

Chapter Twenty-Seven
KERRY

I'm more comfortable today, taking each tentative step
Along a path I'm beginning to accept.
For today, anyway.

We'd chosen Polperrion beach beneath Rico's Bar. It was the closest and not so many families gathered at this one because the sea was rougher on this part of the coast, even on a good day. It was the beach for adventurous souls to go bodyboarding, windsurf or try their hand at proper surfing.

I'm not a confident swimmer and with everything that had happened last year, I was adamant I'd never dip my toe in the sea again. My heart thumped at the thought of Dan wading in, but I couldn't stop him. I couldn't banish fun in the surf because of my hang-up.

There were lifeguards on this beach and Dan and Chloe had life jackets on. And they promised they wouldn't go out far. All the same, my safety radar would be on constant alert.

I tipped my head back and gazed at the sky. It was so lovely to be part of a crowd. I'd missed this. Dan and Chloe had dumped their stuff, picked up their boards and immediately made for the sea. They were a good-looking couple. I was biased toward my son, of course, but Chloe was a petite, attractive blonde although she wasn't vain or obsessed with her looks. Suzie and Greg and I had set up the chairs and commandeered an area for our group.

I shielded my eyes from the sun and scanned the beach. My search settled on a large group playing football. Among them were Gian and Rico. Tina was on the sideline with Tosca and Figaro, cheering everyone on.

Seeing us, Gian waved for us to join them.

'Fancy playing?' asked Greg.

'I'm game if you are. Coming, Suzie?'

'Oh no, darling, I'll watch with Tina.'

Greg and I jogged over, and Gian pulled me toward him while shouting at the group.

'Everyone. This is Kerry.'

There must have been about twenty people in the game; all ages, all sizes, all abilities, and they all greeted me in one way or another.

The game recommenced. I had no idea who was on which team, but I was shown which goal I was aiming for, so just got stuck in. This was beach football at its best: no rules, lots of tackles, almost of the rugby variety and, above all, fun. It's exactly what Adam and I used to enjoy, and I relished the involvement.

Rico dashed around with the energy of a five-year-old. Tina and Suzie enthusiastically lent their support, encouraging us to cheat and trip people up. Tosca and Figaro strained at the leash, eyeing the football and desperately wanting to chase it.

I made a sudden turn, collided with Gian and fell flat on my back, with him tumbling on top of me. He reached out to break his fall.

'I'm so sorry,' he said, hovering above me. 'Are you all right?'

I can't deny that I lingered on those blue eyes a little longer than I should have. Adam had had the most gorgeous brown eyes. That was one of the first things I'd first noticed about him. Unusually, for an Italian, Gian's were as blue as the Mediterranean.

He helped me to my feet. 'I should have told you that we are very competitive.'

'I can do competitive,' I said, loving the sea breeze in my hair and the freedom of running on the beach. 'As long as I know.'

Embracing the spirit of the game, I shoved him to one side and sprinted toward the action. We spent about twenty minutes playing and every so often I sneaked a peek at him and observed how he was with other people. He spent half the time playing chase with the kids instead of kicking a ball.

At one point, I found myself doubled up with laughter, something I hadn't done since before Adam died. Endorphins ran through me unchecked, releasing me into a sense of freedom I'd forgotten was possible. I felt as high as the massive kite that flew in the breeze above me.

Greg announced his retirement from the game, and I did the same. Gian decided that he, too, was ready for a breather. I'm glad we'd asked him to join us. He was quickly becoming a good friend.

Gian, Greg and I made ourselves comfortable in our chairs. Suzie arrived with some takeaway coffees from Rico's and distributed them, along with some sweet croissants. Gian had set up an umbrella under which the dogs could shelter from the sun and had laid down bowls of water for them.

'Darlings,' said Suzie, 'I've just seen Mrs Crowther from the laundrette. I need to see her about our deliveries. See you in a min.'

Greg apologised for being unsociable, but he wanted to finish his John Le Carré novel. 'I've only got three more chapters.'

I, meanwhile, saw a young girl aged about five run over to Gian. She clearly knew him, and her mother stood by and waited while Gian performed the age-old disappearing thumb trick.

I remembered my dad doing this to me when I was her age. Adam did it with Dan and no doubt Gian had done it with his children. He arrived at the part where he'd hidden his thumb and stared at the girl, astonished.

'Where is it? What have you done with my thumb?'

He reached behind the child's ear and retrieved his thumb.

'Oh, here it is.'

The little girl ran back to her mum who mouthed, 'Thank you', to him. He sat back in his chair and sipped his coffee.

'You'll be doing that with your grandchild soon,' I said.

A proud grin appeared on his face.

'Adam always did the three-card trick on Dan,' I added. 'I still have that in his memory box.'

He barely acknowledged me. He was either still thinking about his future grandchild or not wanting to engage. I was sure it was the latter, and I couldn't help but wonder what the problem was regarding the box. Dan and Chloe had left the surf and were grabbing their towels. They would be with us any moment and my chance to tackle this would be gone. Why I wanted to tackle it, I don't know, but I couldn't help asking.

'Gian?' I said, albeit hesitantly.

He tilted his head to make eye contact.

'Why won't you open Lucia's memory box?'

He diverted his attention to the sky. The time he took to think about this felt like an eternity and I wondered if I'd upset him by asking. I didn't push it, although he appeared to be giving the question some thought.

'I am afraid.'

Christ, I wasn't expecting that. I twisted in my chair to face him.

'I am afraid that, when I open it, it will send me back to a place where I don't want to be.'

It reminded me that everyone had their own way of coping; their own way of dealing with grief and he was someone who had perhaps put the barriers up on certain things. Escaping his hometown, not wanting to engage with Lucia's belongings. Yes, he was ahead of me on the grieving journey, but he was also standing still in some respects. Was I doing that? I didn't think so, but standing on the inside looking out, you didn't always see problems.

I rested my hand on his arm. 'Gian, you may find it'll send you to a place you do want to be.'

His gaze was a grateful one but one that told me he didn't think it would.

Chapter Twenty-Eight
DAN

The surf was great. Not too rough but enough to get some good bodyboarding in. Chloe relished it and was now well and truly hooked. She wanted to have a go at surfing, but I told her she should have a few lessons, that it was a totally different skill.

We'd only been down a day, but I felt better already. I think it was good for Chloe, too. She spent so much time caring for her dad, with his MS. Her mum didn't expect her to but, well, Chloe was nice like that. And, if either of my parents had had a disability, I'd have helped them, too.

I felt bad for thinking it, but it was actually good to be away from our house; to break away from the memories there. St Ives was special to all of us, but it was different this time. Maybe it was the weather, the change of scenery, I didn't know. I knew, though, that I was glad I came, and that Mum was okay. She seemed different, too. More her old self. While I was in the sea, I couldn't stop thinking about those pills in the drawer and wondered whether to talk to Greg and Suzie about it. Probably not Suzie. She was great but, if she talked to Mum, Mum would worry and want to talk to me about it.

I should just ask her. We'd talked about all sorts of things, but I couldn't talk to her about this.

Mum and Greg joined a massive football game on the beach. I was half-inclined to do that, too, but I wanted to get in the sea. I was surfing back in when I saw Gian collide with Mum. There was something about the way they were with each other. Chloe and I were having a bit of banter, but I couldn't stop glancing over to see what was going on. I ran back into the surf but kept checking to see if I could spot anything to confirm what I was thinking.

Later, we'd had enough of bodyboarding. Suzie shouted down that she'd got coffee and croissants, so we began making our way back to the group. That's when I saw Mum put her hand on Gian's arm. They were quite intense with each other.

I wanted to sprint over and kick him, tell him to leave Mum alone. Deep down, I knew I was overreacting. I didn't even know what they were talking about. And Mum was quite adamant about dating again. After Colin and Lee had pestered her, it was clear what she thought about dating anyone. But she was different with this bloke. He was nice and everything, but he wasn't Dad.

No one could replace Dad.

No one could be as good as him.

Shit! Why was I getting so angry? Nothing's even fucking happened.

Chapter Twenty-Nine
GIAN

After the morning at the beach, which I enjoy very much, I walk to the newsagent's, and I think about Kerry and how brave she is. She confront everything with no second thought, and I admire her very much for this. But still, I see something in her, something that perhaps frighten her, I don't know. My English is not so good, and it is difficult to explain. I can only think of that first time I see her with the nervous foot tap. That tells me something is not right; that, like me, she cannot confront everything.

When I come out of the newsagent by the harbour, I see Kerry with Dan and Chloe. They stand at one of the places to book the boat trips. Bay Wildlife. They do not see me but Dan, you know, he is a little anxious about what is happening. He try to interrupt Kerry. I squat down to stroke the dogs.

The attendant, he ask Kerry to confirm that she want three tickets.

'No, no,' Kerry said. 'Just one. It's just for me.'

Then Dan, he do something that make me stand up. He pull Kerry's arm, twist her around. 'Mum, no, you can't…'

I wonder what is going on.

'Please, Mum.'

Kerry, she suddenly hold him. Tight, as if she realise a mistake and Dan save her from this.

'Oh sweetheart,' she say, 'I'm sorry. I wasn't thinking. I won't if you don't want me to.'

Dan, he is happy with that decision so Kerry, she turn to the attendant.

'Sorry, I'll do this another time.'

The attendant move to the next customer and Kerry stare out beyond the harbour wall. I make my way home and I wonder, all the time, what is the story here.

Chapter Thirty
KERRY

The challenges differ from hour to hour, day to day
A door opens wide, a door slams shut, a door will sway
The latter is the hardest one
Creating massive indecision.

Later, in my room, I gripped the leaflet about the wildlife boat tours. What the fuck was I thinking, trying to book that in front of Dan? He was wild-eyed. Not in anger; it was sheer panic. He pulled me back and I saw the desperation in him.

I could have kicked myself for being so insensitive, but this was one of my reasons for visiting St Ives. The last hurdle, the last barrier, the demon I'd refused to confront since Adam died. I had to do it. If I went back to Sussex without facing it, I would never forgive myself. I would have failed.

I stared at the cute seal staring out at me from the front of the leaflet and fell into a memory.

As soon as that girl was thrown clear, Adam stripped off and dived into the sea; a choppy sea, the two boats, floundering, the captain yelling, swearing, ordering safety measures, demanding help from the coastguard. I hadn't been worried. Adam was a good swimmer. He would be fine. Everything would be good. Everyone would be safe.

I flopped on the bed. The leaflet had become a ball in my hand. Shit, I didn't want this. I didn't want those images flickering through my head like an old movie winding through an antique projector. I wondered if they would ever burn out and disappear.

Chapter Thirty-One
DAN

Mum was right about Rico's. It was brilliant and me and Chloe got on well with him and Tina. Rico came out bodyboarding with us after he'd finished playing football and he was great to hang out with. Tina is proper Cornish and she and Chloe made a connection, too.

Chloe and I spent most of the weekend with Mum, mainly on the beach and doing some of the coastal walks. It was fun and the weather held out. The evening before we were due to go home, there was drizzle in the air, but Suzie and Greg had booked a table at Rico's and the concertina doors were partly pulled to.

We were drinking beer, eating snacks and having some laughs with Mum. Greg and Suzie were there too, with Gian. Tina was managing the bar and Rico had something else on so he couldn't be with us.

The music they were playing reminded me of Dad: Pink Floyd's 'Wish You Were Here'. He had that song on his playlist. When it finished, an Italian song came on. They were obviously aiming for an Anglo/Latin feel. It was a cool venue, much better than The Greasy Spoon, and I loved that it wasn't full of tourists. Tina told us they put reserved notices on sixty per cent of the tables first thing in the morning and they guaranteed filling those seats with townspeople.

I was having a good time, but I kept toying with the salt and pepper pots and anything else I could lay my hands on. It was obvious that Gian and Mum got on well and me fidgeting like this just proved how frustrated I was about it.

I didn't like it. I didn't want Mum to like Gian. Fucking hell, why not? What's the matter with me? It's the first time I'd seen Mum happy in months. Not just that night but the whole time we were down.

After Dad died, she'd always tried to be positive and upbeat but, down here, it didn't seem put on anymore. It was as if something had happened. The only difference was that she was here with Suzie and Greg and this Gian bloke.

He was nice, I couldn't deny it, but I wanted to slap him. He was right opposite me, so it'd be easy to do. Mum had wanted nothing to do with Colin. She'd wanted nothing to do with Lee either. Admittedly, neither of them were like this bloke. There was a chemistry going on here, it was obvious.

The trouble was, I didn't want Mum even to be friends with him and I hated myself for thinking that. Why would I think that? Why wouldn't I want my mum to have some happiness?

Chloe didn't help. She thought he was cool and good looking and, if she were older, she wouldn't say no. I laughed at her, but it pissed me off that she liked him. Why couldn't he have been a fucking bastard? It would have been easier to explain how I felt.

'It's a shame you are leaving so soon,' Gian said to me and Chloe.

'You'll just have to come back,' Suzie said.

'I will,' Chloe said. 'I'd forgotten how lovely being here is.'

Greg began refilling our glasses.

'I can't drink another drop until I've had a wee,' Mum said.

Suzie and Chloe both went off to the loo with Mum. Women are like that…

Then Greg got up. 'I'll get some more blinis.'

Shit. I instinctively wanted to pull Greg back into his seat. It felt awkward with just me and Gian. He seemed perfectly happy. His dogs had been sleeping by his feet but with all that activity, they were poking their heads out, wondering what was going on.

'There is something you want to say to me?'

I shifted in my seat and shrugged, acting as if everything was fine.

'About your mother?'

Fuck. How could he just ask the question like that? What could I say? I don't like you being friends with her? How childish was that?

'I am no threat, Dan,' he said, calmly. 'I like her. She likes me. We are friends.'

He gave me a 'that's all it is' shrug and it did sort of settle me down a bit. I just sat there like a numbnut, grateful to see Greg return to the table.

Tosca and Figaro gazed up at me from the floor. Bloody hell, even the dogs made me feel guilty about resenting him.

Chapter Thirty-Two
KERRY

Family dynamics, back and forth they go
They hesitate, trip me up, surprise me, retreat and grow.

When we reached The Feather Duck, everyone said goodnight to Gian and entered ahead of me. I instinctively hung back. I enjoyed our goodnight routine and would have missed it if I'd gone through with the others.

'Your son, he's a good boy.'

'I think so but then I am biased.'

'But, look out for him, Kerry. He is still young.'

'Did he say something to you?'

'No. He say nothing. But I understand what he want to say.'

I mouthed a silent 'Ah'. 'He's very protective.'

'That, I think, is a strength. But, also, can be a weakness, yes?' He winked. 'Goodnight, Kerry Simmonds.'

'Goodnight Gianluca Belfiore.' I squatted down to fuss over the dogs. 'And goodnight, Tosca and Figaro.'

He brought out his cigarettes and wandered up the hill.

In reception, Suzie and Greg were making sure windows and doors were locked. Chloe was halfway up the stairs; Dan was about to follow her, but I called him back. He seemed happy and chilled. This break was doing us both good. I didn't want to spoil it but, after what Gian had said…

'Dan, is everything okay?'

'Yeah, why?'

I tilted my head to the entrance. 'He's just a friend, that's all. He's gone through the same as me. It's someone to talk with. He understands.'

Colour crept into his cheeks. Then he hugged me for a few seconds before pulling back.

'What was that for?'

He gave me a sheepish shrug, then jogged up the stairs.

Chapter Thirty-Three
KERRY

Angels on high don't always need their wings to fly,
They can shoot into your heart, like Cupid with his dart.

A couple of days later, Suzie and I ensconced ourselves in a family-run fish restaurant. It was one of those eateries that me and Adam went to, and I needed to tick it off my to-visit list. We'd ordered scallops with black pudding and a hollandaise sauce. I'd never thought about mixing those ingredients before and the dish was delicious, especially accompanied by a glass of chilled Sauvignon Blanc.

Spread out over our table were two piles of property details. We'd spent the morning in and out of estate agents picking up details of those houses and flats I'd marked. Now I had a number that I'd quickly discarded and a handful that I wanted to view. It was still a tentative process but having Suzie along for the ride gave me some moral strength.

We'd been talking about films we'd seen and inevitably discussed *Il Problemo*, agreeing that the film was up there with *Cinema Paradiso* in the foreign film category.

'Honestly, darling, I can't believe Gian didn't tell us he was in that. He was absolutely bloody gorgeous in it, too. Why on earth didn't we work that out?' Suzie sipped her wine. 'I told him off for not letting us know about his glamorous past. I didn't even know the family name was Belfiore. If I did hear it, it certainly didn't register.' She gave me a conspiratorial look. 'He's still very handsome.'

I matched it with a hard stare. 'Don't matchmake. I had a taste of that with Maggie over Christmas and I put her straight.'

'Oh, darling, I wouldn't. That's your call, no one else's.'

Glad she wouldn't interfere, I continued, 'You know he loves Lucia as much as I love Adam.'

'I wonder if anyone else knows? About the film star past?'

'Don't be wicked. He likes to keep it low key. He seemed a bit shy about it when I realised who he was.'

'He's a sweetheart. But, picking up on what you said, I wanted to ask, would you mind if I invited him to your anniversary do?'

My little inner voice whispered that it was likely Suzie was indeed trying to matchmake, despite her protestations. Before I could voice an opinion, she added, 'It would have been Lucia's birthday the day after your anniversary.'

That left me with a whole different perspective on things.

'Really? Oh, God, yes. Of course. We'll celebrate Adam *and* Lucia. That'll be fantastic. It's a shame Dan and Chloe couldn't stay on and join the celebrations.'

Suzie took a swig of wine. 'Dan is so protective of you. It's very sweet.'

'I know. And he needn't be. I'm doing okay, honestly, I am. I've surprised myself coming here.' I squeezed her hand. 'And you and Greg have helped with that.'

I sifted through the handful of property details in front of me. 'I'll make appointments for these when we get back. But I'm not making any decisions without Dan. It has to be right for him, too. I want him settled at uni before I go gallivanting off on my own adventure.'

I gazed out of the window. A funeral cortège was standing in traffic nearby. What it was didn't register initially because I was thinking about properties but then reality struck.

I was thrown back to that day, the day of the funeral. I'd kept my emotions in check until the hearse drew up outside the house. Just seeing it sucked the air from my lungs and I held on to the curtain for fear of falling to the floor. As we came out of the house, I put my arm around Dan's waist. Maggie and Tom were either side of us.

There were three wreaths in the back of the hearse, alongside the coffin. One from me, one from Dan and one from Maggie and Tom. We'd asked everyone else to contribute to the RNLI.

The neighbours had gathered outside to pay their respects. They'd been brilliant when the accident had happened, rallying around and constantly calling in with tea, sympathy and homemade meals.

The funeral director dipped his head to me. 'Would you like to see the flowers?'

I did and I didn't. Deep down, I wanted to walk past the coffin as quickly as possible. With trepidation, I approached the hearse and touched the window. I couldn't hold it together anymore. Silent tears streamed down my cheeks. Maggie sidled in to hold me. I heard Dan crying behind me and was heartened to know that Tom was alongside him.

When I came out of that memory, a tear had escaped. More than one, if I was honest. Suzie brought her chair close and put her arm around me.

'Oh, my darling.'

I leant into her. Perhaps I wasn't as okay as I thought I was.

Chapter Thirty-Four
KERRY

Blossoming friendships bring change, possibility
They elevate a tired song into a joyous symphony.

Two days later, I reserved my place on another poetry workshop. I wasn't sure whether my poetry would improve as a result of these sessions, but it got me out and some words of creative wisdom were sinking in.

Leaving The Feather Duck, I immediately collided with Rico. My notebook, festival guide and pens fell to the ground.

Rico, looking flustered, quickly gathered them up. 'I'm so sorry. Forgive me, please.'

'Are you all right?'

He handed me my things. 'I have a meeting and I am late. I left the groceries at Papà's. Now I'm going to be more late but the chef needs the groceries.'

'Do you want me to get them? Is your father not in? Can't he bring them down?'

He fumbled for his keys. 'Oh, would you please? Papà is in bed with migraine. He will be asleep. The groceries are in the kitchen. Two bags. Could you take them to the bar? They are not heavy.'

I took the keys from him. 'Yes, of course. Migraine? Does he get them often?'

'Occasionally. He will sleep for two, three hours and it goes away. *Grazie mille*. Leave the keys at the bar.'

He turned to go but I stopped him. 'Which is his house?'

'Oh, sorry, yes, La Casa con Vista, the second house on the right, behind the railings.' Again, he went to leave but turned abruptly. 'Kerry. My father. He seem very happy. I think you are good for him.' He lifted a hand to wave. '*Ciao*.'

The comment rooted me to the spot. What did he mean by that?

I pondered the statement as I made my way up the hill. I saw Gian as a friend, a good friend admittedly, who was on the same journey as me. Was he seeing this as something more than that? Or was Rico simply putting two and two together and coming up with some wild figure?

The house came into view. 'Wow.'

I peered through the railings. I'd never ventured up this hill before. Now I saw a scattering of amazing properties, all detached, all individually designed. Gian's was a low-level white Art-Deco house. His Fiat 500 and an old Vespa stood under a carport. I smirked. You could take the man out of Italy but not Italy out of the man. La Casa con Vista. I couldn't speak Italian, but I understood the meaning: the house with a view.

At the front door, I found the correct key, gingerly opened it and peered in. The door opened straight into the lounge. I wondered where the dogs were. God, I hope they didn't start barking. My fear quickly subsided when they quietly scampered over to me as if I was their long-lost friend, their tails wagging with excitement. Have you come to see us? Possible treats? I squatted down to greet them.

'Hello, Tosca, Figaro. You are very good not to bark, aren't you?'

I left my bag and bits and pieces by the door and scanned the room. It was modern, open plan. There looked to be a balcony with sea views, running the length of the building at the back. Gian, I decided, had good taste, decor-wise. He had opted for neutral colours and little clutter. A poster for *Il Problemo* was on one of the walls.

To the side of the poster, I studied a display of family photos. Like ours at home, they spanned the generations from children to grandparents. There was a lovely image of Gian with a child I presumed was Carlotta. She only looked about two years old but was clearly daddy's girl. I felt for him. It was bad enough to lose your wife but to lose a child, too. I couldn't imagine it.

On the cabinet below was a large shoebox sealed with Sellotape, peeling a little with age. The name 'Lucia' was scribbled on the top. The memory box.

I moved to a sweeping arch that led into an office where law and university certificates adorned the walls, along with a graduation photo taken with his parents. He took after his father. The same hairline, the same stance.

On the other side, the lounge opened into a modern kitchen. The two bags of groceries stood on a small island in the middle. There was also a glass jar with dog biscuits in. Tosca and Figaro had followed me everywhere and I'm sure they sensed I'd spotted the treats because their tails were now a blur.

'Well,' I whispered, taking the lid off the jar, 'they say dogs have a sixth sense and I think you do.'

I gave them each a biscuit and picked up the grocery bags.

At the front door, I stopped.

Curiosity got the better of me.

I didn't know what I was thinking. Leaving everything on the sofa, I went to the only closed door that led off from the lounge. Even as I gently pressed down on the handle one thought was prominent. *Kerry, what the fuck are you doing?*

I nudged the door open a fraction. The dogs were immediately at my feet, their noses pushing against the door, wanting to leap up and join Gian on the bed. I flapped my hand for them to retreat. Fortunately, they understood my aggressive stance because they sat down and fixed their sad dog eyes on me. Oh God, they were adorable. I didn't mean to be so aggressive. I was just panicking that I would wake Gian up. Now, I wanted to hug the dogs, but I didn't want to encourage them. I put my finger to my lips with a silent, *sshh*. They seemed to understand, and they lay down.

Inside, I left the door open a little. I was right that the balcony ran along the back of the building. Bloody hell! What a view: a clear expanse of ocean and the coastline leading way up the county to Newquay. The bi-fold doors were open and there was a balmy breeze coming through. On the wall I spotted a professional photograph of Lucia.

On the bed, Gian was fast asleep.

I couldn't lie, I ogled.

He had nothing on, and a sheet just about covered what needed to be covered. I almost gasped. Feelings rose up that I should not be having. Physically and mentally.

Shit, he was hot.

The breeze picked up. The door slammed. The dogs barked.

I dropped to the floor.

Fuck, fuck, fuck.

Shit. Fuck. What the hell!

Gian roused. More asleep than awake, his hair ruffled, he pushed himself up on his elbows and looked around for what had woken him. Then he spotted me crouching on the floor like some ninja.

Sleepy-eyed, he asked, 'Kerry. What are you doing here?'

I felt like a character in a French farce. People in and out of houses and bedrooms, leaping into wardrobes, hiding under beds. How fucking embarrassing was this?

I had no explanation so defaulted to gibbering mode.

'Er, well, I… I bumped into Rico. He said he'd left groceries. Here. Well, not here… not here in the bedroom.'

Fuck.

'Oh, yes,' he said, 'they are in the kitchen.'

'Yes.' I remained on the floor. 'Yes, I said I'd get them. He was running late… for an appointment.'

The amusement in his eyes caused me to babble even more.

'I just thought I'd make sure you were okay, you know. He said you had a migraine; I didn't know if you needed anything.'

'No. Thank you. I just need to sleep.' He frowned. 'Why are you on the floor?'

'What! Oh… I… I dropped something.'

A soppy grin appeared on his face. Oh, how I wanted the ground to swallow me up! I scrambled to my feet, grasping the invisible something I'd dropped.

'All good. I'll leave you to sleep.'

I dashed out and closed the door behind me. The dogs looked curious in the way that only dogs could. I could imagine exactly what they were thinking. What were you doing in there? Why do you look so embarrassed?

I rested my head back against the door. I didn't normally swear this much but, really… 'Shit, fuck.'

Chapter Thirty-Five
KERRY

Just step into the dance, discovering a chance
To take a sole desire and leap into the fire.

That evening, when I arrived at Rico's with Suzie and Greg, I was greeted by the sight and sound of a Latin-American band. They were playing at the far end of the veranda and were excellent musicians, all very Buena Vista Social Club. I began swaying to the music as soon as I heard the percussion and the jazz guitar. There were already two couples on the dance floor, expertly going through intricate salsa moves.

The fairy lights around the veranda were on, although they wouldn't be fully effective until the sun had gone down.

'The group is local,' Greg explained to me. 'They play here every few weeks. And we've got a salsa club down the road, so that lot'll be along tonight, putting us all to shame.'

Rico and Tina had arranged the tables around the edge of the veranda to create a space for those who wanted to dance. It was still early evening, and I would imagine, once everyone had arrived, this floor would be full. It was at times like this that I wished I'd learned how to dance properly and, again, this took me on a nostalgia trip. Fred Astaire and Ginger Rogers in *Top Hat*, Gene Kelly and Debbie Reynolds in *Singing in the Rain*. Not just the professionals, either; everyone back then could jive, boogie and waltz instead of just jigging about like we all did these days. Adam and I had tried dance classes a few years ago but it wasn't a resounding success. He had two left feet and we struggled to get into any sort of rhythm without tripping each other up.

The evening was a balmy one and I was glad I'd opted for smart casual. Most people were just in shorts but some, mainly the women, had made a bit of an effort. Suzie and I had opted for summer dresses. Mine was turquoise with flecks of deep yellow and red. I liked to step up a gear for events like this because there were few opportunities to do so. Most days I easily slipped into casual mode but, this dress tonight, well, it lifted my mood considerably and instilled a sense of pride in me. I'd done a twirl in front of Adam's photo and asked if he thought I'd scrubbed up well. I knew this dress suited me and I couldn't help but lap up the compliments that came my way when we arrived.

Gian had also gone for smart. Did that man ever look scruffy? He was wearing a beautifully tailored summer suit. I couldn't imagine this was purchased off-the-peg at Marks and Spencer. He stood out as the most elegantly dressed man in the room.

A nagging worry entered my head. Would he bring up this morning's visit in front of Suzie and Greg? God, I hoped not.

His arms opened wide. 'How beautiful you both are,' he said to me and Suzie as he gave us each the traditional Continental kiss on each cheek.

'Thank you,' I said. 'And you're very dashing, too.'

He accepted the compliment with a brief nod.

A waiter approached and I ordered a gin and tonic. 'Do you have a particular gin in mind?' he asked.

'Oh, I'm not sure. What do you suggest?'

The waiter listed a selection, many of them from Cornwall. Seeing my indecision, Gian recommended the most popular Cornish one they sold: Tarquin's. Then I had to decide on which flavour! I opted for their Rhubarb and Raspberry gin. Gian ordered a Peroni beer.

No mention was made of my exploits that morning.

I scanned the area as more people arrived. Many of them I'd met from playing football on the beach or Suzie and Greg had introduced them to me. We fell into easy banter and the band continued creating those wonderful Latin-American vibes.

Sometimes, an invisible and unknown entity reminds me that I can exist in the world. At this specific moment, I wanted to fling my arms wide and shout to the sky. I felt normal; I felt part of this crowd, this life, this existence. It was happening more often down here. I felt at home, that I belonged here, as if I'd found my spiritual sanctuary. Someone touched my elbow. It was Gian.

'Would you like to dance?'

'Salsa!'

'Yes. You can salsa?'

'No.'

He chuckled at my panic then steered me toward a space at the edge of the veranda.

'The basic step is very simple. I join the salsa club just a few weeks ago and this is what I learn. Here, let me show you.'

The basic steps were very simple, and it turned out that they were all he knew, but at least we were able to enter into the spirit of the dance. I was always in awe of people who got up and actually danced. It didn't have to be a waltz or a foxtrot. Even modern dancing, if a couple were in sync with each other, it was a pleasure to watch.

I had just one dance with Gian. He, along with Rico and Tina, were perfect hosts. They circulated and mixed with the locals and tourists. I couldn't deny that my eyes kept seeking him out. There was something quite gracious in the attentiveness he showed people, whether friends or strangers. He made you feel part of the group and appeared very welcoming, even to those who didn't appear to be his sort of people. There were a handful of what I would call the 'louder' tourists. That sounded like I was a complete snob, but they seemed more suited to the cheaper end of Benidorm then the higher end of Cornwall. They didn't stay long. I think they were after cheap drinks and a disco. The opposite to what Rico's was offering.

I restrained a grin. Honestly, what did I know? He might have told them to piss off because they were lowering the tone.

The band remained on form and easily slipped from one rhythmic tune to another; each member took a solo on his respective instrument. I'm not entirely sure how they managed to fit into such a small space. There were six of them playing guitar, brass, keyboards and percussion and they'd perfected the art of playing in an area the size of a postage stamp. More guests took to the dance floor and soon it was difficult to allow any more people in. In fact, I think Rico had to turn some people away.

The atmosphere was fun and convivial. We didn't have anyone getting too drunk or showing off. Everyone was there to enjoy the music and, because the music wasn't loud, there was no need to shout to make yourself heard.

The kitchen staff had laid out a buffet and at various intervals they came to replenish the nibbles, consisting of a mixture of tapas-style food. I spotted salmon, shrimp, salami, cheeses, tomatoes, olives and so on, alongside French sticks and pâté. At the far end of the table was a selection of vegan and gluten-free snacks.

As the evening went on and the sun began to sink low in the sky, I thought I would rest my aching feet. I hadn't been dancing much but I had been standing nattering for at least two hours. My daily footwear tended to be flats. This evening, I had my red sandals on with low kitten heels but now even those felt like six-inch stilettos.

As I searched for a seat, Gian appeared. 'I'm so sorry. I invite you to this evening and I neglect you for much of it. Would you like to dance?'

'It's absolutely fine,' I said. 'I can see you're helping Rico and Tina.'

It was a slow dance, and he drew me in. Not too close but this was the closest I'd been to a man, physically, since Adam. If it had been Colin or Lee who'd asked me to dance, I would have been pushing him away by now and probably having a rant, too. But now, I fell comfortably into step.

'Are you having a good time?'

'Yes, I am. Very much.'

He drew me a little closer and I breathed in his aftershave. Aramis. Adam used to splash that on a few years ago.

'*Ah bene. Mi fa piacere.*'

I made the mistake of looking into his eyes when he spoke, and I was such a sucker for beautiful eyes. We made our way around the dance floor among the other guests and all I was thinking was, *fuck, your eyes are gorgeous*. And, like Adam and Dan, he had bloody long eyelashes. A few seconds had passed, and I realised that he'd said something to me. I racked my brains to recall what it was. Had he asked me something? Oh yes, he'd said something in Italian, hadn't he?

'What does that mean?'

He stared into my eyes, taking me in. A few seconds passed, although it seemed like minutes. This was intense. But it was also bloody lovely.

'What?' he asked.

By now, I had forgotten what the hell we were talking about. All I knew was we were gazing at each other, and the seconds were passing by with nothing being said. We were in a world of our own. I think someone said hello as they shuffled by but neither of us responded.

'What?' I finally asked. I'd completely lost track of what we were asking each other.

A voice intruded but, in my head, it was very distant.

'Mr Belforee,' it said in a cockney accent.

I was so in the moment that it didn't register the speaker was right by my shoulder.

'Mr Belforee.'

Yanked out of our mutual reverie, I quickly excused myself and, I had to admit, almost ran to the balustrade to take a breath. Something had passed between the pair of us.

Something more than friendship and I wasn't sure if that's what I wanted. Part of me didn't but, my goodness, a huge part of me did. I listened to the man engage with Gian.

'Mr Belforee. Remember us? We was 'ere just a few months back. Me and the missus. That's 'er over there. We said we'd be back and 'ere we are.'

I looked over. I'm fairly sure that Gian didn't have a clue who this man was, but he hid it well. 'Of course, how nice to see you again. *Mi scusa.*'

He joined me and I couldn't help but laugh at his exasperated expression.

'Do I sense an intolerance of tourists?'

He grinned, then locked eyes with me. 'Not all tourists.'

We leant on the balustrade, and I focussed on the beach and the ocean beyond. In the darkness, I heard the sea lapping at the shore and could just make out the white foam as the waves splashed on the sand. The sun had set. The fairy lights were treating us to their full effect and the band decided to take a ten-minute break. It was just gone ten thirty.

Gian closed his eyes and massaged his forehead.

'You're tired.'

'It is the after-effects of migraine.' He winced. 'It was a very difficult morning for me.'

I turned to face him. Poor thing. I'd never had a migraine, but I knew how debilitating they could be. He appeared pained.

'You know, I found someone crouching on my bedroom floor?'

My concern altered to a sheepish grin. How embarrassing was that? He must have laughed his head off after I'd left. I checked my watch.

'Do you want to go? I would imagine you're ready to drop.'

'But you can stay, Kerry. Don't stop your evening because of me.'

'I'm happy to, really. My feet are aching, and I'll be glad to put my feet up.'

'If you are sure. I would normally take the dogs out and then return but, tonight, I think I need to go to bed.'

I gathered my things while Gian said goodbye to a few people. When he came back, he held out an elbow for me to link arms with him.

I did.

Suzie's conspiratorial expression showed she had witnessed this gesture. I glared at her. No doubt she would conclude more from that than was necessary. Honestly, she was as bad as Maggie.

Ten minutes later, Gian delivered me to The Feather Duck. I hadn't thought about our goodbye. So far, when we'd met for coffee or gone on an excursion somewhere, we'd simply said goodbye. But, after that intimate slow dance and linking arms with him up the hill, a whole new perspective had opened. I couldn't deny it, I was nervous, ready to blurt out my farewell and dash in.

He turned to face me. 'Kerry.'

He brought me close and gently kissed me on the lips.

I thought I would melt. It was tender, romantic and I loved every bit of it. God, how I'd missed this.

Then, the thread of guilt tugged at me. I pushed him back.

He closed his eyes in apology. 'I'm so sorry. I didn't—'

I couldn't stop myself. I moved in and kissed him back. Then I rushed into The Feather Duck.

God knows what he must have thought. I took the stairs two at a time and unlocked my door as if my life depended on it. Had I just made a complete idiot of myself? I threw my things on the bed, hesitantly opened the doors to the balcony and peered out. Would he be there? I bloody hoped not. What would I say, for God's sake?

Shit.

Fortunately, he was making his way up the hill.

I couldn't help it. I couldn't not say it. 'Goodnight, Gianluca Belfiore.'

He turned and waved. 'Goodnight, Kerry Simmonds.'

A minute later, I was sitting on the bed, holding Adam's photo. On my laptop, I had the Facebook page of Rico's Bar open, where I found a photo of Rico with Gian. I zoomed in on Gian.

I studied the two images. I loved Adam. I'd kissed Gian. What the fuck?

I deliberated for what seemed an eternity, then closed the laptop and hugged Adam's photo as I lay back on the bed.

Chapter Thirty-Six
GIAN

My evening with Kerry, it was so wonderful. She is good company, and this is the first time I see her being happy; that sadness I see, it is not there tonight. That is good, I think. I think this holiday is good for her. And she is very social, she speak to many people, and she is popular with them.

I cannot deny that I have feelings for her. She remind me of Lucia because she is fun and positive. Lucia was like this. I never see my wife upset very often and I think that Kerry is like this, too.

But they are also very different. My wife, she is very feminine and never wear trousers or jeans. She love fashion and jewellery. Kerry, she is a tomboy and not concerned about these things. She is feminine in her own way.

When I walk Kerry home, I kiss her. At first, you know, I think she is angry with me. She step back and I feel very bad, that I end this friendship before it begin.

But then, she kiss me!

It surprise me that she do this. That she kiss me. It make me happy, too. When I light a cigarette and I begin my walk home, she call out to me.

'Goodnight, Gianluca Belfiore.'

And I call back to her, 'Goodnight, Kerry Simmonds.'

I think I smile all the way up the hill.

When I arrive home, the dogs, they are all over me wanting to know about my evening and I tell them. I tell them that Kerry kiss me. They do not understand, I know, but they are happy to see me.

I pour myself a whisky and the dogs, they follow me as I go to the memory box. The Sellotape, you know, it is brittle, and it is easy to strip away. I tease the tape, but I make no attempt to tear it off. I don't want to face this. Not at the moment. Not on my own. Not with a drink. That is not, I think, a good way to do this.

I finish my whisky and speak with the dogs.

'We go for a walk, yes?'

I have no need to put them on leads. They are well trained and sit by the door waiting for me.

Before I leave, I kiss my fingers and transfer that kiss to my photos of Lucia and Carlotta.

Chapter Thirty-Seven
KERRY

Open up a door, file away what came before,
Hold life up for real, fall in love with what you feel.

Something unspoken was happening after that night. We didn't talk about that kiss, but we had begun to plan a few excursions, beginning with the morning after the dance. Gian telephoned to ask if I was free, and would I like to take a trip out?

Suzie, of course, overheard the call and immediately offered to look after Tosca and Figaro.

Reading the anticipation on her face, I was quick to state, 'Don't read anything into this, Suzie. It's just two friends spending the day together.'

'Darling, I saw you link arms with him and walk into the sunset.'

'We didn't walk into the sunset. We came back to our respective homes. And friends link arms. I link arms with you, but it doesn't mean I want a relationship with you.'

She waved my excuses away and, fortunately, didn't pursue the topic.

I didn't tell her about the kiss. That would have made her brain spin and she'd spill the beans to Greg and Greg would… well, Greg would tell her to stop interfering and making assumptions. Even so, I needed Suzie here as a support, not as a dating agency. Yes, I was having a couple of good days, emotionally, but it never lasted. I knew something would trigger a slide and I just hoped this excursion with Gian would help me retain the positive energy building inside me for a little while longer.

I hugged Suzie. 'I'll see you later.'

'Drinks on the patio this evening?'

'Looking forward to it.'

Outside, Gian waited with his vintage Vespa that had seen better days. He handed the dogs to Suzie and a crash helmet to me, then told me to hop on the back. I was glad I'd opted for shorts. I thought we'd be going in the Fiat. He wore chinos, sandals and a polo shirt. I was also glad that I was carrying a small rucksack instead of a handbag. I preferred having both hands free and I needed them at that moment.

I climbed onto the seat and searched for how to hang on. He twisted around.

'Kerry, put your arms around my waist.'

I did. Suzie raised her eyebrows. I glowered at her. As we pulled away, I could smell that aftershave again.

'Where are we going?' I shouted.

'What?'

The noise of the engine drowned out my words and shouting louder made no difference.

I occasionally heard what he was yelling at me. Little snippets reached my ears, something about Penzance, something about an island. He took us on the back road toward Penzance, past The Engine Inn in Cripplesease, through the tiny village of Nancledra, passing various pubs and tea rooms on the way. We carried on down narrow country lanes. Occasionally, as the hedgerows parted, there were glimpses of the sea to our left. Most of the countryside either side of us was farmland, accompanied by the inevitable smell of manure at various intervals. As for livestock, I only saw cows, apart from half a dozen donkeys and llamas in a field along the way.

The breeze was warm, and the occasional white cloud obscured the sun's rays. We eventually came to a tiny village and turned off down a tree-lined road that appeared barely wide enough for the tractor that had just trundled by. Then Gian pulled into a tiny gap in the hedge to allow a double-decker bus to pass. How the hell did a bus this size drive around these little roads?

A minute later, we were on the main A30. Ahead, the bay opened up, with the town of Penzance hugging the shore. Just along from Penzance was the fishing town of Newlyn, its houses climbing up a steep hill from the busy harbour. Two miles beyond that, out of sight around the bay, lay the exquisite village of Mousehole.

At the roundabout, I'd assumed we'd be heading for Penzance, but Gian turned left. A minute later and we were on the coast road to Marazion, with St Michael's Mount rising up out of the water of Mount's Bay in front of us.

St Michael's Mount was a unique feature in that when the tide was in, it became an island, at which point the only way to reach it would be by the small wooden boats that ferried people back and forth. When the tide was out, an old stone causeway appeared, allowing access by foot. Currently, the tide was out, and a number of people were already walking across. They looked like little ants from this far away.

Interestingly, Adam had told me years ago, there was a similar structure off the coast of Brittany with the same name, Mont St-Michel, and the same kind of tidal feature.

The island was situated opposite the small village of Marazion which, I'd also learned from Adam, was the main town in this part of Cornwall before Penzance took precedence. Marazion remained, and continued to remain, a village with one road in and out.

Being on the Vespa meant it was easy to park. There were queues to get into the car parks but not for our little scooter. In fact, we went past the parking and turned down a side street with a dead end.

Taking off our crash helmets, Gian placed them behind a wall in someone's front garden. I frowned.

'Will they be all right there?'

'Of course. This is residents only.'

'Won't you get a ticket? I thought they were pretty hot on parking restrictions down here.'

A sprightly lady in her mid-eighties opened the door of the house facing the garden in which he'd left the helmets. 'Gianluca, my lover,' she said, her accent strong, her arms opened wide.

'*Signora* Tremayne.' He kissed her on both cheeks. '*Come stai?*'

'All the better for seeing you, my lovely,' she said in a croaky voice as she handed him something. She then greeted me. 'You his lady friend?'

I wasn't entirely sure what she meant by that, but I said, yes, I was a friend and a lady, and that we were having a day out together. The 'something' she'd given him was a resident's parking permit.

She wished us a good day and told us to come in for a cuppa if we wanted to later. 'I'm doing a house clean today. Got my fella coming down for the week. Ain't only the youngsters who can enjoy a bit of rumpy pumpy.'

I felt like Maggie did whenever I mentioned sex to her. This woman was honestly getting on in years and I couldn't imagine her doing anything but crocheting toy animals.

Gian grinned. 'You be careful, *Signora*. At your age, you could pull a muscle.' He ducked from the clip around the ear she playfully dished out. '*Caio, Nonna.*'

'If I was your grandmother, that slap would've connected.'

Gian took my hand to lead me up the alleyway and into the square at Marazion.

'Who was that?'

'*Signora* Tremayne. She is a friend of Tina's grandmother.'

'How d'you get to know so many people?'

'It is easy. These communities, they are so small. It is like where I come from. Each town, if you spend a little time and talk to people, you get to know them. Keep talking, you know them more and then you know them so well, you spend time and drink coffee with them.

'And then, you receive the favour and, here, in the summer, parking is the favour, *si*? The older generation, they are easy to charm, you know? I treat *Nonna* Tremayne as if she is Sophia Loren, it always work. But I tell you truthfully, I like old people. They have stories to tell. They live a full life.'

We meandered around the few shops that were there, mainly run by local craftsmen and women and very talented they were, too. Artists, sculptors, people who ran antique shops and galleries. It was such a pleasure to do some browsing and all the owners were keen to tell us how they made things and where their inspirations came from.

One shop caught my eye: a jewellery store full of locally made silver rings, necklaces, brooches. You name it, if it was made from silver, it was there. I loved the decor, too. Each display was arranged on sections of polished driftwood with hidden underlighting. The only colour was a subtle hint of Tiffany blue.

Gian had his eye on a ring that had quite a bit of gold in it. 'I like this. Look, it has the coastline carved into it as the design.'

Examining the ring, I could make out St Michael's Mount and the outline of the shore from Mousehole around to Lizard Point. I also checked the price. It was a just over two hundred pounds, but worth every penny. The craftsmanship was outstanding and the design unique.

'Let me buy it for you,' I found myself saying. I had felt good all morning. I'd felt good yesterday, too. I felt normal, alive, as if I was experiencing a routine day for the first time since Adam died and I knew this was thanks to this holiday, staying with Suzie and Greg and meeting Gian. The three of them were helping me more than they would know.

Kiss aside, I still considered him to be a good friend rather than a seriously romantic possibility. The fact that we'd not mentioned the kiss had taken some of the pressure off me and I was grateful for that. I was grateful to have this new buddy showing me the sights and being a companion through this trip, supporting me when I wobbled and not backing away from the uncomfortable topic of death. I wanted to show my gratitude and buying the ring, for me, would be the perfect gesture of thanks.

He had other ideas. 'Are you crazy? *Mamma mia*, you have seen the price of this? You do not buy this for me.'

'A friendship ring.'

'Buy me a coffee,' he said as he steered me out of the store and toward the Mount but not before I'd grabbed a pamphlet giving a potted history of the town, with, conveniently, an advert on its back page for that very jeweller's store we'd just visited.

I bought him a coffee at The Godolphin Arms, the pub overlooking the Mount. Adam and I had enjoyed a crab salad and a beer there several times while admiring the view across to the island. We'd walked over to the Mount a few times but never ventured into the castle at the top or into the gardens. Neither of us was into gardening and although I quite liked old houses, I wasn't fussed either way.

'We go across, yes? To see the island. Have you been? With Adam?'

I described our short jaunts across to it. 'We were big people-watchers, rather than doers, so I haven't seen anything there apart from the harbour and the café.'

'Well, I am not so bothered about the house. I visit many old houses in Italy, and you have no need to pay. My country is full of them. My parents, they live in a house that date from the fifteenth century. In Florence, Bologna, Verona, Rome, we hold the record, I think, for ancient houses. But the gardens, they remind me a little of Italy although you do not have the cypress trees here. I miss those, very much.'

I knew what he meant. I'd only been to Italy once and I was struck by the rows of towering cypress trees lining the roads and avenues. They were quintessential to Italy, like cream teas to Cornwall.

We strolled across the causeway, careful not to slip on any seaweed-coated cobbles and made our way up the slope to the tiny harbour. A row of workers' cottages was set back behind the harbour, still occupied by men and women who worked at the house and in the gardens. The sign on the wall told us that the St Aubyn family had lived at the castle for hundreds of years and still resided there although the building was now part of the National Trust.

Up and up we went, some of the climb being extremely steep. I thought, with Gian so keen to see the gardens, he would know what the plants were. His answer made me burst out laughing.

'This one is a yellow one. That one, over there, that is a blue one with green leaves. Very vibrant.' He bent down and scrutinised one very closely. 'Here, Kerry, I know this one. This one here. You know what this is?'

I leant in. 'I haven't a clue. What is it?'

'It's very rare. In England, I think you call this,' he said, whilst he searched the sky for the answer. It came. 'Oh, yes, this is a weed.'

He grinned and I playfully slapped him on the arm.

As we took in the gardens, a scene from *Butch Cassidy and the Sundance Kid* came into my head, when the two outlaws and their lady friend escape to Bolivia and we are treated to a montage of them all laughing and having fun in various locations along the journey.

We were further up the hill now and he helped me climb onto a rocky ledge. 'From here, you see the entire bay.'

I'd concentrated solely on the gardens and hadn't thought

about how high we'd climbed. Clambering up, my focus was on my footing. When I turned, I froze. I shut my eyes tight. 'Shit.'

'What? What is it?'

In my imagination, I was an inch from plummeting hundreds of feet onto the rocks below and into the ocean.

'Kerry, what's the matter?'

I felt behind me for a plant to grab hold of. Why I thought that would save me I didn't know but it seemed a good idea at the time. My other hand was grasping fresh air, searching for his. 'I don't do heights.'

'Oh!'

He reached out to guide me down. 'Here, open your eyes and look at your feet.'

I followed his instructions. He kept me on the inside of him as he guided me down to a section of lawn.

A nervous breath escaped. 'Sorry.'

'Don't be sorry. I didn't know. Why are you scared of heights?'

I shrugged. 'No idea. I wish I knew but I don't.'

'Well, you know it is good to be scared of heights. That is, I think, a rational fear, yes?'

I supposed it was. 'Are you scared of anything?'

'Snakes. I hate snakes.'

He offered his hand as we negotiated another steep step down. I took it.

'Me and Lucia, we were in Rome one time. We visit my brother and his family, and we go to the zoo there, in the Villa Borghese gardens. We have a good time and I take no notice of where we go when we enter a building because we are talking.

'We enter this building and I finally ask where are we; what have you brought me to and then I see where I am. And I am surrounded by snakes. I tell you, I left! *Pronto*. She thought it would help me. *Mamma mia*. I told her, how do you think this will help me? She think it was very amusing.'

I laughed. Lucia sounded quite a mischievous lady. I reminded him about Adam and his abseiling exploits. 'I think Adam was certain I'd give it a go because I'd gone along with them. But I just went for the view and to write some poetry.'

At the harbour, Gian bought us each an ice cream and we sat for a while. The tide was coming in and we were waiting to get the ferry back. I drifted into a dream, marvelling at the colours reflecting in the ripples of the water, totally mesmerised, the cornet close by my face.

The next thing I knew, Gian had nudged my hand, and I had a face full of vanilla ice cream. I tried to do the same back but, of course, he was on the alert.

The ferry boat moored up and we allowed two elderly couples to go ahead of us. I grabbed Gian just before we went to board.

'Oh, my God.'

'What!'

'A snake.'

If a human had the ability to fly, Gian would have been on the roof of the little wheelhouse. He jumped to the other side of me, scanning the grass and the gravel.

'Where? Where is it?'

I doubled up. Not a chuckle, a smile or a short snigger. This was a proper belly laugh. He gracefully accepted that

I'd executed a well-formed trick as we took our seats on the ferry.

On the short trip back to Marazion, I reflected on the day so far and could honestly say that this had been one of the first days I'd experienced since Adam died where I had relished every minute. I hadn't once sunk into any sort of despair or sadness. Dared I hope that such despair was behind me now?

Chapter Thirty-Eight
KERRY

If you were near to me, if you were here
All my longing would disappear.

That night in my room I cleaned my teeth and prepared for bed. I'd left quite a few clothes draped over chairs and decided to tidy up and put them all away. At the dressing table, I massaged moisturiser into my face and told Adam about my day.

'It's a pity we didn't go up into the gardens when we visited. You get a spectacular view from there although you would have laughed at me when we got too high up.' I sat back in my chair. 'Although, you probably would have been starved of entertainment, wandering around gardens full of green stuff.'

Green stuff. That was Adam's stock phrase for anything plant related.

'Suzie and Greg have booked tickets for the Minack theatre Tuesday night which I'm looking forward to. It's a classical music spectacular. Yes, I know, that's like dragging you to a foreign film but you'd enjoy this because it includes some popular tunes. The '1812 Overture', for one.'

Adam and I had loved the Laurel Canyon Collective; James Taylor, Joni Mitchell, Crosby, Stills and Nash – neither of us had been all that keen on classical music but we did enjoy the popular symphonies and overtures.

I kissed his photo. 'Goodnight, my darling. I love you very much.'

Chapter Thirty-Nine
GIAN

The Minack theatre, it is about a forty-five-minute drive from St Ives and is built on the cliffs above Porthcurno, not that far from Land's End. It make me think of the open-air amphitheatres in Italy. Ours are mostly from the Roman era and this remind me of those structures. Not so big, though. I first came here with Rico and Tina to see a play put on by a local drama school and, I tell you, this place astound me. Even more so when I learn that a woman, almost single-handed, begin work here in the 1930s. She eventually get help, but everything carved with small hand tools. No machine.

This woman, she see the natural curve in the cliff, and she begin to transform it into a theatre. There are several hundred stone seats, a café and toilets all built into this hill. The stage is at the bottom of the seating area and, you know, if you are not so interested with what you watch, you can admire the view toward the Pedn Vounder beach and the Logan Rock. I see, sometimes, dolphins and seals swimming.

Suzie, Greg and Kerry are here with me, and I enjoy the concert very much. I find it difficult not to glance at Kerry. She is next to me, and she enjoy the concert, too. During the concert, I am a little concerned, you know, because she wipe her eyes and I think, perhaps, a tune is prompting a memory for her.

I ask her, are you all right? Is this upsetting for you?

She say no, that she had not heard the song before and that she find it emotional. It was the song 'Vilja', an aria from *The Merry Widow*. Me and Lucia, we see this opera often and Lucia, she also love this song. In Italy, opera is very popular and when I visit my brother in Rome, he always buy tickets. We see Pavarotti perform there in *La Bohème* many years ago.

Kerry feel the emotion. Lucia did, too. Always, she cry if a melody move her, as if it touch her soul. I am like that with 'E Lucévan e Stella' from *Tosca*. It bring a lump to my throat every time I hear it.

When the interval come, we have the picnic. This is what people do who come here often. They come prepared. Suzie and Kerry, they make salmon and cream cheese panini, and we have a glass of Prosecco.

Kerry tell me that her taste in music vary. Very little classical except for the popular tunes but she surprise me, because she like Bing Crosby, Louis Armstrong and Ella Fitzgerald. I examine her.

'I think, Kerry Simmonds, you are born in the wrong era, *si*?'

'Adam used to say that. I'm not keen on the modern world. That's why I prefer old films. The fashions, the music, the culture, the interior designs, the whole ambiance. *Il*

Problemo had that. That's why I'll watch *Brief Encounter, North by Northwest, Summertime*. I hanker after that age.'

'I, too, admire the age of elegance. But, I think, as we get older, we are more nostalgic, yes? You know, my father, he was a handsome man and very much a gentleman, like your Cary Grant and James Stewart. You would like my father. He treat my mamma like the royalty. Every day.'

Then we remember a young man we see in Marazion, in the square. I tell you truthfully, I do not understand the fashion these days. The boy we see, he had ripped jeans. And the girl, she wear a skirt that left nothing to the mind. I turn to Kerry and I say, 'I prefer to use my imagination. A woman with not so much on show interest me more than one that does. And the young man, why does he want to be so scruffy?'

Kerry, she has strong feelings about this, that our young people have lost their style and courtesy, but I disagree.

I remind her. 'Young people are not all like that. Dan is not like that. Rico and Tina, they not like that.' I rest a hand on her arm. 'I suspect you are idealistic for the era, and you see it through the rose-tinted glasses, *si*? You know, it was not so perfect in that time. In Rome, in the 1950s, we have *La Dolce Vita*, but much of our country was still suffering because of the war.'

She sit back and admit defeat to me. 'I know things weren't that brilliant back then. They weren't in England, either, but I can't help but focus on what was good.'

'There are good and bad times for every generation.'

The second half of the performance, it begin. The sun disappear from the sky. There is no moon to speak of, but I am happy with this as the stars are clearer to see.

I enjoy this evening. It is good to share it with someone.

Chapter Forty
KERRY

The hops are in the barrel, the grapes are off the vine
Friends are in the gathering, a moment so sublime.

I didn't think the evening could have been any better. Adam and I had been to a few events at the Minack which we'd enjoyed but we'd never seemed to time our visits for the concerts that appealed to us.

The music I'd heard tonight, well, much of it, was completely new to me and I was overwhelmed with the melodies. Some of them tugged my heartstrings. I couldn't help but shed a tear at how evocative it all was. How could a few random notes strung together make such an impact?

After the concert, we trekked up the hill to the car park at the top of the cliff, all of us enthusing about the evening and the various pieces of music we'd heard.

Inside the car, Greg started the engine and suggested going to the Merry Maidens.

'The Merry Maidens!' I said. This was a stone circle some five miles from Penzance, not far from where we were but not appropriate for us to be visiting at this time of the night. 'What d'you want to go there for? It's pitch black, there's nothing to see.'

Greg tapped his nose.

Suzie was equally perplexed. 'Don't look at me. He obviously has a plan, so let's go with it.'

Fifteen minutes later, we pulled into a lay-by and Greg grabbed some travel blankets from the boot.

'Have you been here before?' I asked Gian.

'No. I have heard the name but have not visited.'

I gave him a brief history lesson. 'It's an ancient stone circle from about 2000 BC.'

Gian wasn't overly impressed. But the man was from Italy, for Christ's sake. He'd grown up surrounded by ancient relics, stones, roads and artefacts.

'It is impressive,' I continued. 'The boulders represent girls who committed the ultimate sin of dancing on a Sunday, so they were turned to stone.'

'This, I think, I have heard before.'

'Darling,' Suzie said, 'I think all stone circles have the same myth attached.'

We clambered over a stile and the slabs of granite, about a metre high, lurked in the shadows.

'Greg, what on earth are we doing here?' asked Suzie. 'I was hoping we'd be on the patio with a G and T by now.'

'Patience, my lovely,' Greg responded, spreading the blankets on the ground.

He straightened up with an expression of achievement on his face. We stared at him. Frustrated that we hadn't caught on, he simply pointed. We followed the direction of his finger and turned our faces to the sky.

'Oh my God,' I mumbled.

'*Mamma mia*,' Gian added.

With no moon or streetlights, Greg had found a dark space where we could watch the stars. We lay down on the blankets and silently gazed at the canopy above us. I swear to God, I had never seen so many stars clustered in the sky, glittering and twinkling. The Milky Way stretched from one side to another like a starry motorway.

Gian selected certain areas in the sky. 'That is Cygnus up there. And to the left, that is Leo and Cancer.'

I turned my head toward him. 'Bloody hell, Gian. Where did you learn that?'

He held up his mobile. 'Skymap.'

I rolled my eyes. 'Here was me thinking you were the new Galileo.'

Lying side by side, our little fingers brushed against each other.

These last couple of days, well, I couldn't explain it. It was as if someone had put me in a rocket and launched me into that universe I was now admiring. I could do this. I could function. I could exist in life and enjoy it. I could laugh. I didn't have to feel guilty about having fun.

Perhaps the black dog of depression would stay in the shadows from now on and no longer leap to devour me.

Chapter Forty-One
KERRY

Some memories make me sad,
some make me smile and laugh
But all in all, I can't complain about my plan,
and where I am.

After the stunning night-sky adventure, we returned to The Feather Duck at well past midnight, and I settled into my night-time routine of moisturising and of updating Adam about my day.

'You know, you and I spent far too much of our time sitting on the beach, Adam. Gian's only been here just over a year, and he's shown me more than we ever saw. Although he didn't know about the Merry Maidens.'

I admonished myself for being so critical and picked up the photo. 'Oh, darling, I'm sorry. It's just that I would have loved to have done these things with you. I wanted you with me tonight.' I replaced the frame. 'But Gian's good company and he's become a good friend. I hope you don't mind me spending time with him. I don't mind being on my own but it's so much nicer to be able to share these experiences.'

Chapter Forty-Two
GIAN

Since Kerry arrive, I enjoy my time with her. I think she enjoy it, too. The first night I see her here, at Rico's, she seem very lost, very nervous and I do not see this in her now.

When I leave Santa Margherita, I think this was good for me. Like Kerry being here. Perhaps, when such things happen in our lives, it is good to change, to start new.

Occasionally, I feel my life with Lucia never happen. That when she die, my life also end; my history with her, my time with her and the children become almost like a fairytale and that I never live that life. I tell you, this is a terrible way to feel, and it make the loss of Lucia more painful because I want to feel that it happen. I need to feel it.

If Kerry move here, I tell you truthfully, that would make me very happy. I would like her to be here.

At the moment, I laugh at her. She is opposite me and, I think, has had a little too much wine and that amuse me very much. I have never seen her like this. I decide that when Kerry has too much wine, she become brave. She lean on the table with her glass and she is very intense. I have my elbows on the table, and I listen to her.

'So, that's what I'm going to do,' she said.

'But the height, it frighten you.'

'Well, yes, it does.' She held a finger up. 'But it shouldn't, should it? I mean, it's irrational, isn't it? That's what they say, whoever *they* are. I should be able to abseil down a cliff. Adam did it. Dan did it. Thousands of people do it. Thousands. Why shouldn't I?'

I bring Tosca onto my lap. 'You are telling me you wish to abseil down a cliff?'

She pick up Figaro and give me a firm nod.

'Yes, that's exactly what I'm saying. They do it just up the road here.'

I hold up the empty bottle of wine. Rico, he think I want another bottle and then he understand that I do not. I think Kerry, she drink enough. I pour water in her glass and she does not notice. She, I think, will have a headache in the morning. So, I hold up the empty bottle to her.

'Not so brave, I think, without a drink.'

She become incredulous. 'I can do it. Don't think I can't. It's time to grab life, even if it scares the shit out of me.' She put her glass down. 'I shall prove to him that I can do it. I'll book it first thing tomorrow.'

I think this is not a good idea, but I know, tomorrow she will be thinking clear and decide not to do this.

'Why don't you do something less dangerous, Kerry? Come on a boat trip with me.'

I tell you, she give me a scorching look, as if I slap her. 'What?'

It last only a second but there is the fear in her eyes. I see that fear before, when she was at the harbour, when she try to buy a ticket. I see that fear in Dan. I understand that I bring back a memory that affect them both and that memory exist here, in St Ives. She bring Figaro close and cuddle him.

'I have made you unhappy,' I say.

She reach over to grab my hand. 'No, no, you haven't. Oh, God, Gian, don't ever think that. It's nothing that you've done. It just brought something back to me, that's all.'

'Do you want to tell me?'

'I will tell you. But not tonight, if you don't mind. I don't feel like going over it at the moment.'

'Of course.'

I order coffee and, I think, we are a little awkward. I am, at least. Kerry, she recover and speak about a poetry workshop, but I find it difficult to focus on this because I know my comment upset her.

Chapter Forty-Three
KERRY

*Digging holes, unnecessarily, confirms to me I'm
bonkers in the nut.
Not brave, not courageous, not confident.
Just bonkers in the nut.*

Shit. I couldn't believe I was standing here even contemplating this. I'd made a trip to Bude, about an hour from St Ives and stood on the top of a cliff face overlooking Crooklets Beach. What the hell was I thinking? All that bravado last night, talking about abseiling. Of course, it was the wine talking, nothing else. I didn't want to abseil down a cliff. Who would want to do that? Who was I kidding?

Now, in the cold light of day, I was standing here arguing with the little voice in my head that continued to goad me. We all had them, these voices. The voice that told you you're useless or incapable. I heard it when I met Adam. I thought he was so handsome and adorable. The little voice popped up then, saying, *why would he be interested in you?*

Now, that voice sneered. I could almost see the lip curling. *Thought you were clever, didn't you? Now see what you've got yourself into. You won't be able to do this. You're going to make a complete fool of yourself.*

Strong character traits are always a weakness. My strength was my stubbornness. My determination to see things through, no matter what.

And, because I'd told Gian I would abseil down a cliff, some crazy part of me was convinced I had to do it.

Anyone in their right mind would have forgotten their drunken bravado and filed it away in a buff folder of daft ideas.

I silently groaned, remembering that Gian had suggested a more sedate activity. A boat trip. Oh, lord, poor thing. He probably wondered what on earth he'd said to upset me. I would tell him, of course I would. I just couldn't go into it last night, not after a few glasses of wine. It would have spiralled into a miserable evening. For me and for him.

My stubbornness had now taken me to the top of this rocky cliff face, dressed in jeans and a sweatshirt. I could still change my mind, but my obstinacy refused permission. I could simply walk just along the coast here and plonk myself on the beach in Bude and eat an ice cream. The instructor checked that my harness was secure, and all the fixtures and fittings attached to it were as they should be.

Me? I was rooted to the spot shivering. Not with the cold, because it was a cheery, warm, sunny day. My legs were simply dissolving from the inside from nerves.

'Fuck, fuck, fuck. Why the fuck am I doing this?'

All the instructor could do was grin. Steve, his name was.

'You know I was drunk when I said I'd do this, don't you? I don't even have any witnesses?'

'You're not the first,' he replied, 'and you certainly won't be the last. And you'll get photos. My colleague over there is taking some as we go down. We can send them over to you.'

That was all I needed. A picture of me resembling a rabbit in the headlights.

'Now, remember what I told you,' Steve continued. 'Just lean back with me. Let gravity take you. You're perfectly safe.'

Bless him. When he'd seen how terrified I was, he'd volunteered to abseil down with me, side by side. There were two other instructors and eight customers; I think I was the only one whose heart was leaping out of its chest as if in a cartoon.

He gently steered me to where numerous ropes fell over the edge. They were reassuringly sturdy and thick but now in my head, they'd turned into flimsy bits of string. What if a seagull started pecking through that rope and it began to fray? What if those metal things attached to me ripped off? What if a rogue wave came and swept us off the cliff face? What if the fastenings holding these ropes at the top here gave way? Oh, stop, stop, stop.

An arm supported my back. Steve's arm.

'Lean back with me.'

A different level of fear presented itself. 'Oh my God. No, fuck, I can't do this.'

'Yes, you can. I'm coming with you, the whole way. Lean back with me. I have you. Gently does it.'

It was gentle, too. We fell back in slow motion and, from that moment on, my eyes were squeezed shut. Every muscle in my face worked to keep those eyes closed while I repeated the same phrase.

'Oh my God, oh my God, oh my God.'

We were now horizontal, and I was at the mercy of a rope and a few clips, all that prevented me from toppling to an early death. I hoped Adam was taking this all in from wherever he was. That sent a tiny shiver of confidence through me but not nearly enough to say I was okay with this.

'You're on the cliff face and you've just done the hardest bit,' said Steve. 'Now, take it slow.'

I almost laughed at that. Be prepared for slow, my friend. There was no way I would be scaling down like a Royal Marine.

'Let the rope feed through a little. Like I showed you.'

I felt for the bit that the rope went through. I couldn't remember the technical term, as I hadn't been paying attention to anything other than what I had to do with it.

I dropped. It felt as if I'd plummeted, but it was probably an inch because Steve didn't move at all.

'That's it. Now let it slide through again. I have you.'

And he did. He kept pace with me. Pace! I was hardly setting records. He remained alongside me, his hand on my back. I was grateful for that, but I knew it wasn't a safety thing. I mean, if that seagull did sever my rope, Steve could hardly hold me.

While I muttered 'Oh my God' and 'Fuck' and a variety of other curses, we inched our way down. My eyes were still clamped shut and I was doing everything by feel and touch. My method of descent probably made this harder but if I were to see how high I was, I'd probably faint.

The breeze was slight and I heard birds calling and the waves crashing on the beach. They weren't crashing but that's what was in my head. Great rollers of surf ready to swallow me up when I fell.

'Okay, Kerry, let's have a breather. Open your eyes. Take a look at the view.'

Have a breather? Look at the view? Was he mad? This wasn't a picnic. I resolutely refused.

He manoeuvred himself behind me.

'Open your eyes. You won't see a view like this again, not from this angle, and I've a feeling you won't be doing this again in a hurry. You're perfectly safe. I have you. The ropes have you and you're already halfway down.'

That stunned me. I thought I'd moved two feet at the most. Relief that I didn't have so far to fall was heartening. Perhaps I could do this after all and not die in the process. A hundred affirmations ran through my head in a matter of seconds. You can do this. Look at the view. It's a few seconds. You're halfway down. Do it for Adam. Do it for you. Blah, blah, blah. All those phrases written in self-help books I never read.

The end result was that I opened my eyes. In front of me, the cliff face. I took the biggest intake of breath I could and looked to my left. My eyes, that had been so tightly closed, were now as wide as dinner plates.

'Oh, wow.'

Weirdly, I didn't even think about the height. I felt as if David Attenborough was giving me an exclusive glimpse into his world, a paradise of nature and wildlife. Ahead of me, a variety of seabirds flew in and out of their nests on the cliff. I'm no bird watcher but I did recognise the common breeds: Herring gull, Kittiwakes and Razorbills. Rocky promontories thrust out into the sea at intervals all the way along the coast. Tufts of colourful seagrasses and plants sprouted wherever they could, clinging to life in the nooks and crannies. The sea, depending on its depth, alternated between a clear turquoise and a cobalt blue. My word, it was beautiful. The crashing waves imagined in my head were simply lapping at the shoreline some distance away.

Then I looked down.

Shit.

Eyes shut.

Steve sensed my nerves. He manoeuvred himself back alongside me. 'You're doing great. You're halfway down. In a few minutes, you'll be on the beach.'

A few minutes!

Continuing at a snail's pace, admittedly with less swearing, we made our way down. I heard my fellow abseilers congratulating one another on a job well done.

I felt Steve pull away from me and I slipped into panic mode. Where was he? I grabbed the rope. Where the fuck had he gone? Instinctively, I opened my eyes.

There he was. Standing on the beach.

I was two feet from terra firma.

Steve grinned as I jumped down. 'Well done, Kerry. You were brilliant.'

All sorts of emotions flooded through my veins at the same time. Relief, absolute ecstatic joy and the inevitable release of adrenalin mixed themselves into a heady cocktail and I yelled at the top of my voice.

'I DID IT.'

Fortunately, Steve had moved away before I released my elation.

I grabbed Steve and twirled him around in a circle. The cascading rush of jubilation was so intense I wanted to the hug the world. Instead, I ran across the beach waving my arms in the air, whooping and hollering like a woman possessed.

I stopped at the shoreline and yelled to the sea and the sky.

'ADAM, I DID IT. I FUCKING DID IT!'

Chapter Forty-Four
KERRY

Ebb and flow, ebb and flow,
An instant high, an instant low.

The adrenalin stayed with me for a few hours afterwards and a permanent grin was on my face for most of the day.

Returning to St Ives, I dashed into The Feather Duck and announced my achievement to Greg and Suzie. You'd think I'd climbed Mount Everest, but this was huge for me. They enveloped me in a group hug, and we toasted my achievement with glasses of Pinot Grigio.

After showering, I cosied up in a luxurious Feather Duck towelling robe and towel-dried my hair while FaceTiming Dan. He was in the kitchen eating some toast. Chloe waved in the background but left us to talk.

'What the fuck, Mum.'

'I know, right?'

'Bloody hell.'

'I had my eyes shut the whole way down.'

'Who cares? You did it! Fuck. I mean… well, just fuck. What made you do it in the first place?'

I briefly closed my eyes at the memory. 'Too much wine last night.' He laughed at that. 'As a result, I bragged to Gian that I could do anything, including abseil.'

I saw the wariness in his face. This is what Gian had seen. The son protecting his mother. I didn't know what thoughts Dan had formed about me and Gian, but he clearly imagined we were an item or something. I decided to ignore the issue.

'The thing is, once you start bragging, you have to do it, don't you? Well, *I* have to. Anyway, next time I see him I can hold my head high.'

It was as if Dan had lost interest, and I couldn't quell the anger simmering inside me. I leant into the screen.

'What's the matter?'

I reminded myself that Dan was still a teenager and still learning the minefield that was emotional confrontation. I softened my approach.

'Dan, what is your problem with him? He lost his wife. He knows what it's like. It's helped, having someone who's gone through the same thing. We've been through this; you have nothing to worry about.'

My assurances garnered a nonchalant shrug. Was that supposed to make me feel better? All it did was prove that nothing would change his mind. Shit. He was as stubborn as me but, at the moment, I found it petulant and childish.

'I'm not discussing this. You're seeing a problem that doesn't even exist.' I changed topic. 'Have you heard from Southampton Uni?'

He gave a curt shake of the head.

'You should have heard by now, surely?'

A shrug. If I'd been there in person, my approach would have been different. I'd be challenging him, I'm sure, but I couldn't do that over FaceTime, not with Chloe there, too. Instead, I switched to mum mode. He was my son. He needed reassurance.

'Dan, whatever I do, I will always consider you, consult with you. I promise. I won't keep anything from you. And I'm not keeping anything from you now. Please believe me.'

I finally received a nod that mildly reassured me; but I sensed he was not entirely convinced.

'Do you want me to come home? Is that what this is about? I can get on a train tomorrow.'

Chloe was influencing his response. He'd glanced away from the screen for just a second and had reacted to her.

'No, it's fine.'

'You're holding back.'

'Mum, I'm fine. Don't fuss.'

I knew I wouldn't get any further with him and I didn't want to argue. Not with Chloe there. 'Okay. I'll call you tomorrow, all right? And if you need to call me, call me.'

'Okay.'

Before I ended the call, he leant toward the screen.

'Mum, well done, with the abseiling. I'm proud of you.'

The elation of the day had been slightly dampened but that comment perked me up. I blew him a kiss.

'I love you.'

Chapter Forty-Five

DAN

Shit!

I knew I'd been off with Mum during that call. She was so happy about the abseiling, and I was amazed about it. But when she told me why she'd done it, that she'd bragged to Gian, I just shut down. I didn't like that he was pushing his way into Mum's life. And she was letting him.

I could kick myself for being such a dick, but I couldn't help it. I couldn't even tell you what I didn't like about Gian. There was nothing to dislike. If it'd been Colin or Lee, I could have given you a list but with Gian, I couldn't. I couldn't give her a reason.

When she offered to come home, I saw Chloe glaring at me and shaking her head. And when I finished the call, she was straight in.

'Why are you giving her such a hard time?'

'I'm not.'

'He's a really nice man.'

I got up in such a temper that the chair almost toppled over. I slammed the laptop shut.

'I see her, Chloe. She thinks I don't, but I see her. She's taking sleeping pills, for God's sake. Crying at photographs, trying to be brave. I don't want her getting hurt. That fucking Colin bloke was bad enough. At least Lee took the hint on the first visit. Colin didn't.'

'But he isn't even in the frame. He never was. Your mum brushed him off ages ago. And Gian is different.'

I went to the window. Why didn't she get it? Why didn't she agree with me?

'Why're you sticking up for him?'

'I'm not sticking up for anyone. But you heard your mum. He's gone through the same thing. He's grieving, too. Let them enjoy each other's company. That's all they're doing. Your mum would say if it was something different.'

I wanted to retaliate but I couldn't. I couldn't because I knew, deep down, she was right. Chloe rested her hand on my back.

'She won't shut you out, Dan. Your mum's not like that.'

I focussed on a photo of Mum and Dad on the wall. I'd not said much to Chloe about this, but I had to say something. 'I just feel as if she's drifting away from me.'

Chloe turned me round to face her. I don't think I've ever seen her so serious.

'Your mum is taking a break that seems to be doing her good. It did you good, too. Being in this house... all your memories are here. You're missing your dad more here. She's in a different place, with different people and it's helping her. Let her enjoy it. Gian is helping her and for all we know she may be helping him. Is it so wrong for her to have a friend she can identify with and talk to?'

I felt like a kid being told off for being selfish. I was

angry but she was right. I was being a dick. Everything she and Mum were saying made perfect sense and yet I couldn't admit it. I wouldn't admit it.

'If Gian was a woman,' Chloe added, 'you wouldn't be thinking like this. Would you?'

Shit. No, I wouldn't. It wouldn't bother me in the slightest. I pulled Chloe close and hugged her.

I was envious. I knew it. I kept pushing back on admitting it, but I had to. I was jealous that Mum had a new friend, and he was a man. And they got on well. I was glad she had that friendship, someone to talk to.

What I was angry about was what it might lead to.

CHAPTER FORTY-SIX
KERRY

Some days my mind is scrambled
Emotions tumble, indecision wreaks havoc
Stay or go, left or right, up or down, forward or back.

That evening, I shed a few tears. The ecstatic joy I'd felt after the abseiling adventure had gradually faded. I wanted to cling to it, bottle it up and be able to drink it every day.

Although we'd ended on a bright note, I was struggling with how to deal with Dan and this simmering resentment he felt towards Gian. I only had to mention his name and his attitude shifted.

Gian was just a friend, I'd insisted, but was I fooling myself? *Was* he just a friend? Was I ready for anything else? If I was honest, I didn't know and, if I didn't know, how could I possibly be honest with Dan? I'd promised to put him first and I thought I was doing that, but *was* I?

I hadn't spoken about these worries with Adam in my nightly conversation with his photograph. Not out loud. I didn't want Adam to know I might have feelings for another man. He knew we were friends, of course, but that was a completely different entity. Friendship wasn't betrayal.

I thought about talking it through with Suzie. I needed validation that it was okay to have feelings for Gian and be open with Dan about it. The trouble was, I thought Suzie was rooting for me and Gian to get together. When we had been at the Latin-American evening, I'd seen the delight on her face during our dance and when I'd linked arms with him. I'm sure she'd already got us walking down the aisle.

I wiped a tear away. Did everyone go through this who had lost their best friend and soulmate? So many people went on to have a second marriage, a second relationship. Did they go through the conflict, the invisible barrier that held me back, that insisted I was being disloyal and betraying my husband's memory?

I stroked his image in the frame.

'Oh, God, Adam, I love you so much. When you died, I vowed that no one would take your place. Ever. Ever. But I miss being a couple. I miss doing things with someone and it's not the same on my own. Even with friends, it's not the same.'

I sat up straight.

'I have to tell you, sweetheart, that I've grown fond of Gian. Lord, I hope you're okay with that. It doesn't mean I love you any less, my darling. Never think that I love you any less than I did when we first got together.'

I kissed the photo.

Five minutes later, I FaceTimed Maggie.

'Maggie, you're up.'

'What's the matter? What's happened?'

'I've been speaking to Adam.'

'What!'

'His photo.'

She relaxed. I described the tension stewing in Dan about my friendship with Gian.

'Tom's noticed a certain animosity toward him. You know what they say about meeting our idols, Kerry. It never works out well. Have you discovered he's terribly arrogant and conceited?'

'But that's the problem, Maggie, he's nothing like that and we're getting on like the proverbial house on fire.'

She beamed.

'Maggie, please, I'm being serious. I don't need you matchmaking. I am honestly…' I choked on emotion. 'I feel I'm being so disloyal to Adam just thinking the way I do.'

Maggie switched to mother-hen mode. She brought her screen toward her. 'Listen to me, Kerry Simmonds. Adam will always be the love of your life. That will never change. But you're here, Kerry. You have a future and a right to do what you want with that future. If that means another relationship, then so be it.

'You'll know when you're ready. These feelings you're having are a surprise to you and it's probably happened sooner than you wanted but you can't deny what you feel, Kerry.'

She tilted her head.

'Does he feel the same way?'

'Oh, I don't know! We haven't discussed it. I don't want to discuss it with him.'

'Well, discuss it with yourself.'

'What?'

'Take a step back and examine the facts. You have feelings for this man. That is the bottom line, isn't it?'

'I suppose.'

'You're on holiday. Enjoy it. You've found a good friend, and you get on well. If he feels the same, it will get discussed whether you want it to or not.'

In bed, I stared at the ceiling. I wasn't sure whether Maggie had helped me or not. She was basically telling me to take it one day at a time and not to analyse everything. That was easier said than done. I had to be honest with myself. I only had another week of my holiday left and, if I still felt the same way I would have to say something.

Chapter Forty-Seven
KERRY

What if this is wrong?
What if I'm stuck in some old romantic song?
Yesterday, I conquered the world, yet today my feelings swirl.
What if this is now a whim?
And Dan? Where does this leave him?
What if this move doesn't suit him?

The following day, Suzie and I had scheduled a morning for viewing the houses and flats I'd listed from the estate agents' details. I greeted the day with optimism and tried to imagine what my life would be like living here. I hoped I didn't fall in love with one property in particular, because I hadn't thought that far ahead. I hadn't even thought about putting mine on the market. There were so many things to think about, the main one making sure that Dan was settled.

The elephant in the room was, of course, Gian. My inner voice and I were waging civil war and neither of us were making any ground.

For now, I viewed a well-laid-out two-bedroomed flat. The balcony gave me a view across the bay. It was spacious, light and airy and would certainly suit my circumstances.

My circumstances.

I cringed at the phrase. How often had I said that to myself? I was now a widow and needed a low maintenance property with little or no garden. This one ticked the boxes, though, and I could see myself here.

Coming from the kitchen, which had all mod cons, we entered the very modern and chic lounge. Even Suzie was impressed, and she could be scathing of home decor.

'Oh, darling,' said Suzie, 'this view. Can't you imagine yourself sitting on that balcony with a class of Pinot and a good book, drinking in the vino and the scenery?'

I appreciated her enthusiasm, and I didn't want to burst her bubble. Yes, it was lovely and yes, I could imagine all of those things, but I was half-hearted.

She slipped an arm through mine.

After quite a pause, I eventually said, 'I'm worried about Dan.'

Her expression invited me to continue.

'He worries about me. Too much. He shouldn't have that responsibility, not at his age. And I am coping. I mean, I have the odd wobble, like the other day with that funeral but it's just a wobble now. I'm not going to pieces like I was a few months ago.'

'He thinks of himself as the man of the house, Kerry. He wants to protect you, to take over from Adam.'

'But that's not his job, Suzie. His job is to live his life and find a career and experience life, have adventures and, if he wants to, get married and have kids.'

'And he'll do those things when the time is right. University will help with that. Being with new friends and working toward a career. He'll get all of that. In the meantime, I think it's sweet that he cares so much.'

I shuffled my feet.

'There's something you're not telling me. Whatever it is, it remains here, with me, unless you particularly want me to tell Greg.'

I bit the bullet.

'Maggie tried to matchmake me with a friend of theirs, Colin, at Christmas and he came around several times wanting me to go out for coffee and stuff. Well, Dan's attitude toward him was… obstructive, for want of a better word. I mean, he didn't even say anything to him, he just had this animosity toward the man whenever he knocked on the door. Then my neighbour, Lee, he came over and made a move on me but, luckily, he took the hint. Dan was the same toward him, too.'

'Did you want to go out with either of them?'

'No! I didn't want to go out with anyone. Dan thought they were both dicks.' I paused. I'd never told anyone this, but I was ready to tell Suzie. 'I did try online dating.'

She gawped.

'I thought that's what you did these days. I mean, I haven't dated for decades. I put my profile up and a photo.'

'What happened?'

'Two men contacted me, and I never responded. I took my profile down. I wasn't ready. I realised I didn't want a relationship then.'

She picked up on that last sentence. 'And now?'

My eyes settled on the horizon. The day was overcast

and there were showers out at sea. Sort of matched my mood.

'Is this to do with Gian?' said Suzie.

I sighed. 'Dan thinks Gian is making a move on me, so he has that animosity toward him like he had with Colin. I could understand it with Colin, but Gian isn't anything like that. He's a nice guy. What is there to get angry about?'

'Is he? Making a move on you?'

'Oh, Suzie, I don't know. It's been nearly forty years since I dated anyone. I don't know the signals. I don't know what happens now.'

'And you think Gian does?'

She sat me down on the sofa.

'Darling, Gian's in the same position as you. He's a handsome film star from forty years ago but it doesn't make him Casanova. He was completely besotted with Lucia, like you are with Adam, and he's struggling to get through this, too. He'd known Lucia since they were fourteen. That woman was all he knew.'

'What are you saying?'

'I'm saying you should take it day by day. Neither of you are pushing for a relationship, are you? You're both breezing along as very good friends and, if there is something between you, well, that's often how it starts.'

I supposed it was.

'Darling, are you hankering for something more than friendship?'

God, why was I so indecisive? I wanted to step outside my body and shake myself. I could go abseiling and confront my grief head on, but I couldn't talk to my son about Gian and I didn't know what I wanted with him. Fucking hell.

'I don't know,' I answered, feebly.

I wanted someone to make this decision for me. I didn't want the chore of having to figure this out for myself.

She took my hand. 'You two have a chemistry but only you know if it's capable of developing into something else.'

'And what about Dan?'

She immediately stated, 'Dan is jealous, darling. Plain and simple.'

'Oh, God.' She simply verified what I already knew. 'But he doesn't need to be, Suzie. I've told him time and time again that he will always come first, and I'll always discuss everything with him.'

'And he'll come to terms with that. Jealousy is a very strong stimulus. Any man, no matter how nice and lovely he is, will be a threat to him. He needs to understand, and he will, in time. You've said yourself; he has a life to get on with. He's young, he may want to travel, he has a ready-made career lined up after uni and he may settle down. You're not going to stop him, and he'll realise that he can't stop you.

'Kerry, it's still early days. Don't force him to think in a certain way. When he sees that you're putting him first and that you have a life to live, he'll come around. It's just taking him a little longer, that's all.'

I appreciated what she'd said. And so far, I'd given Gian no reason to think that what we had was anything other than a friendship.

As my brain sifted through my countless doubts and concerns, along with advice given by Suzie and Maggie, I formulated a tentative decision, one that was sensible and practical.

Friendship was all this would be. It couldn't be anything else.

Dan was my priority, and I was determined to convince him of that. Nothing else mattered. Not at the moment.

Chapter Forty-Eight
KERRY

Feel the fear... Believe in... You are strong...
You can do anything... Release your pain...
Words on the spines of books never purchased,
Although the titles helped instil some purpose.

I couldn't put this off. The reason I'd come to St Ives was to face those hurdles, those barriers, those challenges that I needed to conquer in this place. I'd done it all back in Sussex. After those first visits to our special locations, it was easier to return. It was beneficial for everyone else, too. They knew exactly what I was going through and how to deal with it.

In those early days, after Adam, they witnessed my raw and fraught state. If I'd have avoided making those visits it would have been harder for me to ever go there and the people there would have been awkward, wondering whether to bring the topic of Adam into the conversation.

Because of those initial visits, we were able to talk openly about Adam with ease.

Here, in St Ives, it was different. We knew a few people,

yes, but here it was mainly all about visiting places rather than individuals. I'd done everything except for the boat trip. And I'd only put that off because Dan had been with me when I tried to book it. I'd promised him I'd leave it.

But I promised myself that I wouldn't return home without having done it.

I tapped the telephone number on my mobile and didn't have to wait long. The Harbour Wildlife Tour lady answered straight away, and I asked her if they had any spaces over the next two or three days. I reached over for a pen as she gave me a slot and jotted it down on the leaflet.

'That's great. Thank you. I'll see you then.'

After hanging up, I studied the leaflet for a while. It showed seals and dolphins in their natural habitats, watched by a boatload of happy sightseers. Not wanting to delve into that memory too much, I let the leaflet fall onto the dresser and turned my attention to the matter in hand.

Gian had invited me to a seafood restaurant that evening. Nothing posh, apparently, but he wanted to show me his preferred eating place outside of Rico's. I'd put two dresses on the bed and opted for the one with turquoise and red flecks. It was a 1950's design and my go-to outfit when I wanted to be smart but not too dressy. Especially in St Ives. People didn't dress up in Cornwall. The Cornish fashion was solely casual. If I saw anyone in a suit, I assumed they had a job interview or a wedding to go to. Or a funeral.

I'd only brought two pairs of sandals with me, one for walking and a dressier pair – so that decision was easy to make. The radio played in the background, and I'd been humming along with most of the tunes. The presenter introduced the next track.

'And now, we're taking you back to the seventies with the wonderful Cat Stevens song, "How Can I Tell You".'

The song smashed into me so hard it might as well have thrown me against the wall. The tears quickly followed. I was wrenched away from the here and now and hurled back to square one; back to those first few weeks after Adam had died, weeping and sobbing, tears cascading down my cheeks, my nose running, hiccupping and almost hyperventilating. I slumped onto the side of the bed, the nearby photo of Adam obscured by salty tears. I grabbed the box of tissues from the table and tried to stem the flow, but the lyrics threaded their way into my head.

Blinking to clear my eyes, I went over to the photo of Adam and me in Krakow. The song continued.

Krakow. A sunny evening in the main square. We had drunk a few too many vodkas. There were buskers playing gypsy music. We danced and kissed and broke into hysterics about something. Tom and Maggie were with us and had taken this photo. I couldn't remember what we'd found so funny, but they'd captured the moment perfectly. This was my Adam. Fun, loving, easy-going Adam.

I flopped down at the dressing table; a blotchy tear-stained face stared back at me. An old woman. A widow. The very word made me feel a hundred years old. I hated being a widow. I had loved being a wife. In the drawer to my left, the sleeping pills. How easy it would be to take those and just escape.

The tears returned. What was I doing keeping those pills? Why did I even ask for them? I hated pills.

Would this grief never leave me?

I closed my eyes and saw myself following Adam's coffin into a packed crematorium. Dan was beside me, his eyes focussed beyond his dad, focussing on something irrelevant to stop him from crying.

I should turn the radio off, but I couldn't. This song was a needle in my arm, drip feeding painful memories and emotions. I went to the window. Perhaps something out there would distract me but nothing, nothing, would stop this. I leaned against the wall, slid down to the floor and wept.

I don't know how long I was sitting there. The song had long finished. I ignored the first knock on the door. I thought I'd imagined it. There was another.

'Kerry.' It was Gian.

A gentle rap.

'Kerry, are you all right?'

The sob I tried so hard to stifle echoed out. The door handle slowly moved, and the door was nudged open. Gian peered around it.

'Kerry?' Seeing me, he became urgent. 'Kerry!'

He rushed over and squatted to my level.

'What happened?'

I couldn't lift myself from this despair. It had snatched every ounce of energy from me. I didn't think I had the strength to even answer him.

'Kerry, tell me, what happened?'

'I had the radio on... they played a song... from the funeral...' Just telling him set me off again.

'Oh, Kerry.'

He sat beside me and pulled me close. Of course, that made the tears flow even more. He didn't say anything. He just held me.

Songs set me off easily, but I hadn't had this happen in

a long while. And radio stations rarely played this track so I had never expected to hear it.

After a few minutes, I'd cried myself out and I pulled back. My dresses lay on the bed.

'Oh, God, I haven't even got changed.'

'We are not going out tonight.'

'But you booked a table.'

'Then I will unbook it. How long have you been sitting here?'

I honestly couldn't tell him. It was probably only a few minutes, but it felt like a lifetime.

'Grief is fucking shit,' I eventually blurted out.

Gian positioned himself so that he could talk to me properly. He held my fingers.

'You want to know why grief is so tough for you?'

Fuck, yes. I wanted to know why I had to go through this. Why I had to return to that raw emotion that I'd thought I had under control.

'Because you have loved. You have loved a deep, passionate love. Fierce, infinite, all-consuming. You cannot grieve like this if you do not love with such magnitude. There are men and women who would give anything to have what you have. When they grieve, they don't grieve like you because they do not have this love. Grief is shit, Kerry, but to feel so lost, to feel so desperate, so heartbroken, you have to have loved very much. Do you understand?'

I did and I was so, so grateful for those words. Of course, this devastation was horrid. If I hadn't had that profound love, I wouldn't be feeling like this. We sat for some time on the floor, and I hesitated over my next thought.

'Gian?'

'Yes?'

'After Lucia… did you ever think about…?'

I didn't want to explain. I didn't want to say the word. If I did, and he hadn't had those thoughts, it would mean no one else thought about it; that I was unusual.

He gave a brief nod. 'Yes. I did. I still do… occasionally. I wouldn't! I just think about it. Occasionally. I used to think it will take me to Lucia. But then, I think, what if it does not?'

He stroked my cheek.

'We cannot lie next to them, Kerry.' He pushed himself up from the floor and held out a hand. 'Here, let me help you. We are not going out tonight. We will stay here.'

I frowned. 'Doing what?'

Chapter Forty-Nine
GIAN

It is not right to take Kerry to dinner this night. I think this is not fair for her. I still have moments like this and, when I do, I do not want to see people or go anywhere. But occasionally, it is nice to be with somebody, to not be alone.

I tell her to freshen up and I go get pizza and beer and we sit on the balcony. We eat without cutlery and drink from the bottle. It is a warm evening, you know, and I think this is better for her. To be quiet with a friend instead of in a crowd.

It is not the evening I had expected. I arrive on the terrace at seven and Suzie, she is there, and I ask where Kerry is because I am a little late and she is never late. She say to me once that she did not like it when people are late, that she feel it is rude.

So, I go to Kerry's room and I find her there. I tell you, my heart went to her. She is so upset, and I think she cry for a long time before I arrive.

I think she is happy with my decision to stay here.

When I think it is a good time, I ask her, 'Kerry, what was the song? On the radio?'

'Cat Stevens. "How Can I Tell You". D'you know it?'

'Oh yes. My niece, in Roma, she like Cat Stevens. That is, how you say in English… poignant. Yes, a poignant song.'

She laugh. 'But I have to tell you that Adam insisted on "Always Look on the Bright Side of Life" for the final song at his funeral. You know Monty Python?'

'Oh yes. I like *The Holy Grail*. "It is only a flesh wound", isn't it?' Her reaction amuse me. 'You are laughing at me.'

'I'm sorry. Your accent… it sort of makes it funnier. Adam wanted everyone to leave with a smile.'

Then she ask what I have, at Lucia's funeral. I tell you, I groan. It is not what I want.

'A Catholic Mass. Her family insist. It was very depressing, but I have a memorial for her. She love the opera. We had songs from *La Bohème*, *Tosca*, *The Merry Widow*.'

We sit for two hours, maybe a little more, eating and drinking and I think she feel better now. I finish my beer and tell her I will go. My dogs must have their walk.

We go through to her room, and she say thank you to me.

'What you said earlier… it made a lot of sense. And, Gian, I really appreciate you sitting with me and not forcing anything. People always think they have to keep talking but sometimes you just need company.'

I make a decision. It is not something I expect to ask but I ask because it will force me to do something. It will force me to go through with it.

'Will you come to my place for coffee tomorrow? I would like, very much, for you to help with something.'

I see she wonder what I am asking but I don't want to say. Then she say she will come. This please me. Very much.

'Goodnight, Kerry Simmonds.'

'Goodnight, Gianluca Belfiore.'

I do not kiss her in a romantic way. Not tonight. This would not be right. Her thoughts, they are with Adam. So, I kiss her on the cheek and leave.

Kerry, she wait on the balcony when I am outside and she wave to me.

Chapter Fifty

GIAN

The next morning, I cannot stand still and the dogs, they follow me all around the lounge, wondering what is the matter. I now regret I ask Kerry to come. Not because I do not want to see her. I like to see her. She is wonderful but, last night, I feel brave about this and now I am not so sure.

When she arrive, I make coffee and we sit on the sofa in my lounge and Lucia's memory box is on the table in front of us. I stare at it for a long time, you know, because I am not sure I can open it. The dogs, they stare at me with their ears pricked, curious.

If Kerry is not here, I would return it to the shelf, but I don't want her to see me do this. She know I am frightened because I make no effort to take the lid off so she rest a hand on my arm. She do not say anything. She has no need to. She is telling me that she is here, that she will support me. I like that about her. That she is patient with me and does not tell me I am stupid because I am not as brave as her.

I eventually rip away the Sellotape. Tosca and Figaro,

they put their paws on the table and sniff the contents. Those dogs, they think everything is for them.

When I push the lid away, I am surprised with the photo I take out, one that I forget I have, and I am so pleased to see this again. I share it with Kerry.

'We went to La Scala, in Milan,' I explain to her, 'for Lucia's birthday, her fiftieth.'

I tell you, we look good in this photograph. Lucia, she is not a slim woman, she is big, and she wear a black dress, but she is beautiful in this dress. And she wear a diamond necklace that belong to her mother. I am in a dinner jacket with a bow tie. La Scala is the famous opera house, and we see *Aida* at this venue.

I pass this to Kerry.

'You're like film stars at a première. Did you ever go to a film première?'

'For *Il Problemo*, yes. That film open in Rome and we have a gala evening to launch it. It was fun, you know, but many divas. There are many egos in the film business. That is a thing I did not like. It is easy to believe the things they say about you and with me, they say I am handsome, I am beautiful, all these things. Lucia, she say to me, "Gianluca, I have to keep my eye on you because your head will inflate". She keep my feet on the ground.'

I search in the box again and I bring out a pair of tiny shoes. They are white with silk ribbon on them. Kerry, she is concerned.

'Carlotta's first pair of shoes.' I turn to her. 'You know, she was sick over these things when we first put her in them.'

I think, perhaps, Kerry is right. That opening this take me to a place I want to be. I pull the box closer to me and bring out the next thing. The dogs cannot sit still, and they are sniffing everything I bring out.

'Lucia's first bible.' It is so small, and the type is tiny. I don't know how anyone can read it. I open the cover and show Kerry a dedication written in ink. The writing of a child. 'Look here. "Property of Lucia Rossa, age seven".'

I then pull out her driving licence. 'You know, she almost kill us every time she drove.' I turn to the dogs. 'You know this, too. You witness this many times.'

Kerry, she laugh at this.

'I am serious, always she talk, never does she concentrate on the road.'

'I take it you did most of the driving.'

'I like to drive but Lucia, she tell me I drive too fast and, if she is not driving, she is telling me how to drive. Mind this, mind that, watch this, watch that. *Mamma mia.*'

I complain, you know, but I miss that when I drive now. Lucia, she love to talk, even first thing in the morning, she start. I like to wake up slowly, have an espresso before I begin to think.

Kerry, she pour more coffee for us while I bring out certificates, school reports, old passports and photos. I pass each item to Kerry. She take an interest in everything and does not rush me.

A short time later, I am near the bottom of the box, and I bring out a few wedding photos. Kerry take them from me and we go through them one by one. Lucia, she wear a wonderful dress that she made, with much lace and silk. I wear a suit made for that day, a dark navy suit with a yellow tie. I still have it. I have not changed size since that day.

'I was so nervous,' I say to Kerry. 'I said my names in

the wrong order. And Lucia tripped and nearly fell down the steps.'

'How many names have you got?'

'Gianluca Franco Giovanni Paolo Belfiore.'

'Bloody hell. I'm just plain Kerry Simmonds.'

'These are for my *nonni*, my grandparents. I had *Nonna* Franca and Paola and *Nonno* Gianluca and Giovanni.'

'Is Rico named after someone?'

'Oh, yes, Enrico was Lucia's grandfather.'

Kerry, she see something in the box and hold it up. I have to laugh. It is the ugly ring. That is what I call it and Kerry, I can see that she think this, too. I laugh at her.

'We were broke. When we get engaged. We had nothing and I could not afford a ring so I give Lucia this until we see a ring we could buy.'

I then bring out a pair of very misshapen socks. Carlotta's. One is much bigger than the other. I give a nonchalant shrug. 'Lucia, she's a good seamstress but not so good, I think, with knitting. Oh!' My heart leap into my mouth. The dogs stare at me and wag their tails.

'What?'

I bring out a notebook. 'Her poetry.'

Kerry, she stare at me. 'You never said.'

I don't know why I did not tell Kerry. It was not intention on my part. Perhaps I think I did tell her. It is of no matter. Already, I sit back and leaf through the pages and then read a poem and I throw my head back and laugh. Kerry ask what is so funny.

'One day, Lucia was not well, and I take over the cooking and she always accuse me of putting too much salt in everything. I will translate it. "You world-class son of a bitch".'

Kerry chuckle at this.

'"You ruin my sauce; you ruin my meal. Always too much with the salt. You are impossible and I love you. You world-class son of a bitch".'

I turn to Kerry. 'I am not sure that this is a poem. I think she just wrote a note to tell me how she feel. You know why? We had guests that evening, just family, but she think I ruin the dinner. Because of this, she do not speak to me for the rest of the evening.'

Kerry, she find this very amusing.

I tell you truthfully, I am so happy to open this box. I forget about the items I place there and I enjoy, very much, the memories they bring to me.

Kerry has a workshop to go to and she gather her things, but I draw her close and hug her very tightly.

'Thank you.' When I step back, I tell her, 'If I do not meet you, I do not open the box so I am happy that I meet you.'

'You've one more thing to do.'

I frown.

'Santa Margherita.'

Santa Margherita. *That*, I think, *is a journey I cannot make*, and I think my expression give Kerry my answer to this. She kiss me on the cheek and say goodbye to Tosca and Figaro.

'You just leapt over a huge hurdle, Gian. Think about leaping over another. You've proved you can do it.'

I wave goodbye to her, and she leave me thinking about this but it seem a very high hurdle for me. The items from the box, they are scattered over my sofa and chairs. I decide to make more coffee and choose one or two photos to put on display. I don't want them in the box anymore. I want them out, where I can see them.

Chapter Fifty-One
GIAN

Later that day, the day I open Lucia's memory box, I sit in Rico's at my table and Suzie join me for lunch. I reach down and stroke the dogs and I go deep into my thoughts. Suzie, she notice this.

'Penny for them, Gian.'

'Mmm?'

'Darling, you've drifted onto another planet.'

'I'm so sorry. I didn't mean to be rude. I wonder, Suzie. What happen? To Adam? How did he die?'

'Kerry hasn't told you?'

'She say that she will but, no, she has not and I do not want to upset her by asking.'

'You'll remember this when I tell you. It was around the time that you first arrived. Adam and Kerry were on a boat ride around the bay...'

Chapter Fifty-Two
KERRY

Fear attacks the very depth of my soul
Reaching up with its tentacles from the ocean floor.

I'd booked an afternoon slot on the wildlife cruise with Bay Wildlife, the company Adam and I had chosen that fateful day. What happened to us had been awful, but it wasn't their fault and they'd been exemplary in how they dealt with everything and how quickly they'd mobilised help. I had no qualms about going with them again, and now I stood on the quayside waiting. There were about a dozen passengers milling about ready to board.

The skipper at the controls was the same man who had been in charge that day. A younger man handed out life jackets and made sure we had them on properly.

I swallowed hard as I boarded the boat. Nausea settled in and the temptation to disembark was strong. But that nagging thought kept repeating: if I went home without doing this, I would regret it and it would only make it harder next time round.

I realised the young man was talking to me. 'You all right, miss? If you're worried about seasickness, we've got some pills on board if you want one.'

Did I look that bad? If only it was just seasickness. 'No, I'm fine,' I said with forced positivity. 'Just a bit of a headache.'

The skipper, from his little wheelhouse up front, made a few safety announcements, just as he'd done before. Within a couple of minutes, the engine noise moved up from idling level to a gentle cruise.

I gripped the seat, closed my eyes and whispered silent affirmations to myself. I could do this. I *would* do this. I wouldn't be frightened. I would be proud of myself for doing it. *Think about how you will feel when you've done it*, I said to myself. *You can't get off now, anyway.*

As we cleared the harbour, the noise of the engine changed again, and we made good progress along the coastline of Gwithian toward Godrevy Lighthouse on its island. The passengers were enjoying the ride, the children eagerly anticipating their first glimpse of a seal or dolphin.

The skipper pointed out various places of interest although, in actuality, it was just a huge, long stretch of sandy beach, albeit impressive.

A number of boats were in the vicinity, and I kept my eye on every one. I closed my eyes again and, inevitably, my thoughts took me back.

In my mind, I saw that damned speedboat racing toward us. There were half a dozen people in it and the boy at the controls, who couldn't have been more than seventeen, had been weaving the boat about. He thrust a bottle in the air as he sped by. I remember Adam saying what an idiot the lad was.

The excitement of the children broke my thoughts. 'There's one!'

'Where?'

'There on the rocks.'

'Quiet now,' said the skipper as softly as he could over the Tannoy. 'You shout too loud and they'll be in the water.'

Several grey seals were basking in the sun on the rocks. They had the most lovable faces with those huge black eyes staring out at us.

I relaxed a little. The boats that I'd just seen were now heading further out to sea or back to St Ives.

The young lad helping the captain gave us a commentary about the seals – where they came from, what they ate – and answered a few questions.

After a while, the captain pulled away from the rocks, then asked for those who wanted to see dolphins to raise a hand. The children reacted immediately. Dan had been the same on this trip at their age. Dolphins? Really? A unanimous decision. *Everyone* wanted to see the dolphins.

The captain pushed down on the throttle and we headed out to sea.

I closed my eyes again. The two boats had floundered twenty metres apart. The skipper, in between calling for help from the coastguard, lifeboat and whoever else he could summon, yelled at the boy in the other boat, blasting him for being such an idiot. The boy, so full of bravado just a few minutes ago, now stood stunned at the consequence of his actions. The skipper returned to the radio, demanding the police attend the scene.

I'd been so confident about Adam. He was doing okay at first and I had no reason to doubt his strength. But that strength began to fade and those ten to fifteen metres between me and him might just have well been as wide as the English Channel.

When I jumped in I was of no use. All I did was splash about and get colder by the second and add to the problem. The rest of passengers on our boat were frantically rowing, life jackets were thrown as far as they would go but nothing worked. With every stroke of the oar, the water seemed to push them back. Every jacket flung out seemed to catch the wind and land short.

Only Adam lost his life that day. A needless death.

At the harbour, I'd been too shocked to react to anything or anyone. But, later, even months later, even now, if I were to see the lad responsible for driving that boat, I honestly thought I'd kill him.

Chapter Fifty-Three
GIAN

When Suzie finish her story, I sit back in my chair. This story, it horrify me. It did at the time and, Suzie is right, it happen just after I arrive.

'I remember this. The young man, he take his father's boat and he and his friends, they have been drinking, yes?'

'Yes. The boy was charged.'

I understand now why Kerry react like she did when I suggest a boat ride.

Chapter Fifty-Four
KERRY

If I face that fear, look it in the eye
I have to ask why. Why did I do this?
Will it make a difference? I think it will.
I'm sure it will.

When we moored up in the harbour, I remained in my seat, my thoughts tumbling with memories I'd brought back by taking the trip. Even worries that I hadn't had for months resurfaced. What would I do now? Why exist without Adam?

And, my God, I ached. I realised that my body had been tense during the whole trip and, only now, back in the safety of the harbour, did I relax.

I watched, aimlessly, as the skipper went through his routine checks around the boat. He spotted me and I could see he was trying to work something out.

He suddenly dropped the rope in his hand and came across. 'I know you,' he said in a broad Cornish accent. 'You're the lady... your husband.'

He bobbed his head toward the open sea. He didn't need to say any more. I gave a very brief 'yes that's me' nod. He took a seat next to me.

'I'm sorry, pet, I didn't recognise you. If I'd realised, I would've had someone sit with you.'

That small act of kindness caused me to well up a little. 'I wanted to do it on my own. I needed to do it on my own. I'm a bit of an idiot like that.'

I wasn't crying but tears weren't far away. He opened his arms wide, and I accepted the offer of a hug. I think he held me for about a minute, and I was grateful for that support. When I was ready, he helped me out of the boat, and I went up the steps to join the hustle and bustle of the town.

As I took a deep breath, I spotted Greg chomping on a pasty. He'd seen me get off the boat and very quickly concluded what I'd done. The pasty went straight in a bin as he dashed over and scooped me into his arms.

I almost fell into them. When I'd planned to do this, I hadn't thought about how I'd feel when I got off the boat. I'd imagined I'd be overjoyed at having faced the monster head-on, maybe running around the harbour waving my arms in the air like I did after the abseiling.

I hadn't bargained on the emptiness, the loss and the despair.

Greg was an unexpected and welcome guardian angel. Once in his embrace, I hugged him so tightly, every fibre of my being needing the warm comfort of this man.

'Don't let me go,' I said. God knows what passers-by must have thought. We stood like this for ages, and I felt the desperation and horror of those memories fade, retreating to where they should be.

Replacing them was a sense of pride. I'd done it. I'd met the challenge. I broke through the wall. The worst possible memory that I had had of losing Adam was conquered and when I eventually pulled back from Greg, I couldn't hide the satisfaction in my face.

Chapter Fifty-Five
KERRY

The flow of conversation, the sound of laughter
The songs of love and happy ever after.

Early that evening, on the patio, I walked into a scene straight out of *Cinderella*. Suzie was putting the finishing touches to decorating the area, ready to celebrate what would have been mine and Adam's thirty-fifth wedding anniversary and Lucia's birthday. It was a perfect evening weather-wise, with gentle warmth in the air and wispy white clouds in the sky. The evening promised to remain dry.

Later, when the sun had melted into the ocean, the lanterns, candles and fairy lights would enhance an already magical grotto. I noticed some incense burners, too. Additions for the night included some beach-themed bunting and a two helium balloons: one bearing the message 'Happy Anniversary' and one 'Happy Birthday'. Suzie had borrowed the cork board from reception, and this was propped on an easel. I went over to examine the photos of Adam and Lucia that she'd arranged on it in an artistic way. Their smiling faces were surrounded by red and purple hearts.

A small buffet table was already set up ready for the food.

'Oh, Suzie, this is lovely.'

'Well, if Adam and Lucia are looking down, they're going to have a wonderful evening. And we have fireworks.'

'Fireworks!' I couldn't help but be impressed.

'Not from me, darling. It's to mark the end of the festival. We'll have a perfect view from here. Greg's popped out to get some spliffs.'

'Oooh. Nice.'

'Adam would approve, I'm sure. I don't know if Gian smokes it, but he can give it a try tonight if he wants to.'

Butterflies had launched in my stomach and chest, not because of nerves, but happiness. I was overwhelmed by the effort she'd put in to make this evening the best it could be. And, knowing Suzie, there would be some wonderful treats in the buffet.

I took her hands. 'Thank you. For this. For everything. But, especially for this.'

She hugged me. 'And well done on the boat ride. Greg rang and told me. Kerry, you are one fucking amazing woman.'

I had to chuckle. I didn't often hear Suzie swear. She must be impressed.

Chapter Fifty-Six
DAN

I had a brilliant day with Chloe today, down at the beach at Littlehampton. She took my mind off things. It was like being back in Cornwall.

The only person who knew what was worrying me was Greg.

I knew Mum was having a good time in St Ives, but I wondered if she'd still got those pills. I worried that she might have a bad day and decide she'd had enough. Part of me was angry with myself. 'The little voice in your head', Mum called it. Well, I had it going on in my head all the time, telling me not to be so stupid; that she wouldn't do that.

I needed to be sure that everything was okay with her.

When I left Chloe, I went straight back home and got on the phone to Greg. I FaceTimed him on his mobile and I saw he was in town.

'What're you saying, mate?' he said.

'She had a stack of them, Greg, in the drawer.' I saw the frown as if he didn't believe me. 'I'm just worried, you know...'

'Yeah, well, don't be. She wouldn't do that, Dan. You're worrying over nothing. I'll take a look around but I'm not rummaging around in your mum's things. After today, well…'

'What. What happened today?'

'She took the boat ride, Dan.'

I stared at the screen. I didn't know what to say. I didn't know whether to be angry or ecstatic. Angry because she told me she wouldn't do it or ecstatic that she was brave enough to go through with it.

'Listen, mate, I gotta go,' Greg said. 'And Dan, don't worry. Your mum's brilliant and I don't reckon she needs those pills for anything and certainly not for what you're thinking.'

I waved goodbye; no sooner had I ended the call, then another came in. It was Mum connecting through on FaceTime. I pressed Accept and saw she was in the bedroom.

'Just a quick call, my sweetheart. How're you doing?'

'Yeah, good.' I told her about my day with Chloe, how I'd enjoyed hanging out with her and that we'd had fish and chips out and that we were going to the cinema that night.

'We're going to see one of your stupid films.'

You'd think I'd told her I was having dinner with the queen.

'No! Which one?'

'*An Affair to Remember.*'

'Cary Grant. Oh, how adorable. What made you want to see that?'

'It was you telling Chloe about the films you like to watch. She'd seen it advertised at the arts cinema. Did you know *Sleepless in Seattle* was based on that film?'

'Yes, I did, but as much as I love Tom Hanks, the Cary

Grant one has far more romance, elegance, charm and all those other things you don't get these days.'

I tutted at that.

'And the comedy, too, especially on the ship when they're trying to avoid one another.'

'I'll take your word for it. I'll probably be bored stiff.'

'Like father, like son.'

I grinned at that. Dad had always moaned about having to sit through those old films, but I knew he enjoyed it really. He wouldn't have gone if he didn't. There was a *ping*, and a message came through on the screen.

'I've sent through a photo of the patio. Suzie transformed it. I wish you could have stayed. We're just waiting for Gian.'

I knew I'd reacted because I felt my jaw clench but, after Chloe had had a go at me, I tried to keep it hidden. I hope it hadn't shown in my face. I didn't want to spoil Mum's night. But I saw her frustration. I knew she'd seen something.

'It would have been his wife's birthday tomorrow, so we thought it'd be nice to invite him.'

I should have said something. I should have been more upbeat, and Mum was in there, straight away.

'Honestly, Dan, what is it about him? He's just a friend.'

'Nothing, it's fine. Honestly, Mum, it's fine.'

'Right, well, I'd better get ready. I'll speak to you tomorrow and I'll be home in a couple of days. I've lots to tell you but I'm running a little late.'

'Mum?' She waited. 'Greg told me. About the boat ride.'

'Oh, darling, I'm sorry. I know I said I wouldn't, but I had to. I would have kicked myself if I came back home without doing it.'

I nodded. 'I know.'

'I'll tell you all about it tomorrow. I promise. I can't think that I'll be fit for anything except a long natter. Suzie is determined to make this a celebration for your dad and for Lucia so the wine will be flowing.'

'Okay. And Mum? Happy anniversary. I hope you have a good night.'

'Thank you, sweetheart. I love you very much. And enjoy the film. I want to know what you think.'

I couldn't help but grin at that. She blew me a kiss and signed off.

I couldn't deny I was pissed off that Gian was going to be with Mum tonight. I understood why he was going, and Mum kept telling me he was just a friend. She promised she would always been honest with me.

But then, she'd never told me about the pills.

And she'd promised she wouldn't go on the boat ride.

So, was she being honest about Gian?

Chapter Fifty-Seven

KERRY

*Choices, memories, nostalgia, future, past
Depending on the day, they're as strong as a diamond
or fragile as glass.*

I pursed my lips. I knew Dan would react when he found out. He might have tried to hide it, but it was written all over his face. Admittedly, the expression only lasted a second, but I saw it. He didn't like that Gian was coming tonight.

Well, tomorrow, I would have a long talk with him. Not about the serious stuff, but lately our video calls had been quite frantic and short because we'd both been busy. No, I'd spend time just catching up and focussing on what he'd been doing.

Dan was getting out and about and I was so pleased that he had Chloe in his life. She'd been an absolute rock for him over this awful time and I knew she'd helped where I couldn't. No matter how good a relationship Dan and I had, sometimes a young man needed someone other than his mum, especially at his age.

I didn't want to wish life away, but I secretly hoped that she and Dan stayed together. They were good as a couple. Of course, when they got to their respective universities, they might well go their separate ways. But whoever Dan ended up with one day, I hoped it would be someone like Chloe.

I chose my dress for the anniversary night. It was the one I had been going to wear the previous week, the night of the meltdown, a flattering '50's-style cotton dress. When I bought outfits like this, I always took Maggie along with me to tell me straight. Did I resemble mutton dressed as lamb? I was all for being young at heart, but I couldn't bear it when older people dressed too young.

In Brighton, there was a man who'd been a Teddy Boy in his youth. He was now well into his seventies and still styling his thinning hair into the Elvis quiff and wearing a drape jacket. I always grimaced when I saw him.

Maggie, fortunately, had given me the thumbs up on this dress. I slipped it on and started applying some make-up. Not much. I'd never been one for plastering myself with greasepaint. A touch of mascara, a bit of lippy and eye shadow. I turned Adam's photo so that I could see him better.

'Thirty-five years, my darling. We'll be raising a toast to you and to Lucia. I hope you'll both be looking down on us. And there's spliffs and wine. Two of your favourite things.' I picked out a pair of dangly earrings. 'Darling, I don't know if you have any influence on things where you are but please get Dan to stop this animosity toward Gian. The poor man hasn't done anything to deserve it. He's been the perfect gentleman and a wonderful companion during this holiday.'

Checking myself in the mirror, I was happy with my efforts. I wanted to look good for Adam. I wanted to look good for me. And, if I was honest, a small part of me wanted to look good for Gian.

I kissed Adam's photo, grabbed my clutch bag and left.

Chapter Fifty-Eight

GIAN

Tonight, we celebrate Lucia's birthday and Kerry's anniversary. I think this is a nice thing to do and, in my bedroom, I check that I am smart.

I have chosen, for tonight, a dress suit, a tuxedo. My wife, Lucia, when it was her birthday, we always have an intimate meal, just the two of us. We have other celebration with family, but I always insist on a meal for two, and we wear our best clothes and eat at the best restaurant.

I struggle with a bow tie. I try to fold this and always I fail. Lucia could do it but, she is not here so I have cheated and bought one that is already tied. My tuxedo, it was made by a tailor in Italy. It fit me well and I am happy with it. I polish my shoes and splash aftershave and, *pronto*, I am ready. Rico and Tina, they have the dogs for the night and that permit me to stay longer this evening.

In the lounge, I pick up the bouquet of flowers that I buy for Kerry. Carnations and roses. For her anniversary. I am about to leave when I see something on the doormat. I get closer and find it is a ring box.

When I open it, I see it is the ring from the shop in Marazion. The one Kerry want to buy for me. I take it out and put it on and I love it. It is very stylish, very unique. I know this is from Kerry and I am grateful to her for this.

Then, I grin to myself. I like to have fun and to tease people if I can. I have an idea form in my head about this ring and decide to play a little joke with it.

I keep the ring on my finger, pick up the flowers and head out. Already the plan, it run in my head.

Chapter Fifty-Nine
KERRY

People in our company are easy
The time we have we'd like to share freely.

Greg finished mixing a gin and tonic for me and Suzie. He opted for a beer. It was going to be a longish evening and I was sure that by the end of it we would all be a little tipsy and mellow. Especially as there were a few spliffs waiting in the wings. If the wine didn't get us, the spliffs would.

Suzie had laid out the buffet: French bread, pâté and salami plus a few blinis with salmon and cream cheese. There were ripe tomatoes, prosciutto ham and various salads, along with raw vegetables, dips and hummus. She'd provided a good selection of Mediterranean treats that blended well together. At the moment, those nibbles remained under net protectors, safe from wasps and flies, awaiting our appetites when they surfaced.

Suzie had thought along the same lines as me and dressed up, although she always had a sophistication about her. She suited flowing outfits, and she wore bright colours that showed off her complexion. She honestly did just seem to float everywhere and, this evening, she was wearing some dark coral-coloured culottes with a loose-fitting shirt a shade darker. She could have just walked out of a 1960's flower power movie.

Greg had, for the first time during my holiday, switched to quite smart trousers and a cotton sweater.

I wondered what Gian would be wearing. I didn't have to wait long to find out as he'd just arrived.

Bloody hell. A tuxedo. My goodness, he'd taken the unwritten dress code to a whole new level.

My admiration turned to a quizzical frown as he strode purposefully toward me. Greg asked him what he wanted to drink, and he curtly asked for beer.

'I told you not to buy that ring,' he snapped. 'What are you doing spending that sort of money on me?'

I couldn't believe he was being so disagreeable. 'I wanted to buy it.'

'I said specifically not to buy it.'

'It's nothing to do with what you want. It's a gift.'

Then he stabbed a finger at me! 'When I say no. I mean no.'

I almost snarled but quickly stopped. Did he just wink at Greg? Had I imagined that?

'This is...' My eyes flicked between Greg and Gian. I couldn't ignore what I'd seen. 'Why did you do that?'

'What?'

'You just winked at Greg.'

'I did not.'

Greg had an infectious laugh and was hopeless at hiding it. And, Gian, well he was struggling, too, although his eyes remained stern.

'You're trying not to laugh.'

'I am being serious.'

'No, you're not. You're winding me up.'

Greg couldn't help himself and Gian completely failed to hide his amusement. The punch I delivered to his arm landed a little harder than I'd intended. He genuinely grimaced and clamped his hand on his arm.

'Kerry!'

By now, Suzie and Greg were lapping up the entertainment we were providing. Gian's giggling turned into a laugh. I was, for a split second, annoyed at being caught out.

'You bloody toerag.'

'Toerag? What is this?'

'Look it up.'

'You know, you look very beautiful.'

'Oh, don't put on the charm.'

He rubbed his arm. 'If you are going to punch me again, stick to the same arm, it's numb already.'

'Good.' I turned my back on him. I had to retaliate somehow. Inspiration landed and I grinned at Suzie and Greg as I put on the best injured tone I could.

'This is supposed to be a celebration and you come in here trying to start an argument.' I sniffed and thought I might have gone over the top until I heard the panic in his voice and felt his presence behind me.

'Oh, Kerry. I'm so sorry. It was just a joke. I didn't mean to upset you.'

Suzie and Greg settled back in their seats, enjoying the exchange. He obviously saw it, too.

'Wait a minute,' Gian said, turning me around. I proudly grinned at him. 'You're not angry.'

Bless him. The relief on his face was palpable and I couldn't help but laugh. He joined in with the jollity, pleased that he had not completely destroyed the evening.

Greg returned to preparing Gian's drink. 'If you're planning that another time, Gian, let me know and I'll sell tickets.'

I noticed the ring on his finger. 'You're wearing it.'

'Of course, I'm wearing it. I love it. But, Kerry, you should not have spent so much.'

'Can I say something, in all seriousness?'

He waited.

'This holiday... I don't think I've had this much fun since... it's just a way of saying thank you.' I reached down to the table and picked up a card that I'd chosen earlier in the day. 'Happy birthday to Lucia.'

He appeared genuinely touched by this and signalled for me to wait. He dashed back inside and quickly returned with a lovely bouquet of flowers.

'Happy anniversary, to you and Adam.'

'Oh, Gian, thank you.'

He kissed me on both cheeks before giving me a hug.

'And,' he whispered in my ear, 'you are very beautiful.'

'And you are very handsome.'

'Right, come on,' said Greg. 'Let's get settled and start on this food. I'm bloody starving.'

Before I had a chance to move, Gian pulled me back. 'Kerry. Suzie, she tell me... about Adam... about how he die. I'm so sorry. I would not have asked—'

I stopped him. 'You weren't to know. And anyway, it's not a problem anymore.'

The confusion on his face quickly cleared. 'You took the trip?'

'Yes.'

I felt pleased with myself but, beneath that, I was also delighted that he was gazing at me with enormous pride.

Chapter Sixty
GIAN

I think I spoil the evening when I play the joke on Kerry. I like to see the fun in things, but I think, this time, I go too far. Then I find she is fine with it. Lucia, she would go crazy with me when I do these things, but I can't help it, it is part of me. I like to have fun and this, I think, is fun.

We spend this first hour chatting and drinking and Suzie prepare a buffet; very tasty and it was good that she provide French bread and pâté. This I enjoy very much.

We have more drinks and, Greg, he purchase *spinello*, in English I think you say 'spliff' and I am already halfway through mine. I tell you truthfully, this make me very dreamy, and I grin like an idiot but it also make me mellow. It is some time since I smoke it and it make me notice things that I don't normally consider, like the twinkle of the fairy lights and the lanterns and candles, too. In the distance, I see the lights in the cottages that hug this hill. It remind me of Santa Margherita, the way the buildings cling to the hillside. I notice this more with the *spinello*. The colours are more intense.

Greg, he bring the drinks trolley over so we help

ourselves. I think we all get a little tipsy. The ladies, they joke to me about my time as a film actor and they discuss the films they like. I notice that Kerry always pick the older films.

Suzie disappear for a minute and she come back with a book, a big book full of photographs of the old film stars and we start to play a game; marry, kiss or kill. I think this is the name, but we change the kiss to sex. We are not permitted to choose; the book is opened at a page by one person and the next person have to make the decision. We have a lot of fun with this and the spliffs and alcohol contribute.

The first person to open the book is Suzie. It is a photograph of Bette Davis. She is a very old film star, and this is not, I think, a good image of her. And she show this to Greg. 'Sex, kill, marry.'

Greg and me, we are of the same opinion.

'Kill,' Greg say.

'I don't blame you,' I say.

I take a drag on my cigarette and chuckle. Kerry is amused at the effect this is having. She pick up the book and she search for a page.

'You are not supposed to search,' I say to her. 'You are supposed to pick at random.'

She ignore me and she show me a picture; the caption below it says Ethel Merman. I am not sure exactly who this is, but I know my answer straight way.

'Kill.' Then I select the actress on the page opposite. Grace Kelly. 'But then I would have sex with Grace Kelly because she will be hiding in my wardrobe.'

The game, it come to a natural end and Greg, he suggest a complete change.

Chapter Sixty-One
KERRY

High up in the evening sky, the constellations roam,
Picking out the shooting stars that offer up a show.

As the evening went on, a sense of contentment washed through me, as if I'd come out of a coma and everything was right with the world – and always would be. Of course, having the spliffs helped each of us. Suzie became even more chilled with the effect. From what I could see, Greg didn't appear to be any different although I knew he partook quite often. Gian slid into a similar state as Suzie, but it was accompanied by a dopey expression that just made everyone want to smile.

The sex, marry, kill game created much hilarity and it quickly became apparent that I was the old film fan. I knew all the film stars in Suzie's book. Gian knew some of them, but Greg and Suzie only recognised the mega-famous ones; Marlon Brando, Audrey Hepburn, Yul Brynner.

The end of the game signalled a further round of drinks. Gian and I transferred to the edge of the double-bed lounger.

Suzie was draped on a single lounger and Greg had opted for a luxurious bean bag. He climbed out of it and hauled Gian to his feet. 'Let's sing the girls that song.'

I looked sideways at Suzie, who was equally clueless.

Gian, still with that dreamy look on his face, was happy to go with it. 'All right, ladies. Something romantic for you. Sicilian.'

I suppressed a laugh at the false starts while they fumbled around for the right key. I recognised the tune, 'Luna Mezzo Mare', which featured in *The Godfather*.

We settled back to listen although I had no idea what was being sung because it was all in Italian. Greg, bless him, sang with great gusto and his broad Cornish burr added an unusual and amusing aspect to things.

Gian had a resonant baritone voice. I recognised a handful of words from the part he was singing: *pesce, calamari, pomodori* and so on.

They wrapped their arms around each other's shoulders and very dramatically broke into what appeared to be the chorus. Repeated phrases of, '*Oh mamma, patate e cipolle*' followed by lots of *la la la*'s and a final hug.

Suzie and I applauded enthusiastically, and Gian returned to his seat next to me.

I had to ask. 'Romantic? *Calamari* and *pomodori*? Isn't that squid and tomatoes? And *patate*? That's potatoes, isn't it?'

'Yes. Not romantic at all. But is a good way to teach Greg Italian.'

He reached for his drink, and I couldn't help but look on fondly.

The evening slipped into a chilled vibe. The sun sank

below the horizon and the lights of St Ives twinkled. Suzie had requested a selection of Ella Fitzgerald songs on Alexa, and she was singing about someone watching over her. She and Greg had curled up together on the swing chair.

Gian and I settled back on the lounger. We'd ditched our usual drinks in favour of a liqueur each. It was a period of quiet for all of us. We'd laughed, talked, sent Adam and Lucia our love and reminisced about them for some time. Now it was almost eleven and we were all very sleepy.

Gian spoke quietly to me. 'Kerry? Do you have to go home on Wednesday?'

'Well, yes, I do. I need to get back for Dan.'

'Can't you stay a little longer.'

'How much longer?'

'Very much.'

Every organ that could perform somersaults in my body did exactly that. He wasn't just suggesting a few days, he was proposing a much longer period. And, deep down, where my instinct lay, I welcomed that suggestion. I wanted to stay. I wanted to get to know him more, to spend time with him.

He'd been so kind and thoughtful during this holiday, recognising my feelings and moods and helping me through that bloody awful meltdown. And I liked to think that I'd helped him, especially with that memory box. That had been a huge barrier for him, and he'd overcome it.

I'd grown fond of him as a friend but there was an added element now. These feelings weren't only to do with friendship. Something else was brewing and I knew it had simmered for some time. I'd relegated that emotion to the back burner but now I was being confronted with it.

Before I could formulate an answer, a loud bang shattered the calm.

We instinctively looked to see a fountain of fireworks exploding over the town. What a display! I don't know how much the town had spent on them, but we were treated to a good fifteen-minute show of zooming rockets and cascading chandeliers of colour and sound. Even the characteristic smell of gunpowder reached us on the breeze. My frequent *oohs* and *aahs* amused Gian.

'You are like a child,' he said.

'Adam and I used to take Dan to Florida, to the theme parks. We stayed in a hotel once that overlooked Disney World. Every evening, without fail, I got to see the most spectacular firework display and I never tired of it. I was just as excited as Dan was. Adam said it was like having two kids in tow instead of one.'

Gian snaked an arm around my shoulder, and I leant into him as the fireworks came to their climactic conclusion.

I was aware of voices, but they were way in the distance and my eyelids were so heavy I had no desire or motivation to open them. Nothing registered in my foggy head. Greg was saying something about waking them up. I felt a blanket being draped over me and sleep beckoned but not before I heard Suzie's response.

'Gian had two spliffs. Nothing biblical will happen.'

If she said anything after that, I didn't hear it. I was dead to the world, in a gin-infused slumber.

Chapter Sixty-Two
KERRY

Never in one lifetime will your every dream come true,
But now it seems that all my dreams have come with you.

I woke bleary-eyed and disoriented as the sun shed its first light on the day. Where the hell was I? I certainly wasn't in bed. Was I at home? No. No, I was at The Feather Duck. Or was I? What happened last night? Did I go out?

Those questions whizzed by in a second and my brain finally came up with the answer. Of course. We'd celebrated Adam and Lucia; we'd drunk too much and shared an extra spliff when we shouldn't have done. There were wonderful fireworks and…

And Gian had asked if I would stay.

I hadn't responded to the question, and I hadn't gone to bed. My sleepy eyes flew wide open, and I froze. I was still on the double-lounger. A sideways glance confirmed that Gian had also fallen asleep there.

Shit!

His bow tie was discarded, the top two buttons of his shirt

were open, his hair was ruffled and, thank goodness, he was fast asleep. We'd had a brilliant night and he'd been wonderful company. Suzie and Greg were perfect hosts, and I couldn't have asked for a better way to celebrate my anniversary.

But I hadn't anticipated spending the night with another man. I knew, effectively, I hadn't slept with him in the biblical sense.

Biblical.

Gian's had two spliffs, nothing biblical will happen. Suzie's comment from last night had clearly lodged in my thoughts. It must have been Suzie who put the blanket over us.

Weirdly, I hadn't scurried off the lounger in horror. Nothing biblical *had* happened. We just happened to fall asleep on the same bit of furniture. Yes, I was initially startled but that vanished in the blink of an eye.

What I didn't want was for him to wake up with me lying next to him. I wouldn't know what to say.

I craved a shower and clean teeth and I'd promised to check in with Dan. First, though, I had to negotiate getting off this lounger without waking Gian.

I shifted to the side, trying my best not to disturb him. There were a few creaks and I winced at every one. He must have felt something because he turned onto his side, facing me. His arm flopped onto my hand. Shit. Now what? If I moved too quickly, I'd wake him up.

Oh God, it was that morning all over again, when I'd picked up those groceries and made the mistake of going into his bedroom. Another moment like that didn't bear thinking about.

I left it a few seconds. Satisfied he was still asleep I gently slipped my arm from under his and slid off the lounger and onto the patio like an anaconda. I went to get up but stopped. My eyes ranged freely up and down his body. I couldn't help it. I leaned across and kissed him on the forehead.

I got to my feet then quickly closed my eyes and held my head as the world spun for a few seconds before settling. Happy that the nausea had subsided, I edged slowly through the doors and into reception, my hand on the wall to help my progress.

The clock told me it was just gone seven. What the hell was I doing waking up at that time? Suzie was at the reception desk, equally hungover. She'd put the flowers Gian gave me into a vase.

'Oh, hello, darling. You look like I feel.'

'What are you doing up?'

'I'm always up early to prepare breakfast. I know there's only you here but it's now inbuilt, no choice in the matter. Do you want breakfast?'

'Yes, but not just yet. I thought I'd freshen up first. In fact, I may see if I can get a couple more hours' kip.'

She studied me. I kept fiddling about with things on the reception desk. Her eyes posed the question 'What's up?'

I was sixty-five years old and, despite the hangover, felt like a giddy teenager. Christ, just tell her. I blurted it out. 'Suzie, I think I'm in love with him.'

Suzie barely reacted. 'Oh, darling, he fell for you the day he met you.'

I gawped. 'Why didn't you say something?'

'Not my place, darling. After what you said about Maggie, I didn't want to push in on the matchmaking front. It's clear the pair of you have a connection. You'd be the perfect couple.' She held my forearms. 'Adam would be over the moon.'

I could almost hear my brain clunking and spinning, thinking it all through. I returned to the entrance to the patio and observed Gian, who remained in dreamland.

Careful not to turn too quickly, I made my way back to Suzie, a little light-headed. She had rather a smug I-knew-this-would-happen look on her face.

I checked my phone. 'Oh. I missed a couple of calls from Dan last night. I'll try to get another hour's sleep and then freshen up. Shall we say ten for breakfast? That gives me time to turn into a human being!'

'Perfect.' I looked back to the patio and then at Suzie with a coy smile.

Chapter Sixty-Three
GIAN

I feel movement on the lounger, but I do not think about it. I think perhaps I dream so I continue to sleep. When I wake up, I am confused about where I am. Then it come to me. The patio is empty, and my eyes settle on the board with the photos of Lucia and Adam. The celebration. We have a good evening. I enjoy it very much. I think I must have been very drunk to have slept here all night. And, of course, I have the spliff. That also make me sleepy.

I check the lounger and try to remember. I don't recall Kerry going but she must have gone to bed. Or did she stay here?

I get up slowly and grab my jacket and the card that Kerry give me for Lucia.

In reception, Suzie is there, and she laugh at the state I am in. I see myself in the mirror and shrug because I have something else on my mind.

I stare back at the patio and then at the stairs and then at Suzie. She examine me this whole time.

'Was Kerry…?' I tilt my head toward the patio.

'She was. All night.'

That cause me to swallow hard. I don't want Kerry to think I take advantage. But, Suzie, she come to me and take my hand.

'It's absolutely fine, Gian. I think Kerry is very fond of you. Actually, darling, I don't think it. I know it.'

I know I have the stupid grin on my face last night with the spliff but it return to me now. I cannot help it. I think I wear that expression all the way home.

Chapter Sixty-Four
KERRY

I focus mainly on my mood being up
But, sometimes, my mood brings me down
I try to keep them the right way round, otherwise
things get messy.

After an hour dozing in bed, a cup of tea and two paracetamols, the fuzz in my head began to clear. I might have been feeling better but my reflection in the mirror reminded me of a zombie from *Plan 9 from Outer Space*, a sci-fi movie of the 1950s. I had panda eyes and my hair appeared to have gone through electric-shock treatment.

A refreshing shower and a strong coffee worked wonders.

On connecting with Dan, I was all set to tell him how wonderful the evening had been and that we'd celebrated our anniversary in style and how much his dad would have loved it.

We hardly got past hello when he landed a bombshell on me. His application to Southampton had been declined.

'What!' I leaned forward to study his face on the screen. 'What? What d'you mean, declined?'

I struggled to find the words. His grades were excellent, I reminded him.

He shrugged. 'Everyone gets good grades, Mum. I'll have to rethink. Maybe get a job locally.'

'What! No. Dan, listen, we'll talk this through. You have plenty of options.'

'Not if I can't get into Southampton. Ocean Marine will pull out.'

'No, they won't. Have you even spoken to them? I mean, you have the grades, you've done your bit.'

I desperately tried to formulate my thoughts, but they tossed in my head like clothes in a washing machine. I'd been absolutely sure that getting in was just a formality, that he would be travelling to Southampton and starting the next stage of his life. It had never crossed my mind there was a chance he wouldn't be accepted.

What the fuck?

The decision to get a job locally was, I knew, a knee-jerk reaction. As far as Dan was concerned, all was lost, but it wasn't. We needed to sort this out. Before I could respond, he asked:

'Mum? I'm sorry to ask, but can you get back earlier?'

I was already thinking the same. 'I'll come home today. I can be with you tonight. We'll sit down and think about the alternatives. All right?'

My answer lifted him.

'I'll call you when I know what train I'm on.'

He gave me a quick wave and cut the connection. The news took the wind from my sails. I'd been looking forward to a long conversation with Dan about his days and his trips out with Chloe. I was going to describe my abseiling adventure, the concert at the Minack, the stargazing, the sculpture park. I'd touched on all of those things, of course, but our calls were always short because we both had stuff going on. All of this was now firmly stored away as I focussed on the news.

Over breakfast, Suzie and Greg offered their opinion.

'It ain't the end of the world for him,' said Greg. 'Loads of kids don't get the place they want, they just go on to a different uni.'

'Darling, perhaps he was so excited about Southampton, he feels it's useless,' added Suzie. 'You know what teenagers are like. Everything is black and white. If something won't happen the way they want it, it's the end of the world.'

'I didn't think Dan was like that,' I said, feeling the need to stick up for him. 'He always seems so mature, and he thinks things through.'

'This time next week, it won't be such a big deal,' said Greg. 'He'll be thinking more clearly and realise he's got choices.'

'Greg's right,' said Suzie. 'You go home today and talk it through with him. And I hate to quote a cliché, but this may have happened because he has something more fitting coming along. He'll probably end up going to a uni that suits him better.'

Yes, there were plenty of good universities around, but Southampton was considered the best for those studying to become marine engineers. And one of the first things he needed to do was contact Ocean Marine. I wondered if they might have any influence with the university or could suggest another. Surely, if he was studying for the same degree, it wouldn't matter where?

I checked my watch. I'd rung Gian earlier and asked him to meet me for coffee. My call had been rushed. I hadn't said why I needed to meet straight away, but I couldn't just up and leave without saying goodbye.

Chapter Sixty-Five
GIAN

The call I receive from Kerry, I don't know, it seem a little rushed, you know? I hope she is not upset about last night, about sleeping with me. I can do nothing about this except to say I am sorry, that I did not mean to do this. I just fall asleep. I didn't realise she is still there.

When she arrive, she is flustered. She sit down beside me but refuse a coffee and is far away in her thoughts. Even Tosca and Figaro do not keep her attention for long.

Then she say, 'Do you mind if we go for a walk?'

The back of my neck tingle. She, I think, is going to give me bad news but I do not know what this could be. I lead her out of Rico's, and we go along the path that overlook the beach. The dogs enjoy this but my mood, it sink very low.

After a few minutes, we stop and she turn to me. 'I'm sorry, Gian, but I'm cutting my trip short. I'm going home today.'

'Kerry, last night, I didn't—'

'Dan didn't get his place. At uni. He's so down about it

and he's asked me if I'd come back early. I can't say no. I need to be there for him.'

I am confused with this decision. It does not have to be made today. 'Just two days more. That is all you have here. Let him sleep on it.'

That, I see, is not an option. I tell her, this is not the end of the world for her son. There are other universities that do the degree he want. I feel helpless about this because there is no need for her to return today.

'Kerry, give him time to think. This is not a disaster. He has the options.'

'I'm not letting him down.'

'I'm not telling you to let him down. I am telling you to give him time.'

She is taking hardly any time to breathe. 'He's still struggling, Gian, I see it all the time. He's still processing losing his dad and now this has happened, and I'm worried about him and, to be honest, I can see he worries about me. We've not been apart this long and—'

'Kerry, you have to let go of each other.'

I see that I say the wrong thing. She is a typical mother. My mamma, she is the same with me. Lucia, she is the same with Rico. One piece of criticism about their son and that make them angry.

She frown at me. 'What's that supposed to mean?'

I have the Italian temperament and I fly into a rage at times. It means nothing but, the English, they don't cope so well with this, so I try to be calm.

'I see how protective he is of you. With everything… everyone… but he is blind to where *you* are. Here. Now.' She is puzzled so I try to explain. 'The boat trip. That was the last thing for you, wasn't it? The thing you fear the most. And you did this. You conquer your fear, your grief. This moves you forward. Emotionally. Your son, he need to see that. He need to see that you move on. That your emotion is not tied so strongly to grief. You two dance around each other, all the time dancing around in a circle and not getting to the core of things. Let him know where you are. He is too protective of you.'

Her voice has an edge to it, and I think she want to hit me. 'Don't tell me how to deal with my son. You're not his father.'

I cannot help it. I raise my voice to her, and I demonstrate with my hands. The dogs, they wonder why I am angry.

'I'm not trying to be his father, Kerry.'

'Well, you're acting like it. You don't know him. You don't know what he's gone through.'

I can't help it. I yell at her. 'Open your eyes, Kerry. You both speak but you do not talk. Not about the things that matter; that really matter. You are frightened to upset him; he is frightened to upset you. What happens then? I tell you what happens, nothing is solved, nothing work out and then you come to this. You cannot run to him every time something happen.'

She glare at me but I have said this now. I can't go back with my words, so I continue.

'Let *him* face this. Give him time to think. On his own. He is not a child. A few days and he will think this through. He will arrive at a solution that will suit him but, he need time for that, on his own.'

Then she yell, '*You're* on your own. That didn't help you. You couldn't even open a fucking memory box.'

This take my breath because this hurt me. Deeply. She

walk away. The dogs run after her and they realise I do not follow so they return to me. Then Kerry turn to shout.

'And you haven't made it to Santa Margherita.'

I have no words.

Me and Lucia, we argue all the time, sometimes we rage at each other, but we never hurt each other, we are never vindictive. Never. I feel perhaps I lose a friend that I have grown to love.

Chapter Sixty-Six
DAN

I felt bad about asking Mum to come back. I knew she was having a good time down there and I knew she only had a couple more days but...

My phone rang and it was Greg FaceTiming me. He was on the patio.

'Your mum told us. About uni. I just wanted to say that it's not the end of the world, mate, so don't go making rash decisions.'

'I won't.'

He grinned at me. 'If the worst happens, come down here. I could do with someone doing breakfasts. Save me getting up early.'

I laughed. I wouldn't mind doing that. A bit of cooking and surfing in the afternoon.

'What I'm saying, Dan, is you have options. You have choices. Your mum'll tell you that. And your dad would've said it, too. So, don't be making stupid decisions. Oh, and by the way, those pills you were worried about? The empty packets are in the bin. I reckon she flushed 'em down the loo. D'you want me to have a word with her?'

'No! No, please, don't. Anyway, she's coming back today.'

'Yeah, I know. We'll miss her. She's at home here, Dan. You sort out your university stuff and get your lives on track. It's a time for moving forward and that's what your dad would want.'

I just gave a nod and ended the call. That's easy for him to say.

Chapter Sixty-Seven
KERRY

At the best of times, parting is difficult
At the worst of times, parting is painful.

I didn't tell Suzie and Greg about the altercation with Gian. I'd tell them later, when I got home. Inside my head, I raged. However, I put on a carefree 'everything is fine' show as I embraced the pair of them and loaded my case into the taxi.

'Darling, call me as soon as you get home.'
'I will.'
'And promise you'll be down later in the year,' added Greg.
'I promise,' I said.

My heart had been pounding as I marched away from Gian. Who was he to say those things? He had no right to wade in like that! How dare he? In the taxi to the station, I furiously replayed the scene in my head.

But now, an hour after leaving him stranded on the

clifftop, I stood on the platform at St Ives station and found my anger turning into a different beast altogether.

Shit, shit, shit.

I couldn't believe I'd said those things. How cruel. How hurtful. To criticise his grief, to mock him about not facing his own battles. Could I have sunk any lower? I wanted to rush back with a thousand apologies, to tell him that it was a rush of blood, that I wasn't thinking, but the train was due any minute and I couldn't miss my connection. I thought about calling him when I found a seat but that was too public. An email? Yes. No. I'd write a letter. An old-fashioned letter apologising for being so unkind. Oh, God, that would take an age. I had to telephone. I'd do it when I got home.

Our altercation remained front and centre, and I continued to deconstruct every sentence I'd spoken, every retaliation; all of them were being recast. Why didn't I say it like this? Why didn't I answer like that? Why did I react like a teenager having a tantrum? How childish to hit back with hurtful jibes! God, I wish I was better with confrontation.

Most of his comments had been constructive. Why had I taken them so badly? The Latin temperament hadn't helped. Arms thrown up, head thrown back, exaggerated rolling of the eyes. I wasn't used to that, and it made the whole argument so much more than it was. I'd seen Gian and Rico rage at each other a few days ago and it was over as quickly as it started; all forgotten, and they moved on. Had he already forgotten about this?

Had I seethed at him because there was some truth behind the words? Already I was analysing my relationship with Dan. It was a good one. Who was Gian to tell me that me and Dan didn't talk? *Of course* we talked. All the time.

I further scrutinised the words he had used. Suggesting that Dan and I skirted around the big issues. No, we didn't. How dare he say that! I railed against the whole concept.

But that little voice was worming its way in. Did we talk to each other? Had we had an in-depth, open and honest dialogue about how we both felt?

I closed my eyes. No. If I was totally honest with myself, the answer had to be no. I was the adult in this relationship. I was Dan's mother and focussed on not upsetting him. I didn't want to make him face the things he needed to face. I wanted to shield him. Fuck, I was always complaining about parents who didn't allow their children to make their own decisions and there I was, doing exactly that.

The train pulled into the station and a mass of tourists disembarked. I stood back to allow them all to disperse.

I took a deep breath. I didn't want to go home. I still had two days booked with Suzie and Greg. I wanted to find Gian and clear the air. I hated the thought of leaving on bad terms.

I happened to look down the platform.

Shit!

Gian was making his way through the crowds. He wasn't rushing and I got the impression he was hesitant about my reaction. God, I hope the argument wasn't going to continue. Had he come here to tell me a few more home truths?

Why couldn't the train have come in five minutes earlier? I didn't want to face him. I'd made my mind up to telephone when I got home. I wasn't prepared for another confrontation.

Standing alongside me now, he said my name so softly, I barely heard it.

I didn't give him the chance to continue. 'Gian. I'm so sorry. I didn't mean to say those things. It was unforgiveable.'

He grabbed my forearms and locked eyes with me. They were intense and almost took on a new shade of blue.

'Kerry. I want you to know this. To believe this; to remember this. I love you. Very much. I want you to be here, with me. Will you think about this?'

My jaw dropped. Fuck. That was the last thing I expected.

'I know you have to sort things out. With Dan. With your life. But please believe these things I say to you.'

The whistle blew. We embraced. I was so grateful that he'd forgiven my outburst and overwhelmed that he felt this way about me. About us.

'I will think about it. I promise.'

He placed my bag on the train, then cupped my face and gave me a long, lingering kiss. Fuck, it was good.

The timing couldn't have been worse but the only way I was going to think straight was to be as far away from Gian as possible.

Seeing him every day was not conducive to resolving matters at home. He'd be a distraction and that would result in me putting Dan second, something I vowed I'd never do.

The whistle blew and, on the train, I stood by the door. We were both close to tears. Shit, I'd arrived here holding the tears back, now I was leaving doing the exact same thing.

Why was life so fucking complicated?

I remained by the door as the train departed and I stayed there until I couldn't see him anymore.

ACT THREE

SUSSEX, SOUTH-EAST ENGLAND
ITALY, EUROPE
MAY–OCTOBER 2021

Chapter Sixty-Eight
KERRY

The art of conversation can be difficult
We sometimes lack the skill of discussion
There is no fault
Like the tuning of an old wireless, the wavelength isn't right.

I arrived home at just gone five in the evening to find Dan had prepared a lovely dinner: crab linguine with Prosecco and a sprinkling of Parmesan. He normally did this on special occasions, and I think this was his way of compensating for the fact that he'd asked me to come home early.

We decided, when I arrived, that we'd catch up on each other's news first before tackling the serious issue. I described in more detail what I'd done in Cornwall: the galleries, the workshops, the Minack, the abseiling. Everything. I slipped brief mentions of Gian into my account but no more than necessary. I didn't want to spoil what was a lovely dinner and a good atmosphere.

Dan updated me on his trips out with Chloe, a book he

was reading, hanging out with friends and spending some time with Tom and Maggie.

'And I hate to admit it, Mum, but I enjoyed *An Affair to Remember*.'

'Ha! I knew you would. You may have your dad's devil-may-care, adventurous spirit but I thought you must have inherited something from me and now I know what. Liking old films.'

A sheepish grin. 'We're going to see *The Umbrellas of Cherbourg* next week.'

'Ha!' I repeated in triumph. 'A foreign film. Oh my God, I don't believe it!' I gave him a warning. 'Be prepared to cringe at that one. You might get fed up with the singing.'

'Someone else said that. It was Chloe's choice so I can blame her. I've put in my request for the next one.'

'Which is?'

'*Rear Window*.'

'Hitchcock. Oh, Dan, that's a good choice.'

'Come along with us.'

We talked for some time because I think, subconsciously, we were putting off the inevitable. I knew Dan wouldn't bring it up, so it was up to me to make the first move.

'Right, come on. What's going on? Talk to me.'

I think I surprised him with my tone. I surprised myself. I'm not normally abrupt, however, we needed to sort this out. We needed to move on.

'Hang on,' I added, 'before we go into this, you do know that you can reapply, don't you? Have you spoken to them?'

I noticed a shift in Dan's body language. Where he'd been open with me over dinner, he had now closed down a little. The reaction to my question was a simple shrug.

'There are other universities.'

He swirled the wine in his glass and made little attempt to engage. I waited an age and the frustration in me began to build. I forced it down.

'Why don't you take a break and apply next year? I know you've already delayed things but, there's no rush to—'

'I've applied to Brighton,' he interrupted. 'I'm staying local. All my friends are here; there's a good social scene.'

'Brighton! Do they even do engineering? Have you spoken to Ocean Marine?'

When he didn't react, my frustration turned to anger and, again, I suppressed it. I wanted to knock his head against a brick wall, to yell and scream, *What the hell are you playing at? This is your future we're talking about.*

I didn't, of course. That would only have made things worse.

'For God's sake, Dan, at least speak with them. You're acting like you've given up. People have their first application refused all the time. It doesn't mean you won't get in later or into an equally good uni. I'm not saying Brighton is bad but it's not on a par with Southampton. Not for what you're doing. What about Imperial College? It's in London, that's no distance from here.'

He just sat there chewing his lip and staring at the table. I tried softening my approach.

'Sweetheart, Gian said something—'

If looks could kill, I'd be dead.

'What the fuck's he got to do with it?'

'Nothing, and that's not the issue.' I said, watching him collect the plates and take them to the sink. 'The issue is that he said the same as your dad would have said. Sleep on it.

Don't make a rash decision; you'll think more clearly after a few days.'

'Yeah, well, he's not my dad.'

Before I had a chance to respond, he stomped out and took the stairs two at a time. Determined to get the last word, I followed him and shouted, 'Greg said exactly the same. Suzie too.'

I closed my eyes and leant against the wall. Christ, why did I do that? Why did I want the last word? I felt like a five-year-old trying to get one up on a peer. My dad's better than your dad. My bike's better than yours. What was the matter with me?

I returned to the kitchen and snatched up my phone. I needed moral support.

The following morning, I ensconced myself in Maggie's and Tom's kitchen, cradling a mug of coffee.

'You really do have feelings for him,' said Maggie, more as a statement than a question.

Typical of Maggie; I'd gone over the issues about Gian and the problem with Dan and his choice of university. The latter, for me, was the important issue but, of course, Maggie had latched on to the former.

She continued, 'This isn't because it's Luca Belfiore?'

'Maggie, I'm not a teenager. I'm not at school lusting after Donny Osmond or Rod Stewart. And, anyway, that's not important. None of that's important. Dan has to be settled. I made that promise to him.' I sat back. 'The problem is I wasn't expecting him to stay here.'

Tom brought his chair closer. 'Is Dan adamant about Brighton?'

'Yes, and it's the wrong choice, Tom. He's not taking second best; he's taking fourth or fifth.'

'It's not a bad university, Kerry.'

'But there are others that specialise in marine engineering.' I felt myself bristle with frustration. 'You know, if he stays here, all of my plans for St Ives are finished. I can't leave him here.' I pulled myself up. 'Shit, that sounds bloody selfish, doesn't it?'

'No, it doesn't.' Maggie said, topping up my coffee. 'You've every right to worry about your own future. When did he hear?'

'Over the weekend.'

'Leave it,' she said in a very matter-of-fact way.

'Leave it?'

'Maggie's right,' said Tom. 'It's too soon. This is hasty, impulsive. He's not thought it through, and he has time to do that. Don't push it. Let him stew on it a little. A few days makes all the difference.'

Maggie suggested to Tom that he take Dan aside, but Tom dismissed it.

'When I was that age, the last thing I wanted was a pep talk from a parent or suchlike. I made mistakes at that age and most of them I worked out for myself. That's part of growing up. I'll happily take him for a pint, but it'll be up to him to bring the subject up. If I do it, he'll think you've engineered it, Kerry.'

He was right, of course. Perhaps time would smooth things over. Knee-jerk decisions were not the best and, if I didn't badger him for a few days, Dan might well work it all out. I wondered if Chloe had shared her views with him.

It would be nice to speak to her but that was inconceivable. What on earth would Dan think if he discovered I'd brought my worries to her? I mentally threw that thought into a blazing inferno.

'Okay,' I said. 'I'll leave it a few days and see what happens. Like you say, we've got time. At least he doesn't want to delay things. He wants to get on with life and that's a good sign. That, at least, tells me he's moving forward.'

Maggie hugged me. 'If there's anything you think we can do to help, just pick up the phone.'

'And if we think of something,' said Tom, 'we'll be sure to let you know.'

I was no further forward, except that I'd shared the problem, and it was true what they said. A problem shared and all that. It didn't feel quite such a burden.

Chapter Sixty-Nine
GIAN

The warmth of the summer sun feels nice against my face and the tourists begin to flock to the town. I am not so keen when they do this. I prefer it out of season, when it is quieter.

Rico's is very busy at the moment, but I like that Tina insist on the tables for the locals because I always have someone to talk with, although I do not have the desire to talk today.

After Kerry leave, I become a little depressed, you know. Nothing is the same without her and I miss her when I have coffee. I think the dogs miss her too. Today, they sniff around the chair opposite me as if searching for her.

I am glad I go to the station to say goodbye. I did not want to end on an argument. And I need to tell her my feelings and that I know she do not mean the words she say. But I am not so sure that it will make a difference.

I just know that something disappear from my life. Like it did when Lucia left. When Carlotta left. Something leave and it is difficult to replace it or fill the hole that open up.

I stand for a while and watch my friends play football on the beach. One of them, Joe, he wave to me.

'You coming down for a game?'

'Not today, Joe.' I don't tell him why.

Rico, he come to stand next to me. 'Papà. Why don't you go down? It's not good to be moping about.'

I don't answer.

'Papà?'

I turn to him. 'Rico, I am fine. Really. Don't worry about me.'

But I know he worry. Tina, too. I see it in their faces.

Chapter Seventy
KERRY

Water can save my life, quench my thirst
But it can also build a river so wide, it's impossible to cross
Then where will I be?

Things didn't get back to how they were after the altercation Dan and I'd had the day I got home. Two weeks passed. Something had wedged itself between us and wasn't shifting. Oh, we were being civil to each other and occasionally having a laugh, but it felt forced, as if we were having to make an effort. Dan had slipped a little into teenage disinterest and I was squashing feelings of frustration and rage.

I groaned to myself. This is what Gian had observed about us. That we spoke to each other, but we never really talked.

This particular morning, I was putting the finishing touches to a pie. Dan came in and came straight over to see what I was doing.

'What're you making?'

'Chicken and leek pie.'

'Nice.'

It was one of his favourite dishes and his response was upbeat, positive. Perhaps the ice was thawing today.

The doorbell rang.

'Would you put it in the oven for me?'

'Sure.'

I was only gone a couple of minutes. The postman had delivered a parcel for next door. I placed it on the stairs and returned to the kitchen.

'Post for next door. Are you okay with corn on the cob, with the pie?'

The thawing ice had refrozen. Why, I didn't know.

'Me and Chloe are heading into town. I'll be back for dinner.'

When the door closed, I plonked myself down at the table in a sort of helpless heap. I had to figure out a way to reach him. What I was doing wasn't working. Leaving it a few days hadn't made any difference to his decision.

How long should I leave it until I intervened?

It wasn't just that he'd given up on his education, his career. It was if he'd given up on everything else as well.

Chapter Seventy-One
DAN

Shit. I wanted to punch the wall so fucking hard I wouldn't care if I broke every finger doing it.

I knew Mum was upset with me and it was all my fault. All of it. I was being such a fucking moody idiot. I didn't want to be like that, but I couldn't help it.

That morning, I'd given myself a lecture on everything I was doing wrong. I told myself to grow up and stop acting like a fucking prick. I was okay when I got to the kitchen. Mum was making a chicken and leek pie. I love chicken and leek pie and she made great pies.

She hadn't mentioned the university stuff and that bothered me. That wasn't like her. I thought she'd keep going on about it, but it was as if she'd accepted it. She was disappointed, though, and she had every right to be. I was letting her down.

It wasn't her fault. She was just trying to help but I didn't want her help. I didn't want her to… shit, it didn't matter. Southampton was history. Brighton was my choice.

I didn't want to go there but it was local and that was the main thing.

When Mum went to the front door, I saw a photo processing envelope. She'd had some photos developed from her phone. I flicked through them. They were of the anniversary night and Suzie and Greg were glammed up. Mum, too. She was wearing that summer dress she liked. She didn't look her age at all. They were nice photos and probably going up on the cork board.

Then I saw one of her with Gian. He was wearing a tuxedo and had his arm around Mum's waist. I honestly wanted to tear it into the smallest pieces and set fire to it.

I heard the door close, and I dropped the photos back on the surface. When Mum came in, I told her I was going into town with Chloe. I wasn't. I wasn't doing anything. I didn't have any plans. I just wanted to get out and think things over.

Fuck, I wish Dad was here. None of this would be happening if he was here.

Chapter Seventy-Two
KERRY

When the boats moored by the river are derelict
The journey cannot be completed
Is there a bridge somewhere to deliver me
To where I need to be? I don't see one.

The pie was a success. Dan complimented me on it and praised my culinary skills. When he'd arrived home from meeting Chloe, he seemed more himself. I suspected it was an effort, but I went along with it. It was better than being at loggerheads.

That was all well and good, but this meant I was forcing it, too. We were back to skirting around the issue. If I tried to engage with him about university and making a different choice, he'd tell me he didn't want to discuss it; that he'd made his mind up and that was that. Maggie and Tom, although wonderful, loving and caring friends, were struggling to make meaningful suggestions. They'd never had children so probably weren't the best people to confide in.

When I got into bed that night, I gripped Adam's photo. 'Honestly, Adam, what the fuck! If your soul does go on to some other plane and you're listening to me, please put some sense into his head. It's like he's given up and I honestly don't know how to get through to him.'

How *could* I get through to him? I had many ideas, from ranting and nagging to begging on my knees. I had no appetite for any of them.

I decided to bring up an old film on my laptop. *The Philadelphia Story* with Cary Grant and Katharine Hepburn. Fun and light: that's what I needed at the moment. Something to escape into.

Chapter Seventy-Three
GIAN

It is several weeks now since Kerry leave and I do not hear from her. I am upset about this. I know she want to help her son, but I hope she do not travel the wrong road. I went to call her a few days ago but I only go as far as the third number, and I stop. My heart was in my mouth. Excitement to call her but also worry that it will anger her.

Fortunately, I receive some consultancy work. An Italian couple who wish to buy a home in this country. I help them with the legal side of things to ensure they understand. At my desk, as I finish paperwork, I hear someone open the front door. It is Rico.

He call out, 'Papà.'

The dogs run to greet him.

'In here,' I reply.

He come into my office with a newspaper and a croissant. 'I thought you were coming to the bar.'

I check my watch. I didn't realise I spend so long a time here. 'I'm so sorry.' I lead him through the lounge to the kitchen. 'You want to have coffee with me here?'

'I would but I have a dentist appointment.'

'*Va bene.*' I begin to make coffee for myself and my son, he does not move.

'Papà.'

'Mm?'

'Papà. Kerry. Why don't you call her?'

'No.'

'Why not?'

'She knows how I feel.'

'But it's been weeks now.'

I give a shrug, like it is of no concern.

'She made you the happiest I have seen you since Mamma.'

He's a good boy and he understand me. And he is right, you know, about Kerry. But I don't want to talk about it, so I give him another shrug. Then I think he does not deserve this, so I turn to him.

'Rico, I'm fine. Stop worrying about me. I'm grown up, I can deal with this.'

I see that Rico is not so happy, but he cannot do anything. He kisses me on both cheeks. 'I love you, Papà.'

'I love you, too.'

When Rico leave, I take my coffee and paper through to the lounge and switch the radio on. The dogs, they follow me and watch as I look at the photo of me with Carlotta. The presenter, he introduce the next song, 'She' by Charles Aznavour.

I tell you, that song seep into me like salt into an open wound. I was there, with Carlotta, in that photograph. I remember it like it was yesterday. We play in a small garden that overlook the sea. She was always laughing, always, and she run around to play hide and seek. I scoop her into my arms and tickle her and she giggle so much. Lucia, she bring out homemade lemonade and see us and take this picture.

I bring myself back to this room, but I focus, then, on the photograph beside it, with Lucia.

It is the photo that I find in the memory box. Of me and Lucia arriving at La Scala. Lucia, she is so beautiful, and I was so proud to have her on my arm that night. I love her so much and I miss her more than my words can describe.

We enjoy that opera very much and, after the performance, we go to an expensive restaurant with friends. I arrange a surprise for her, for her birthday. The restaurant, they prepare a dessert, and it has a small firework in it. They dim the light and everyone in the restaurant, they sing happy birthday to her. This was, I think, a happy day for her.

I sit down on the sofa, and I know that I am not far from tears. The dogs, they jump on the sofa, and they come close to me. They sense my mood and they try to console me. I take them in my arms, rest my head back and close my eyes and relive a scene that repeat itself in my head many times; in the hospital, reading to my Lucia and not knowing that she had left me. When the nurse touch my arm, then I realise…

The tears roll down my cheek and I sit up to wipe them away. Tosca and Figaro they climb up and try to lick those tears. On my finger, I rotate the ring that Kerry give me.

I think of my time with Kerry. That first meeting at Rico's, the sculpture park, our visit to Marazion, the party at The Feather Duck. I have many wonderful memories of her in so short a space of time and I wonder, you know, will I see her again?

The song, it ends on the radio and I bring the dogs close to me.

Chapter Seventy-Four
KERRY

My son, my pride and joy, my one reason now for living
What path have you taken?
Is there a map, a signpost, something to let me know
where you are?

I stood for some time in the kitchen gazing at a photo of Adam and me on the wall. An older photo, taken when Dan was five years old, when we were standing on the promenade on Brighton seafront.

Dan was making tea. I wonder how often he stood here studying these images.

He joined me, handing me my mug.

These last few days, we had tolerated each other more than anything else. I'd thought grieving for Adam was bad enough, but this was upsetting me just as much.

Yesterday, I'd suggested we sit down and have an in-depth discussion about his future. Predictably, he'd said he didn't want to talk about it.

'But we need to talk about it,' I said.

'No, we don't, Mum. We don't need to talk about this.

I've made my mind up. I'm going to Brighton. Why're you making such a big deal out of it? It'll be cheaper anyway.'

'Money is not the issue. We can afford it.'

'Just leave it. Stop going on about it. I'm happy with the decision. Why can't you be?'

We went around in circles for some time, and we never jumped off the carousel. How could he be happy with that decision? Perhaps I should have stayed in Cornwall for my last two days and come home when I was supposed to. Because my coming back early hadn't changed a thing.

Dan grabbed his keys. 'I'm popping over to see Chloe. I'll be back in about an hour.'

At least he was okay about normal things. I mean, a lot of teenagers just went without a by-your-leave. Dan was still okay with day-to-day stuff. Just exceptionally touchy about his future.

The door closed and the house was silent. My phone pinged. Suzie. I sat down with my tea and read the text, 'Hope you're okay. Thought you'd like this. I forgot to send it to you at the time.'

I opened the attachment. How wonderful. A picture of me and Gian on the anniversary night. We were goofing about on the patio. Gian had that dreamy grin on his face after his first spliff. What a lovely time we all had.

I recalled the mock argument over me buying that ring and let out a little chuckle. The chuckle, however, was half-hearted. That underlying sadness that I had squashed almost to non-existence was making a guest appearance. How I longed to be in St Ives. Now. I wanted to have a coffee with Gian on the terrace at Rico's. I wanted that easy relaxed lifestyle that I'd got used to down there.

Shit.

The tough months were supposed to be behind me. How long was I going to keep feeling like this? How much more was going to be thrown at me? Why didn't Dan get that place? If he had, we'd be making plans and getting ready for the next stage of our lives. Because this wasn't just Dan's life that had been upended, it was mine, too.

I returned to the photo, wondering what Gian was doing at that moment.

Chapter Seventy-Five
GIAN

In the reception of The Feather Duck, I go through the schedule that Greg have for his tour; his tour with the senior rugby team in Italy.

Because I have decided that I go with him. I think it will be good for me to have this break and I can visit my brother in Rome and see my nephew and niece and their families.

Suzie help me with my jacket as I confirm things with Greg.

'So, I will be able to watch your first two games in Milan and one game in Bologna. Then I go to Rome, and you go to Napoli.'

'That's brilliant, mate. I'm right glad you're coming, and you can help me with the lingo. I'll come to yours tomorrow and bring the flight details. Hopefully, you can get a seat on the same plane.'

'*Molto bene. Ciao.*'

'*Ciao.*'

When I go outside, I look towards the balcony where Kerry had her room. I do that many times when I pass by.

Tonight, I whisper to that balcony. '*Buona notte*, Kerry Simmonds.'

Chapter Seventy-Six
KERRY

Friends do what they think is best for you
Sometimes, their best is just a pile of poo.

I was sitting in a café in Littlehampton. There wasn't much to the town and during the summer it relied heavily on its long, wide sandy beaches to help the economy. Families loved it because of the small fairground on the seafront and because it was a safe place to bathe. To swim in the sea at Littlehampton, you had to walk ten minutes for the water even to get up as far as your knees.

The café was on the promenade and offered a good view of people, so I entertained myself with the 'security' game. Adam was still very much alive in my head and, occasionally, I would whisper 'security' if I spotted someone I thought would have amused him.

My phone pinged. It was Jenny, who ran The Java Jive café. She was the one I was waiting to meet.

'Can't make coffee but I've sent someone in my place. His name's Eddie.'

Jesus Christ! Her matchmaking strategy was as far removed from subtle as humanly possible.

What was it about people thinking they could run my love life for me? How dare she? How bloody dare she? I twisted in my chair. Was she watching from a far-off table? I couldn't see her.

I turned back to see a man about my age standing there. He was slim, wearing jeans, a leather jacket, a flat cap and lost expression.

'Hello. Are you Kerry?'

Shit. I couldn't just walk away, could I?

'Yes,' I said. 'I'm supposed to be meeting a friend.'

To be fair to him, he pulled a face as if he knew what had happened.

'Yes, I know. Jenny. She sent me in her place, and I feel a bit awkward.' He sat down opposite me. 'I thought it was a bit weird when she asked me to come in her place. Who does that?' He winced. 'She's set us up on a date, hasn't she?'

I had no need to answer. The tilt of my head probably spoke volumes.

'Oh, God, I'm sorry.'

I half-chuckled. 'It's okay, it's not your fault. For some reason, people think I can't exist without a man.'

'The same with me. Except a woman, not a man. I mean, I'm not against… it's just that—'

'No need to explain. Let me hazard a guess. You've lost someone, split up with someone, you're divorced, separated, lonely or you're one or all of the above and your friends want you to be happy and don't think you can be until they help replace what you've lost.'

He brightened. 'Yes.' He gestured at my cup. 'D'you want another? I promise I won't hit on you. I'm Eddie, by the way.'

Eddie, it turned out, was relaxed and easy to talk to. He'd gone through a messy divorce three years ago and had tried a couple of dating apps with no success.

'Have you tried dating sites?' he asked.

'Yes,' I responded. 'I quickly discovered that I can't make a decision based on a photograph and a few hastily written likes and dislikes. And, anyway, I haven't been ready for a new relationship.'

'Me neither.'

'Do you have children?'

'Yes. A daughter, she's nineteen.'

Ah, serendipity. My immediate thought was to run a scenario by him where he had to imagine that his daughter had given up on her education choices. Perhaps he would have an answer for me.

'She's not talking to me at the moment. She blames me for the divorce. Well, it was my fault. I had an affair.'

The best laid plans! Doris Day singing 'Que Sera Sera' drifted into my head.

Unfortunately, following that announcement about his daughter, this quickly turned into an agony-aunt session with me being the aunt. I gave him twenty minutes of my time and empathised with his situation but I couldn't bear it any longer. I made my excuses and left.

I wasn't ready for that. For having to get to know someone from scratch all over again.

Heading to my car, I dissected my last thought. I'd got to know Gian from scratch. I guess it all depended on chemistry.

You either clicked or you didn't. And Gian and I had clicked. Eddie and I did not.

My hopes of moving to St Ives and a possible relationship, however, were becoming a distant memory. I'd not heard from Gian. It had been two months since our parting at St Ives.

I put all thoughts of contacting him aside.

I'd left it too long.

I got in the driver's seat and stared through the windscreen at nothing in particular. Tears blurred my vision. Would I ever find someone like Gian again? Men like that are so few and far between.

Later that day, I changed the bedding in our bedrooms.

In Dan's room, I stripped away the bedsheet and duvet and threw them in the corner with some other washing. The disturbance of air caused papers to fall on the floor. I quickly gathered them up and put them back on his desk. To the side of those papers, I glimpsed the letter from Southampton University.

It was half-open.

I read it.

Chapter Seventy-Seven
KERRY

The biggest barriers can form from the smallest of things
The mountain from the molehill,
And it can be the smallest of things that topples the mountain
And then you can begin, you can start again.

From the kitchen, I fixed my attention on the garden. If I'd had lasers for eyes everything in that space would have been annihilated. My lips were clenched, my jaw tight, my body tense. Anyone would think I was waiting to go ten rounds with Mohammed Ali. Every fibre of my being was itching to trash the house just to release my fury.

What was he thinking of? What could he possibly gain from this? How could he be so deceitful?

The ticking clock distorted time. Waiting, waiting, waiting. In my head, the tick-tock increased in volume. The louder it became, the slower the time passed.

Eventually, I heard the front door open and close. My heart thumped. I took a breath. Be calm. Don't overreact. Don't do anything to make him clam up or, worse still, storm out.

He entered the kitchen. 'Hey.'

I swung around and glowered. I didn't have the words. All I had was seething anger. He frowned at me. To clarify my mood, I jutted my chin at the letter on the table.

The letter that revealed the university's delight at being able to offer him a place.

Dan shifted his gaze to it and paled. He didn't step back physically but he certainly did in his head. This, he wasn't expecting. This, he couldn't get out of. This, he had to explain.

The silence continued, for seconds, for a minute. The clock ticked. Tick-tock, the pair of us facing off against each other. I wasn't going to break it. I wasn't the one deceiving his mother. I wasn't the one stopping us from moving on with our lives. If he made any attempt to get out of this, I'd lock the door until we'd cleared the air. We were not skirting around this any longer.

Tick-tock. The wheels almost visibly whirred in his head as he formulated a response. What could he say? Sorry wouldn't be enough. I needed more than that. I wanted explanations.

His mortified expression eventually turned to resignation. His shoulders fell and his eyes filled with tears.

'I didn't want to leave you on your own.'

Fuck.

Shit.

I wasn't expecting that.

An invisible broom swept away my anger.

His face flushed as he wiped a tear away. 'You're missing Dad. I—'

I rushed to him, all thoughts of admonishment forgotten.

'Oh, Dan, of course I miss him. Every day. That doesn't mean putting your life on hold.'

'I'm not leaving you to cope on your own.'

'You don't think I'm coping?'

He met my gaze. 'I see you crying, Mum. I see you when you're looking at photos. When you hear a song or see something. I see how sad you get. I don't want to leave you like that.'

Oh my God, my poor boy.

Fuck, this was a conversation we should have had the moment Adam died. A discussion about the grief: the despair, the heartbreak, the sadness, the emptiness, the colossal loneliness that can strike you down when you least expect it.

We'd avoided all of that for fear of upsetting each other.

I stroked his cheek. 'Sweetheart, that will always happen. Even when I'm an old woman, there'll be something that'll remind me that your dad's not here. That's part of grief. You can't just turn it off like a tap. Yes, I get upset but that'll happen whether you're here or not.'

He swallowed and his eyes darted everywhere. Up, down, side to side, anywhere but at me. There was more to this. We'd scratched the surface. He stared at the floor, hesitating.

'Dan, tell me. What is it?'

I didn't push it. He had to do this in his own time. I hoped to God our phones wouldn't ring or someone knock on the door. He was so close to opening up.

He met my gaze. 'I saw the pills.'

'What?' What was he talking about? 'Pills?'

Realisation dawned. I gasped at the conclusion he'd drawn from that.

'Oh my God, Dan. You th… Dan. Fuck, Dan, I would never do that. Never in a million years would I have done that to you. No matter how low I felt, I'd never have left you to deal with that on top of everything else.'

He tried to turn his head, but I forced him look me in the eye. I needed him to see I was being honest.

'I flushed them down the loo. You know I hate taking pills and they kept coming on repeat prescription and I never got around to cancelling it. Fuck. Oh, my darling. I'm so sorry. Why didn't you tell me?'

He shrugged. This was like peeling off layers of wallpaper that had been hanging for decades. I thought I'd reached the end, but I hadn't. There was something else and I was being extremely dense about it. I liked to think I was switched on, savvy, but I couldn't figure out what he was holding back.

'Dan, please. Talk to me. Please don't hold it in.'

I could almost see the conflict eating him up.

Tick-tock.

Oddly, the film *Zulu* came to mind. The British soldiers, outnumbered a hundred to one, waiting for the onslaught from the tribe surrounding them on the hills. The drums beating in the background. Waiting.

Tick-tock.

There were a few photos on the table. I hadn't got around to framing them. There was one in particular he had his hand on, aimlessly sliding it back and forth, back and forth.

The insight I sought arrived.

Booking the boat ride, the stash of pills, the potential dates with Colin and Lee. My friendship with Gian.

I held his hands. 'You think you're going to lose me. You think I'm going to abandon you in some way.'

The wall of emotion he'd been fighting to hold up collapsed. Tears streamed down his face and onto his shirt.

'Oh, sweetheart, sometimes I forget how young you are.' I pulled him close.

'Your dad will always be a part of my life. Our life. And you, Dan Simmonds, will always be a part of my life. Always. It doesn't matter where we are geographically, we will be there for each other. Always.'

'I miss him, Mum.'

Now my tears began. 'So do I, love.'

We held each other for an eternity as if letting go would break a spell, undo the bond that had reconnected. When I felt the time was right, I pulled back from him.

'You know, he was so proud about you going to university. No one in our family's been to uni.'

'Dad went, didn't he?'

'Polytechnic. Not quite the same thing.'

He chuckled between the occasional half-sob.

'Darling, if we stay here, like this, we'll end up stagnating and hating each other, resenting each other. Look at where we've been these last couple of months. You can't tell me that things have been normal. Get out there and live your life. That's what your dad would want. That's what I want. I don't want you fussing around me. I'm sixty-five, not ninety. I still have a life to live and none of this means that I miss or love your dad any the less.

'And you are not going to lose me. This is just a big, big hurdle for us to jump, but we have to jump it. Together. Even if it scares the shit out of you.'

Dan joined in on the last part of his dad's mantra and laughed. He wiped his tears away.

'I'm sorry. For being an idiot.'

'You're not an idiot, Dan. You're a kind, caring and

considerate young man and I love you for that. This grief, it's a part of us now but we must grow around it.'

He stepped forward and hugged me.

This was his hug, and I didn't step back from it. I left that to him. Finally, he did release me and he asked a question I had never expected to hear from him.

'Tell me about Gian.'

Chapter Seventy-Eight
KERRY

As I'm getting older, the best thing by a mile
Was having had you in my life. You made it all worthwhile
And the road I'm travelling on is all the better now,
because of you.

I sat in bed with a mug of hot milk and updated Adam about what had happened between me and Dan and how everything had come spilling out of him once he allowed himself to open up.

'He knocked me for six when he told me why he'd done it. I knew he was protective but to be willing to change his plans, I mean, well, I couldn't be angry with him. I could have kicked myself for not recognising it.'

I hadn't realised how much Dan's attitude had affected me until we'd cleared the air. The heaviness had lifted. I had my son back. I had the optimistic, laidback, beautiful Dan that I thought I'd lost.

The first thing he did, without any prompting from me, was telephone Southampton University. If I'd have had any more tears left, I would have cried. Instead, I opened a bottle of Prosecco and poured a glass for each of us. I think we both got a little tipsy and we spent the next couple of hours rummaging through the memory box and reminiscing about Adam. Chloe came over too. She guessed that something had happened that day and I'm sure Dan would tell her in time.

'So,' I said to Adam, 'that's where we are, my darling. Your son is off to Southampton and I'm… well, you know what I'm going to do, and I know you're okay with it.' I puffed my pillows up. 'I wrote a poem earlier and it flowed out of me without any thought. After I'd written it, I realised it was from your point of view. That's bizarre, isn't it?'

I picked up my notebook.

You now have your life to live,
This is now your time, love,
One day you will join me,
And I'll be waiting here, love.

I kissed the photo. 'Thank you, my darling. I will always love you and you'll always be my number one.'

Chapter Seventy-Nine
DAN

I couldn't believe it. University. Southampton University. Marine engineering. Fucking brilliant.

I stood on the concourse of Brighton railway station with a rucksack and a suitcase. Mum, Maggie and Tom had come to see me off.

I didn't know what the fuck I'd been thinking when I'd lied to Mum. It was like I'd shut the door on reality and disappeared into an alternative universe. I was convinced I was doing the right thing, that it would make things better for Mum but all I was doing was making everything worse and stopping her from doing stuff. Honestly, what a fucking idiot.

Even spending time with Chloe had changed a bit because I'd put myself in a hole and just kept digging.

We argued about it a couple of times. She was right. I was being a complete tosser. We didn't split up or anything. I liked her, and I wanted to keep seeing her. It would have been difficult with her going to Scotland, but she'd changed her mind. It wasn't St Andrews now. It was Exeter. That wasn't far away at all so we could still see each other. She'd travelled down to her digs a couple of days ago.

And Gian must have thought I was a selfish prick after meeting me. I had such an awful attitude towards him. I hoped, when I went down during the holidays, he wasn't going to say anything. I got the impression he wasn't that sort of bloke, but I wouldn't blame him if he did.

I hoisted my rucksack onto my back. Mum had paid for a first-class seat which was awesome and now this was the bit I was dreading. Goodbye. The house was on the market which I found odd. I'd grown up in that house, but Mum and I had discussed it.

'The memories are in your head', Mum had said. The materialistic stuff that you want to keep, keep. Bricks and mortar were just bricks and mortar. But Dad had built that house. It was built for us. We talked about renting it out but that would have been worse, going back there every now and again and seeing other people living there.

She said there were things we had to let go and this was one of them. A clean break. Dad would be with us no matter where we were. He didn't live in this house, he lived in our hearts.

Before I went through the ticket barrier, Maggie and Tom held me as if I was never going to see them again.

'We're so proud of you,' Maggie said. 'You call and let us know how you're getting on.'

I promised I would. Tom shook my hand.

'Enjoy university, embrace the whole thing but, above all, make your dad proud.'

'I will, Tom. Thanks.'

Mum fussed over me like she always did.

'Call me when you get there. Let me know you've arrived safe and that you're okay.'

'I will.'

I quickly hugged her.

'Thanks for everything, Mum. I love you loads. And I'm okay with Gian.' I turned once I'd gone through the barrier. 'Really, I am. He's a nice bloke, not like that dick, Colin.'

We laughed at that. We hadn't seen him for months but his interest in Mum was still a source of fun for us.

I waved and headed off to my platform and the train taking me into my future.

Chapter Eighty
KERRY

Love.
Love is a funny thing.
Heightens your emotions and it gives you everything.
You don't need a book to tell you what love can bring.

The house sold almost immediately. It didn't surprise me. Adam was a fantastic builder, and this was a well-thought-out property. The rooms were all a good size, we had a utility room, a downstairs cloakroom and shower. The garden was landscaped and there was a double garage. And we weren't too far from the shops and schools.

Because of all those things, I could expect to get the asking price and I did. That had given me plenty of scope for purchasing a decent property in St Ives.

I was on FaceTime with Suzie, describing what I was planning. While we were talking, she moved from reception to the patio. The lanterns flickered behind her, and she switched on the little heater as she made herself comfortable. The lights of St Ives twinkled in the background. Greg was on his way to Italy for his rugby tour. I was ready to meet Maggie and Tom for a meal.

'I'll probably rent somewhere for a few weeks to give myself time to get the right property. I don't want to rush into anything.'

'Darling, you're staying here while you do that. No arguments.'

'But your guests?'

'I still have three rooms. I'll take your room off the schedule until you find somewhere. Stay for the winter.'

I could have hugged her. Well, that was one thing I didn't have to worry about.

'Are you drinking wine?' I asked when I noticed the glass in her hand.

'Yes.' She held it up. 'Pinot.'

I held mine up. 'Me too. Cheers.'

'Cheers. Darling, I'm so pleased that everything's worked out. Sounds like Dan got himself in a state. Especially about Gian.' She moved closer to the screen. 'I have to tell you, Kerry, that man is missing you. He's not been the same since you went.'

'Oh, Suzie, I think that bird's flown. We haven't spoken since I came back.'

'The bird hasn't flown.'

I sat up.

'He talks to Greg more than me and I can tell you he's wanted to call you a few times but was wary about doing so.'

'Why? Oh, that's a stupid question, isn't it?'

'He didn't want to interfere.'

'Well, now I've made my mind up about moving, I'll give him a call and reconnect.'

'Oh, darling, he's not here.'

'Not… what?'

'He's on his way to Milan. With Greg. For the rugby. I think he's staying a couple of months.'

'A couple of months!'

'He's going to see his brother in Rome – and you have yourself to blame for this – he's going to Santa Margherita.'

'What? Really?' I was delighted, of course, but devastated that he wouldn't be in St Ives.

'D'you want me to find out when he'll be back?'

Inspiration dropped into my head.

'No,' I replied with a sense of determination. 'I want you to find out when, exactly, he's due to arrive in Santa Margherita.'

Suzie resembled the scheming cat that pinched the cream. 'On it.'

When I finished the call, I pulled out an atlas. I never used digital maps. There was something of the explorer in me when I opened an atlas. I still didn't have a satnav in the car, preferring, instead, to use a map.

I found the north-west of Italy and traced my finger down the coastline. Where the hell was Santa Margherita?

I finally found it. The nearest airport would be Milan or Genoa and I could get the train across. Easy-peasy.

My heart skipped. I hoped this would work out. What if he went to Santa Margherita and decided he wanted to move back? What if he met a woman in Milan? And fell in love with her?

Oh, for God's sake, Kerry, stop putting obstacles in the way! Stop trying to pre-empt what might or might not happen.

An hour later, I was sipping wine with Maggie and Tom and enjoying a lobster thermidor. Delicious. And the evening was a long one.

We would see each other a few times before I moved but this was the farewell meal; Maggie and Tom's treat, and we'd talked the whole evening. We'd reminisced the whole evening. How we'd met, the memories we had, the excursions we'd been on and the countless evenings out we'd enjoyed over the years.

'How many films do you think we've seen in that arts cinema?' I asked.

'Hundreds,' Maggie said. 'We go at least twice a month and we've been going for twenty, twenty-five years.'

'You'll miss that in St Ives,' said Tom.

'Yes, I will, but my most cherished films are all on DVD or I can stream them from some platform or another. I'll not be starved of nostalgia. I may even start up a classic film club in St Ives.'

Maggie took my hand. 'And there you are, a character in your own screenplay. Who'd have thought that when we came out of that cinema a couple of years ago, you would meet Luca Belfiore.'

'And strike up a friendship with him,' said Tom.

'A relationship,' Maggie corrected him.

'It's early days, Maggie,' I said. 'I'm not losing myself in fantasy until I see him. He may decide otherwise and that'll be disappointing, but I have to accept that he may have moved on.'

'That's not what Suzie seems to think.'

'Suzie's as bad as you. I want it to happen, of course I do, but this is real life. Not everything works out the way we want it to.'

My statements were sensible, practical and commendable. What I wanted to do, however, was sing from the rooftops. To stand up, throw my arms up, like Mitzi Gaynor did on the beach in *South Pacific*, and declare that I was in love with a wonderful man.

'You do it in your own way, Kerry,' said Tom, 'and don't let anyone tell you otherwise. When you are settled, we'd like to be your first visitors – after Dan, that is.'

'I'd love that. We mustn't be strangers.'

'That won't happen. Maggie's already insisting we buy a holiday home down there.'

'Oh my God, that'd be brilliant.'

We continued reminiscing until close to midnight. We toasted Dan. We toasted Gian. We toasted old films and memories.

And we toasted Adam.

Chapter Eighty-One
GIAN

I enjoy the rugby very much and Greg's team, they are very good. I am not sure that the Italian team is a good match for them. We play rugby in my country, but I think we need more instruction because we always lose when we play other countries.

When the team move on to Bologna, this is when I separate from them and make my own way. I plan to visit my brother in Rome, and I also visit Mamma's and Papà's graves.

I promise Rico that I return for Christmas. I try to convince them to come here, to Italy, for Christmas but they said no, not this time. Tina, she say she want to wait until after the baby is born. I will be back in time to see him being born. They know the baby will be a boy and they will call him Giovanni, after my father. My heart fill up, to be a grandfather. I hope they have many children.

Now, I sit on the train to Santa Margherita. I have Tosca and Figaro with me. They are company, especially for this journey. Since Kerry help with the memory box, this journey is always on my mind. A constant thought that I must visit and exorcise the sad thoughts of this place. I have many good times here and I want to reconnect with these.

I tell you truthfully, I do not want to make this journey alone. I want Kerry to be with me, for support, you know? But I travel alone and, I think, this is not a good thing. I worry about how I react. Perhaps I do not get off the train. Perhaps I go straight to Rome.

Chapter Eighty-Two
KERRY

You are my world, you're the centre of my universe,
You're the sun in the sky, you're the free bird as she flies,
You are my soul, you're the beating of my heart,
You are loving, you are kind, you send tingles down
my spine.

I didn't think I'd ever seen such a beautiful town as the one I was visiting now. I'd arrived the previous day and begun exploring. Santa Margherita truly did hug the coastline and the hills above it. The more modern part of the town was elegant and classy, definitely a cut above St Ives. It was chic, upmarket and clean. And what was it about Italians? I'd seen it in Milan when I flew in, and I saw it here. Even in casual clothes, they were stylish.

The houses and cottages on the hillside were painted in various pastels but mainly beautiful shades of yellow and copper but it was clear why Gian referred to this as the town where the rainbow fell. It was magical in every sense of the word.

The sky was cloudless, the sun was hot, the sea was made up of shades of blue that I'd only ever seen on an artist's palette and so, so clear, it was easy to peer down to the ocean floor. I passed numerous lemon trees. Above me, on the hills, vineyards and the food and drink on offer in the various stores and restaurants all seemed to be locally made or sourced.

Tranquillity hung in the air. The Italian trait of being in no rush whatsoever even trickled down to the dogs and cats, who were happy to simply sprawl in the shade of olive trees.

Today, I headed toward the train station. Beyond the rails, the sea sparkled. A few boats pottered around the coastline. Within a few hours of arriving here, I'd slowed my pace considerably although, at that moment, my heart was a beating drum.

At the bottom of the hill, I went through the station entrance to the ticket office. I bought a return ticket to the next station so that I could get on the platform. It was four euros well spent. I made my way on to the platform.

Suzie had found out which train Gian had caught. Greg had texted her after he'd waved him off at Bologna.

Butterflies swooped in my chest, and I honestly couldn't stay still. I didn't know whether to sit, stand or walk. I ended up doing all three. God knows what anyone was thinking, although there were only a handful of people on the platform. It was out of season, so I guessed they were mostly locals.

An announcement came over the Tannoy. My heart switched gears from pounding to a thrumming crescendo. I didn't speak Italian, but I knew this was Gian's train approaching. There was one every half hour; this had to be it. I took the deepest breath. I'd positioned myself at the end of the platform so I could see the length of it as people got off.

Running through my head was the scene from the end of *The Railway Children*: Bobbie standing on the platform and her father appearing as the steam disappeared. Bobbie running to him shouting, 'Daddy, my daddy!'

The train appeared around the bend and began slowing down. By the time the front carriage reached me, it was coming to a standstill.

About twenty passengers disembarked and my eyes searched for Gian. I spotted him in the middle. He'd got off where the exit was. Oh, bless, the dogs were with him.

I willed him to turn this way, but he didn't. As I walked slowly toward him, I could see that he was rooted to the spot. He looked beyond the station roof to the town, and he didn't seem keen on going any further. He put his suitcase down, took out a cigarette and lit it.

A woman at the little news stand suddenly shouted, 'Gian. Gianluca Belfiore!'

He seemed pleased to see this rotund, elderly lady and he gave her a big hug. I was too far away to hear what was being said. I wouldn't have understood it anyway, but I got the impression that she was telling him off for leaving it so long.

All this time, I continued to make my way slowly toward him. I now didn't want him to see me until the last minute. I wanted to see his face clearly when he turned to me.

A few customers at the news stand called the woman back. '*A presto,*' she said to Gian.

I knew what that meant. See you later. A man recognised Gian and he was given an enthusiastic welcome. They talked for a couple of minutes before he, too, left.

I was now just five yards away and a little behind Gian. I stopped. Alone with his thoughts, he appeared anxious, as if wondering whether he could go through with this. I moved a little to enter the field of his peripheral vision. It was Tosca who saw me first. Then Figaro. They pulled at their leashes.

The tugging on the leads caused Gian to glance in my direction.

Oh, if only someone could have filmed this! It was as if he'd seen a UFO land beside him.

Barely audible, he said, 'Kerry?'

I hadn't thought this far ahead.

I simply gave him a half-hearted 'here I am' smile.

The pleasure on his face was worth it.

'Kerry,' he said again, as if not believing I was there.

The dogs pawed a greeting.

'I thought you might want some company,' I said.

It's difficult to explain how I could perceive the jumble of emotions that tumbled in his head. Within the space of two seconds, I made out love, desire, gratitude, relief, shock, surprise, plus a whole load more. He said nothing but I didn't think words could describe what we were both feeling anyway.

He drew me close and wrapped his arms around me so tightly I thought I'd lose my breath.

I closed my eyes and hugged him.

I'd made the right decision.

When I opened my eyes, I spotted a movie poster on the advertising board and smiled. It had seen better days and had paled in the sun.

The movie? *Il Problemo, La Soluzione*, starring Luca Belfiore.